ANNALS OF THE NAM SOLDIER, OUTLAW,

Book Two

MOUNTAIN OF MADNESS

Awakened from an induced year-long slumber, the Nameless Dwarf is tortured with memories of slaughter and must come to terms with who he has become: an outcast, a butcher, the most reviled of dwarven-kind.

As forces of unimaginable destruction coalesce around the mountain fortress of a mad sorcerer, the philosopher Aristodeus puts together a team for a last desperate attempt to avert the coming cataclysm:

A knight besieged by doubts, who has been prepared since a child for the current crisis, yet is crumbling under the pressure of the task before him;

An albino assassin who denies the truth of what he really is;

A woman with a black sword as disturbing as the axe responsible for the massacre at Arx Gravis;

And a dwarf with no name, who will either carve out the path of his own redemption or condemn the world to a night that will never end.

Soldier, Outlaw, Hero, King:
Annals of the Nameless Dwarf

BOOK TWO

MOUNTAIN OF MADNESS

This is a work of fiction. Names, characters, places, and incidents are products of the author's imagination or are used fictitiously and are not to be construed as real. Any resemblance to actual events, locales, organizations, or persons, living or dead, is entirely coincidental.

MOUNTAIN OF MADNESS. Copyright © 2019 by D.P. Prior. All rights reserved. No part of this book may be used or reproduced in any manner whatsoever without written permission except in the case of brief quotations embodied in critical articles and reviews.

ISBN: 9781795520577

MOUNTAIN OF MADNESS was originally published in a substantially different form in GEAS OF THE BLACK AXE and was also included as part of the box-set LEGENDS OF THE NAMELESS DWARF: THE COMPLETE SAGA.

www.dpprior.com

CERRETH, THE FORBIDDEN LANDS

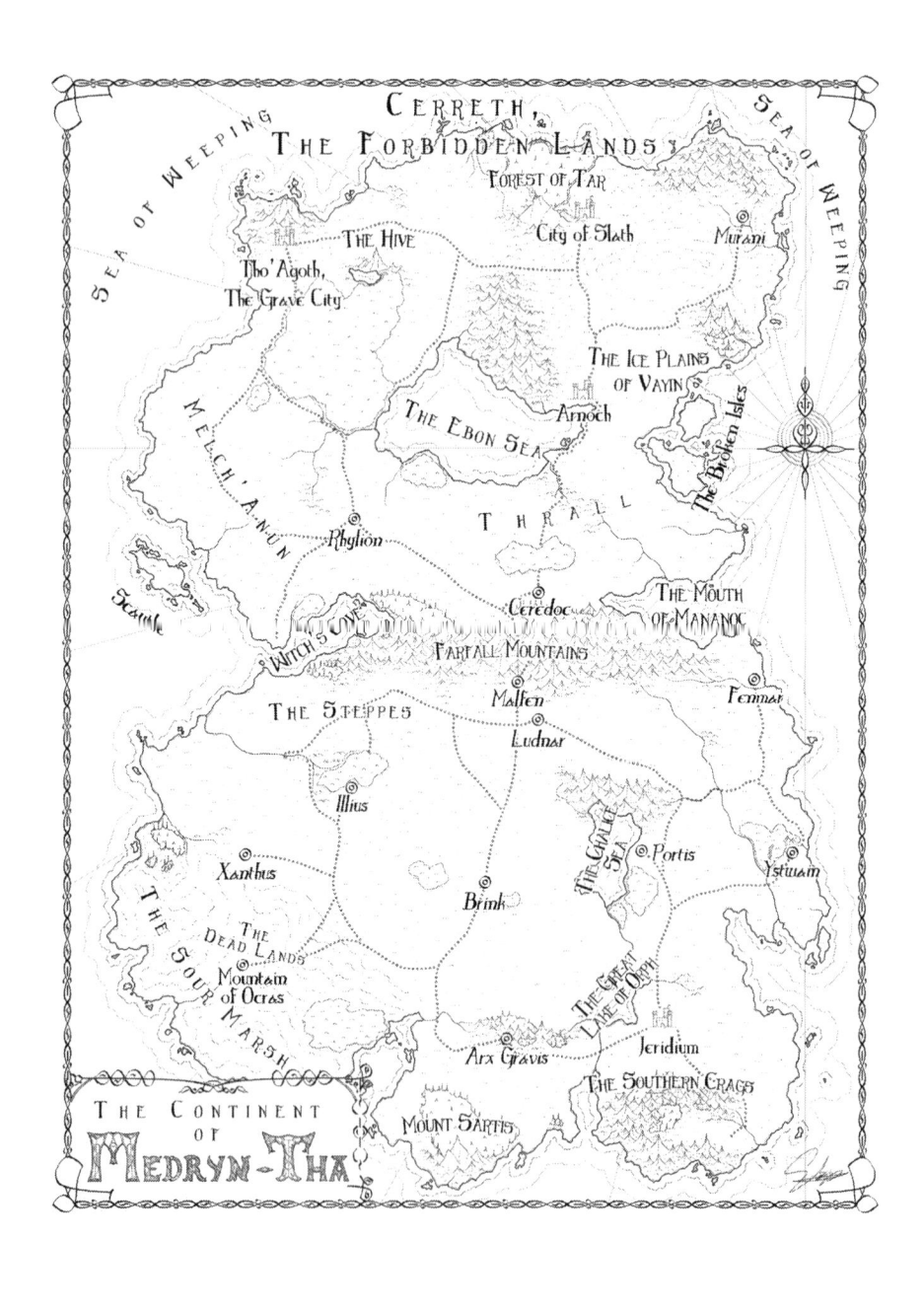

The Continent of MEDRYN-THA

- Sea of Weeping
- Forest of Tar
- The Hive
- City of Slath
- Murani
- Tho'Agoth, The Grave City
- The Ice Plains of Vayin
- The Broken Isles
- Melch'Anun
- The Ebon Sea
- Arnoch
- Rhylion
- Scatule
- Thrall
- Ceredoc
- The Mouth of Mananoc
- Witch's Cove
- Farfall Mountains
- Malfen
- Fennar
- The Steppes
- Ludnar
- Illius
- Xanthus
- The Chalice Sea
- Portis
- Istiuam
- Brink
- The Dead Lands
- Mountain of Ocras
- The Sour Marsh
- The Great Lake of Orth
- Arx Gravis
- Jeridium
- The Southern Crags
- Mount Sartis

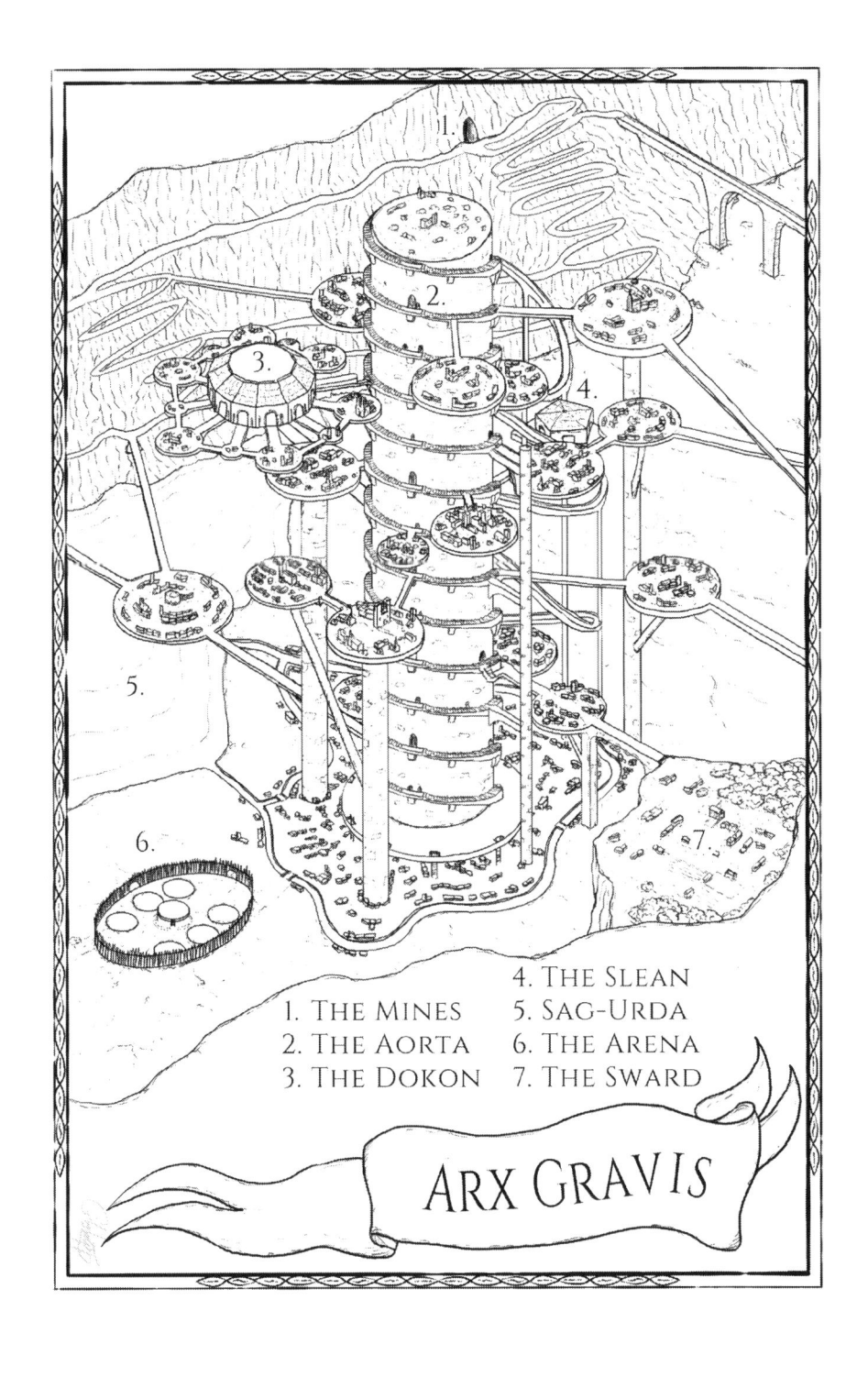

4. The Slean
1. The Mines   5. Sag-Urda
2. The Aorta   6. The Arena
3. The Dokon   7. The Sward

Arx Gravis

PROLOGUE

Sektis Gandaw stood high upon his *ocras* mountain and gazed out over the bleached bones of the Dead Lands toward the Sour Marsh. His coat whipped and snapped behind him in the breeze. In his metal-clad hand he held the stone statue of a serpent, sunlight glinting from its amber eyes. His desiccated lips curled into a smile. They had not done that for quite some time. Years. Centuries, even.

And so, he smiled and he chuckled, though it seemed to him a gurgling, rasping thing. And he held the serpent statue aloft in triumph, brandishing it against the world he had judged and found wanting.

From so high up, he could see it all laid out before him: the fetid tangle of the swamp, the clumping of the clouds, the jagged teeth of distant mountains—all so flawed in their design; all so imperfect.

But that would change now he had the statue, for it was no ordinary statue; it was the fossilized remains of the serpent goddess Etala, and at last his agents in Vanatus had brought her to him.

The Mad Sorcerer, they called him. Well he would show them who was mad. The people of this continent of Medryn-Tha, same as the people of the Vanatusian Empire and all the peoples of the whole sick world of Aosia, were blinded to the imperfections all around them, imperfections mirrored in their very selves. Instead, they heaped praises upon imperfect gods for making such a mess out of the primal dark they had slithered from.

That was madness, in Sektis's book. Madness and collusion with the malign powers behind the world. But he had questioned, and he had carved out answers. He knew just what to do to set things right, how to unweave the tangled threads of chaos and set them straight; and now he held within his grasp the power source that would enable him to do so.

He had tried once before and come up short.

This time he would not fail.

ONE

Albrec clung to the crystal-spangled plinth as the room tilted. His legs scissored in the air behind him, loose change cascading from his trouser pockets like hale on a tin roof. A klaxon blared briefly and then shut off as the floor came level once more. Albrec heaved a sigh of relief. He should never have stowed away! Whatever had he been thinking?

But Shadrak the Unseen had entered this strange craft with a man and a woman, and Shadrak never did anything unless there was money involved. Money and murder. Neither did Albrec, which is why he had snuck aboard when no one was looking. It seemed like a good idea at the time.

"Nooo!" Albrec wailed as his feet flipped over his head and he found his face pressed against the cold hard surface of the black mirror atop the plinth. The glare of dozens of crystals blazed across his vision in a kaleidoscopic blur, and acid bile swilled into his mouth.

"Stop it moving, stop it moving, stop it—" A particularly pungent reflux stopped his prayer before it led to rapture. Not that he was praying to anyone in particular, mind; it was more like a message in a bottle.

The room slammed down again, and Albrec shot across the floor arse over head until his feet hit the wall. He couldn't quite situate the rest of his body: his paunch was practically smothering him, his chin was in his chest, and his trouser legs were cutting into his knees where they had run up his shins. Just his rotten luck if someone came in right now and caught sight of his lily-white calves hanging like bloated sausages behind that infernal strip of black hair that was forever slipping towards the nape of his neck.

But at least it had gone still.

Before he dared move, Albrec's hand crept into his jacket pocket in search of the reassurance his cheese-cutter always brought. It was an old friend, a faithful aid, equally at home in the kitchen or wrapped around a victim's throat. He inside-outed the pocket, scrunched at the fabric, did the same with the other pocket and then, in a paroxysm of terror far greater than he'd just experienced, he flopped to his side and flipped to his knees all the better to pat himself down.

The cheese-cutter was gone. The pats turned to slaps, which turned to thumps, the last of which was aimed at his forehead. This was insufferable, intolerable, inconceivable. He never ceased fiddling with the cheese-cutter; it was always between his thumb and forefinger like a holy man's prayer cord, only infinitely more useful. The habit was so ingrained as to be unconscious. Perhaps it was so unconscious as to have been forgotten. Albrec glanced around the chamber, dived in amongst his scattered coinage and put his face to the ground like a bloodhound.

"Bloody shitting hell, Albrec, you stupid, silly cun—" He clamped his mouth shut before he could say the unmentionable word. Even now, so many years after her unfortunate death, he winced at the slap Mumsy would have given him—right on the lug-hole, as she would have put it, sending shock waves through his skull that would gradually ebb away to a persistent ringing. He was sure she'd dislodged a year's worth of memories with every clout. If nothing else, the recollection of the old trout gave him pause for thought and allowed him to reassert the rational over the primitive mind. It took a lot these days for Albrec to lose control, and loss of control was a habit he couldn't afford to slip back into. Not in his line of work.

"Master poisoner," he reminded himself. "Deadly assassin."

He stooped to roll down his trouser legs, tugging them smooth over the tops of his ankle boots. His heart still ricocheted from the loss of the cheese-cutter, but his mind was back where it belonged, firmly grasping the reins.

The crystals on the plinth winked out one by one, and then the silver wall in front of him parted with a whoosh.

"It wasn't me. I didn't do—"

Before he could complete the same automatic response he'd always blurted out as a child, Albrec caught a whiff of fresh air coming up the passageway beyond. When he'd entered the room with the plinth mere minutes ago and the wall had closed behind him, he feared he would never get out alive. Which is why he'd twiddled several of the crystals on the plinth, just to see if any of them opened the walls; and everything had gone to shit in an instant.

Before the wall could close up again, he hurried out into the passageway then followed the same maze of silver corridors he'd entered by, until he arrived at the entrance to the craft. The silver door must have slid open of its own accord because there was brilliant daylight coming through the rectangular opening. Albrec almost wept with joy as he crossed the threshold and stepped outside.

And gasped.

He'd expected to see the verdant hills above Vanatus City, which is where he'd followed Shadrak and the others into the strange craft; but instead ocher terrain spread as far as the eye could see, and here and there outcrops of what looked like limestone stood as high as a man. There were craters dotted all over the place, reminding him of that perforated cheese they produced in the provinces.

He stepped out onto the desert sand and scanned the horizon. Way off in the distance he could just about make out the hazy peaks of a mountain range.

Albrec hadn't felt so crushed since Dana Woodrum had scoffed at the beautiful cupcakes he'd presented her with for her birthday. Unbidden came the vivid recollection of his revenge: Dana's red face and swollen lips; her hands clutching uselessly at her throat as yellow drool dripped down her chin; the stench of her shit as her organs collapsed and she slopped to the floor like a drowned invertebrate. Oh, the gloating satisfaction. He'd observed her for weeks, haunted all the parties she attended, endured her scathing remarks, but it had been worth it to find out that she couldn't resist sugared cherry tart with a dollop of cream and chocolate sprinkles.

Albrec became aware of his fingers questing through his jacket pockets. He could almost feel the wooden ends of his cheese-cutter and started to run his fingertip along the wire—but it wasn't there.

Miles and miles of ocher desert.

He could have a concussion, he supposed. Maybe someone was playing a trick on him—Shadrak most likely. *The pallid little shit doesn't want anyone muscling in on his profits.*

He stared down at the ground, back up at the suns, the far-off mountains. In the opposite direction, light shimmered and sparkled where the horizon became a faint strip of blue. Off to the left, a fair few miles away, was a vast city surrounded by white walls with tall towers and minarets poking their heads above. Whatever it was, it wasn't Vanatus.

When he glanced behind, he gasped again. The craft was gone. He reached out and recoiled as he felt the cold surface of the craft's hull, but he could see right through it to where a trail of dust snaked along a broad road. There were wagons and pack horses amid the dust—a caravan of some sort, and it was heading his way.

Albrec crouched down and gathered some pebbles into the shape of a cross to mark the entrance. Brushing the dust from his palms, he straightened up and found his eyes drawn to one of the craters.

It was one of those things he knew he shouldn't do, but there were times his curiosity was irrepressible. *It'll be the death of you*, Mumsy always used to say. Funny that, he thought as he set off toward the crater, because her favorite saying had certainly rung true for her in the end.

The blasted crater was farther off than it looked. Sweating so much his finely tailored jacket and trousers were positively drenched, he scrabbled up a scree bank and saw that what he had thought was a crater was actually a large hole set into a gentle incline where the ground had blistered into a low mound. Hole probably wasn't the best way to describe it either. Cave mouth might have been better. It was as wide as a house and the height of two grown men. The edges of the entrance glistened with what looked like dew, but on closer inspection he saw it was metallic.

Oh my gilded backside! Gold!
Be careful... All that glitters is not—
—*Not in my experience.* He soon shut that train of thought down. He wouldn't be who he was today if he gave in to that kind of negativity.

The moment he stepped across the threshold, the stench struck him like a slap round the face with a dead fish—a cross between putrefying compost and off-meat. He whipped out his handkerchief and held it over his nose and mouth. The damned thing still stank of snuff. Washing seemed to have no effect, and yet he couldn't bring himself to throw it away. It was the only thing of Papa's left.

He took a couple of wary steps into the cave mouth, marveling at how the specks of gold, or whatever it was, continued to sparkle even out of the sunlight. When he went in deeper, it was like walking on golden stars that wound downwards into the receding distance. Not a cave, then, Albrec mused: a tunnel; and a big one at that. It hardly looked natural, the way the width remained uniform; the smoothness of the walls.

He pressed on until the light from outside was lost around a bend. The steady downward gradient became more sheer at that point, and he had to touch the lefthand wall for support. He'd gone no more than a few steps when he trod in something sticky. His foot came free, sock and all, and he had to balance on one leg and bend from the waist to retrieve his shoe. It came away from the ground trailing a thick rope of goo. He scraped off what he could against the wall and then dropped it so he could put his foot back down. He was still wiggling his toes and straining to get his heel in fully when a blast of wind rushed past him from the depths. Rotten wind, if such a thing existed, like a belch from a toothless crone with a mouthful of vomit. Not wind, then, he realized.

An exhalation.

The ground shook as something squelched and rustled down the tunnel to the accompaniment of an echoing hiss. The darkness ahead shifted and then got a whole lot darker as the specks of gold winked out or were smothered.

Albrec took a step back, crouching so he could use his finger as a shoehorn, and then he was retreating up the tunnel. More of the gold flecks were swallowed by shadow, and another rush of fetid breath blasted over him and sent Papa's handkerchief into a crazy spiral. He watched it like an enraptured child at a puppet show, reaching out a lazy hand to catch it.

In that instant, a colossal maw ringed with serrated teeth opened right in front of his face. Albrec whimpered, broke wind, and stumbled backwards at the same time. The handkerchief hit the ground, the monstrosity roared, and Albrec squealed his most high-pitched squeal and ran back up the tunnel as fast as his legs could carry him.

When he reached the cave mouth, he glanced back over his shoulder.

Papa's hanky—

A gargantuan flat head surged into the light, trailed by a purplish segmented body. A dozen yellow eyes flickered open and locked onto Albrec. He stumbled outside, not daring to take his gaze off the thing as its sinuous body coiled into the cave and then undulated towards him.

Albrec half-slipped, half-rolled down the scree slope, leaping to his feet with the grace of a far more agile man. The monstrous worm roared from just above him and Albrec never stopped to look back. He scanned the ground for sign of the pebble cross he'd left, heart galloping so fast he feared it would burst.

There! He spotted the cross and started toward it, but the earth ruptured in front of him, and another giant worm started to emerge.

Shit!

He turned and ran to the left, figuring he could cut a semicircle behind it, but another wriggling body burst from the earth to block his way.

Double shit!

Albrec whirled and sprinted in the opposite direction, even as the first worm slithered down the scree slope in a cloud of dust and rubble. A fourth head split the ground ten yards in front of him.

Shitting, shitty shit!

Dozens of the things were surfacing all over the place. Albrec just kept moving, jiggling and wobbling this way and that, screeching and whimpering every time a new worm emerged. He was done for, he knew it.

Curiosity will be the—
"Oh, fuck off!"
Didn't I tell you? All that glitters—
"Shove it up your arse!"

He cut a zigzagging course between the monstrous worms, and suddenly he was through and pelting along hard-packed earth towards the dust cloud following the caravan he'd spotted earlier.

TWO

Someone had spoken, which must have been what had awakened him.

It was black as the Void, and it stank like a gibuna's mangy hide.

Or bad breath.

His breath.

His heart lurched, and he gasped.

He must have fallen asleep in a tavern somewhere, drinking himself into oblivion, because he was sitting upright on what felt like a bench. He tried to open his eyes, but the lids were stuck together. He went to wipe away the gunk of sleep, but a chain rattled and his hand came no more than an inch off the bench.

Cloth rasped. Boots scuffed on stone.

Panic bit and he would have stood, but his legs were chained too.

"Who's there?" he wanted to ask, but his lips were as sealed as his eyelids. Ice sluiced through his veins. What if they meant him harm? What if they had come to kill him? But who? And more importantly, why?

And then it hit him: the realization that not only did he not know where he was and who was there with him, but he had no idea who *he* was.

A ruddy haze came into view behind his eyelids. Or was it a stain?

MOUNTAIN OF MADNESS

Blood.

He could smell it now.

It had drenched his skin and soaked right through. He saw it in his mind's eye: rivers of blood, and him bathed in it from hands to elbows, from feet to knees. It spattered his face, matted his beard. He remembered chopping. The rise and fall of an axe. Screams. Mountains of the dead. Demons. He thought he had been killing demons, but they had been dwarves.

And he was a dwarf.

A dwarf with no name.

They had taken it from him, shamed his family forever, made him an outcast lower than even the baresarks who lived at the foot of the ravine—Arx Gravis, the city he called home.

Made him a nameless dwarf.

Which meant things were bad. Things were very bad. Or had it all been a dream? Was he still dreaming?

He needed light. He needed to see. There was something covering his head, which is why it was so hard to breathe.

His eyes strained open, but through the stringy muck that clung to the lashes, all he could see was a strip of grey bordering on black. He blinked and refocused. It was the grey of the walls: finely mortared bricks. Good stonework. Dwarf stonework. But he could hardly see up or down.

He dimly remembered a helm being settled over his head; relived the sensation of it meshing with the flesh of his neck, never to be removed. That's how they'd done it, how they had stolen his name.

A bald human… That was it: the philosopher who had encased him in an *ocras* helm. The helm that had belonged to…

It was there one instant, gone the next.

But the voice that had woken him—that stayed with him clear as anything. He knew that voice. It had been the last thing he'd heard before falling into an unnatural slumber.

The philosopher's voice.

The man who had put him here!

His lips came unstuck and he roared. Fired flooded his veins as he strained every muscle. Bolts shrieked, chains snapped, and he stood.

The Nameless Dwarf swiveled the helm, searching for a toga and a bald head. But the eye-slit came to rest on a brown coat, worn over a white surcoat with a red symbol on the front—a stick person with curves for legs and a horn-topped circle for a head, within which was a single crimson eye. Chainmail glinted beneath the surcoat.

He craned his neck until he saw a lean, angular face beneath a broad-brimmed hat, and dark hair that fell below the shoulders.

The man in his field of vision stepped back, and the Nameless Dwarf pivoted the helm to track him.

There was an iron door in the background, with a grille at head-height to a dwarf, but chest-high to this human. The room itself was circular, the ceiling festooned with cobwebs. Dust was steeped about the floor.

The man's hands came up, and the Nameless Dwarf raised his fists instinctively. Fear or rage glinted in the human's eyes. It was difficult to say which, given his stony face. Rage then, the Nameless Dwarf decided, advancing a step, for the man had the look of a fighter.

The human feigned one way then darted the other. The Nameless Dwarf slung out a hook that should have pulverized him, but his timing was off and he struck the wall instead. Pain flared, and the skin of his knuckles split. He went for an uppercut, but the man was fast and twisted aside. He backed the shogger against the door, saw the rage turn to fear in his eyes. But then he saw something else: stone manacles on the man's wrists, connected by a short chain. A prisoner, then, as much as he was.

"Do I know you, laddie?" The Nameless Dwarf's voice came out a rasp, his throat was so dry. "I thought you were someone else, but he's a crusty bald bastard, and you must be half his age with ten times his hair."

The man made an effort to relax, but his eyes betrayed a sense of horror.

"I am Hale Zaylus, a knight from—"

"Never heard of him."

"This philosopher," Zaylus said. "His name wouldn't happen to be Aristodeus, would it?"

"Aye, that's the shogger. Worked his fancy magic and left me to rot." He dipped the helm and saw through the eye-slit the dark stains on his boots, the grisly film coating the front of his chainmail.

"It was Aristodeus who put you here?" Zaylus asked.

"Him and the Council of Twelve. Half of them wanted to kill me. Might have been better if they had." He angled the helm to get a good look at his forearms. They were crusted over with dried blood, all the way to the elbows.

"I know him," Zaylus said. "In Vanatus he was my mentor."

"Ah, he means well, laddie. He might be a lying, flatulent windbag, but his heart's in the right place. Least that's what my pa told Thumil, and that's good enough for... Oh, my shogging fruits! Thumil and Cordy—they were married. Her wedding dress was drenched in blood. They were both in the Dokon when Aristodeus put this bucket on my head."

He rapped the helm with his knuckles and then raised his bloodied hand to the eye-slit. "Must have cut myself when I punched the wall."

"Thumil?"

"Marshal of the Ravine Guard. I served under him, and he is... was my friend."

"I've met him," Zaylus said bitterly. He made his way to sit on the bench. "You know a way out of here?"

"If you want to try breaking that door down, don't let me stop you."

"How often do the guards check on you?" Zaylus asked. "Bring you food?"

The Nameless Dwarf sauntered over and sat beside him. "I'm not sure they do."

Zaylus grew agitated. "They must feed you, surely. How long have you been...?" His voice petered out. "The dust on your helm and armor... A first I thought you were a statue, and then that you were dead. And the blood... all over you. What happened?"

"You mean, what did I do?"

Zaylus watched him intently, but even if he could have

21

remembered everything, the Nameless Dwarf couldn't speak, in case the words he uttered made it true.

"Then, at least tell me your name," Zaylus said.

The Nameless Dwarf chuckled. "Ah, you got me there, laddie."

Zaylus frowned, but before the Nameless Dwarf could explain, the grille on the door slid open. Muffled voices came from outside, followed by the grinding screech of bolts being drawn back.

The door opened a crack and Thumil entered the cell. He was wearing the white robe of a Councilor. Of course he was! Thumil had been made Voice of the Council following the death of Dythin Rala.

At Thumil's nod, the cell door closed. There was a resonant clunk from the lock, and the grate and thunk of three bolts being snapped into place.

"Precautions," Thumil told Zaylus. "I'm sure you understand."

Thumil looked worn and haggard, his beard lank, and there were bald patches in his hair.

"My companions?" Zaylus said.

"One is safely locked up like you," Thumil said. "But the other eludes us still. You should not have come here, Hale Zaylus. You're lucky to be alive."

He wasn't wrong there. The Black Cloaks at the top of the ravine were ruthless when it came to intruders. Maybe the Red Cloaks had found them first.

"I see you've met," Thumil said, staring at the Nameless Dwarf seated on the bench. He scratched at his beard, and a clump of hair came away in his hand. "Tried talking to him?"

Zaylus glanced at the Nameless Dwarf and started to reply, but Thumil spoke right over him.

"Me too. Used to come daily. Then days turned to weeks, and weeks to months. I guess I just hoped he would…" He stopped and stared at the sheared bolts on the floor beneath the bench. The color drained from his face, and he backed away toward the door.

"Hoped he'd what?" the Nameless Dwarf said as he pushed himself up from the bench.

Thumil yelped, and his knees buckled. He slid down the door to the floor.

"Hoped I'd say something?" The Nameless Dwarf stepped toward Thumil. "I would have, if I'd known you were here. Weeks, you say? Months? How long has it been, for shog's sake?"

Thumil was shaking, and his eyes were wide with fright. "It's not possible. How can you be awake? Aristodeus said only he could... Do you remember?"

"Aye, Thumil, I remember."

"Your name?"

"No, not my name. Other things, though. Things I'd sooner forget."

"But *you* remember his name, surely?" Zaylus said.

Thumil shook his head. "It's gone. Gone from all time, past, present and future, as if it never existed and never will."

The Nameless Dwarf flopped back down on the bench. "You should have let the Council kill me."

"I couldn't," Thumil said. "You were my friend."

"Were?" Zaylus asked.

Thumil grimaced and chose not to answer. "They call him the Nameless Dwarf now," he said. "We are a people steeped in tradition, Zaylus, in history. Names are very important to us. They are recorded by our families, all the way back to the Founders of Arx Gravis. One gap in the roll of names brings dishonor to the whole lineage. Most dwarves would prefer death."

"There's still time," the Nameless Dwarf said.

"Stop it," Thumil snapped. "Just stop."

The Nameless Dwarf gave a mock salute and lay back on the bench.

"I need to think," Thumil said. "I wasn't expecting this. *They* were not expecting this."

"By 'they,' he means the Council of Twelve," the Nameless Dwarf said. "A bunch of prevaricating old idiots who can't even decide what day it is. About the only thing they can agree on is what to do with me. For once I'm on their side. Forget your veto, Thumil. Go with the majority vote."

"Please," Zaylus said. "There isn't the time for this."

"I agree," the Nameless Dwarf said. "Fetch a spear, Thumil. One quick jab here." He thumped his heart.

D.P. PRIOR

Thumil gritted his teeth and answered Zaylus. "So you say. The Mad Sorcerer."

"Sektis Gandaw," Zaylus said. "Doesn't that worry you?"

"Out of sight, out of mind is our way," Thumil said. "We're no threat to Sektis Gandaw and his experiments."

"This is no mere experiment we're talking about," Zaylus said. "This is the Unweaving, the unmaking of all things, all worlds. Even you, Thumil. Even the dwarves."

"I know my history," Thumil said. "The Mad Sorcerer tried to unweave all of creation before. And you want to know why he was able to? Because of Maldark the Fallen, that's why. One of our own, a dwarf, and the main reason we have kept ourselves apart from the world ever since."

"Be fair, Thumil," the Nameless Dwarf said. "According to the *Chronicles*, Maldark played a part in defeating Sektis Gandaw and preventing the Unweaving."

"Maldark made amends, yes, but he never forgave himself for delivering the goddess Etala to the Mad Sorcerer, despite being the one to ultimately save her and hide her away from the world."

"Sektis Gandaw has the Statue of Etala once more," Zaylus said. "His agents found it hidden away in the Empire. We pursued them here from Vanatus."

"No, no, no," Thumil said. "If Gandaw really had the Statue of Etala, how come we're still alive? Don't you think he'd have unwoven us all by now?"

"Maybe he's running it past the Council of Twelve first," the Nameless Dwarf said, "which should give us a fair few years."

Thumil shot him a withering glare.

"I think he's started," Zaylus said. "When we left the Sour Marsh there was a brown cloud above the Mountain of Ocras."

"You've been there?" Thumil said. "Then why didn't you put a stop to the Mad Sorcerer, rather than bring your problems here?"

"The mountain is guarded by silver spheres that spit fire," Zaylus said. "The only way inside is through the tunnels you dwarves used for—"

"The *ocras* mines?" Thumil said. "You want to use the tunnels that run from the mines to the Mountain of Ocras? They've been closed for years."

"But you can get us into them?"

Thumil rubbed at his beard, frowning as strands came away in his fingers. "They could be unblocked, I suppose, but shog knows what you'd find inside. According to the *Chronicles*, back when we were mining for him, Sektis Gandaw had the tunnels infested with giant ants to keep the *ocras* from being stolen. The only reason our boys weren't eaten is because he made an ant-man to control them. Horrible thing, by all accounts, and I pity the poor bastard he took and melded into it."

"I'll deal with that hurdle if we cross it," Zaylus said. "The question is, will you help us?"

Thumil puffed his cheeks up and blew out a big breath. "That's putting the cart before the goat, I'd say. I cannot act independently of the Council. There will have to be deliberation, a vote."

"No time," Zaylus said. "Convince them they need to act now."

"You've yet to convince me," Thumil said, "and I can assure you, the Council will take a lot more persuading."

"Turn a blind eye, then."

"Let you and the woman go?"

"Woman?" the Nameless Dwarf asked. "Does she have a beard?"

"Better still, get us into the tunnels," Zaylus continued, ignoring him. "You're the leader of the Council, aren't you? The Voice. Surely you have connections."

Thumil looked horrified. "That's the sort of attitude that leads to tyranny. I'll not do it. No dwarf would." He turned away and raised his fist to knock on the door.

"I would," the Nameless Dwarf said.

Thumil spun round to face him.

The Nameless Dwarf stretched, yawned inside his helm, then swung his feet to the floor and stood. "Seeing as you won't kill me, I might as well make myself useful."

"No," Thumil said. "No, that won't do at all."

Thumil turned back to the door and knocked three times.

"I'll speak with the Council, Zaylus," he said, "tell them of the urgency, but don't get your hopes up. Nothing happens quickly here. And first off, they'll have to know about our friend here being awake. If they ever recover from the news, there will be endless debates about what to do about him. Endless."

The door swung open, and spears bristled across the threshold.

"Everything all right, my Lord Voice?" a gruff voice asked.

"No, everything is far from all right." Thumil stepped between the spears and out into the corridor.

"Shog, he's awake!" someone yelled. "The butcher's awake!"

THREE

"Here, catch," Buck Fargin said, flinging something shiny across the kitchen.

The cretinous rogue had driven one of the wagons in the caravan Albrec had spotted. Like had recognized like, and Buck had offered Albrec a job. Only Buck wasn't a fully fledged guildsman, as Albrec had supposed. He was a lowly dogsbody, and the job had been as a kitchen hand in the excuse for a restaurant in which Buck worked.

Albrec caught it on instinct, turned it over in his hand. "A potato peeler. Why, thanks."

Smoke wafted up from the brazier atop the clay oven. Whatever was sautéing (if one could stretch the meaning of the word) in the cast iron pan was charred black on the outside and no doubt completely raw in the center. There was a steaming cauldron beside it, bubbling and spitting with far too much vigor for the sludge congealing inside. The stench was hard to discern—lamb, perhaps, but with more than a hint of tarragon (*not right at all*) and so much turmeric that the water had turned yellow and stank like an Ashantan brothel.

Albrec coughed into his sleeve, wincing at the memory of poor old Papa's hanky.

Twisting plumes of dirty smoke wound their way up the crumbling brick flue, but much of it still wafted out into the kitchen, probably because the four-legged carcass turning on the spit obscured the opening.

Albrec had to admit, though, it was a curious contraption. The spit was connected to a vertical shaft coming down the flue. Where spit met shaft, there was some kind of primitive gear. The shaft seemed to rotate of its own accord, and as it did, the spit turned, too.

"What makes it turn?" he asked, stepping closer and waving steam out of his face so he could crane his neck for a better look.

"Don't know and don't care," Buck said, thrusting his hand into a pail of carrots and proceeding to butcher them with ham-fisted chops of a blunt knife. It made Albrec wonder at the quality of the cuisine if Buck was the best sous-chef they could come up with. "Spuds are behind you."

"Spuds?" Albrec turned to look. "Oh, potatoes."

"Not much for peeling, eh?" Buck said. "I'll swap you. Come here, I'll show you how to chop."

Oh, please, Will you?

Albrec made a show of awed fascination as the cretin hacked away at the carrots as though he were quarrying granite.

"See," Buck said, handing Albrec the knife and relieving him of the potato peeler. "It's all in the wrist."

Yes, I'm sure it is.

Albrec took up a position in front of the chopping board, set the knife down like a surgical implement, shrugged off his jacket and handed it to Buck, then delicately took the knife back up again.

"Don't be shy, now," Buck said. "Bit firmer. That's it, show it who's boss."

Albrec held up a finger for silence. "Now, Master Fargin, wait, watch, and learn. Handshake grip on the knife, index finger to the top and side of the blade, tip down, and rolling chop. Forward and down, forward and down."

Buck was looking at him as if he were mad. "But you ain't cut nothing yet. It ain't like we got all day for your poncy shenanigans."

"Stage two," Albrec said. "Make a claw of your subordinate hand…"

"Eh?"

"Claw on carrot." He started to demonstrate as he spoke. "Slice down the middle; take one half, keep the blade rolling—forward and back—feed it the carrot, root at the top. Chop away from the root, always away. Chop, chop, chop chop chop, chopa-chopa-chop-chop. Aaaand the other half." He made short work of that one, too. "Rinse and repeat. Cut down the center, chop away from the root…"

He could tell Buck was gawping, even without looking at him. Years of practice, two years sous-chefing for the great Maurice Mouflet—the Way rest his soul—then a decade as the most acclaimed head chef in Vanatus City, until that business with the *boeuf à la mode*. The guilds had demanded it: Mouflet had upset someone very important, and for a copious purse Albrec had abandoned a flourishing career to return to his first love of poisoning.

"What's your game?" Buck said, a wary look coming over him. "You been shitting me?"

"Not at all," Albrec said. "You shrewdly discerned my talents when we met. Suffice it to say that I have many skills with which to serve your ambitions, Master Fargin."

Buck bit down on his top lip and nodded. "That's all right then. Just like we agreed. You scratch my back…"

And I'll ram a knife in yours, you cretinous moron.

"And I will most definitely scratch yours," Albrec finished for him.

"Good. I was hoping you'd say that. See, I knew you was gonna turn out a dab hand in the kitchen. Just wanted to see for myself. Thing is, I'm expecting someone. Magwitch the Meddler. He should be here any minute to collect the *ocras*, you know, from the back of the wagon."

"How could I forget?" The ride to Jeridium cooped up with that flatulent, snoring, hairy midget was going to be difficult to forget. The little man had slept most of the way, only ever waking to relieve himself and bemoan the lack of booze. Albrec still couldn't shake off the stench of his stale beer belches. "Is he still…?"

Buck nodded towards the restaurant—if you could call it such.

Dougan's Diner was more of a soup kitchen crossed with a spit-and-sawdust tavern. "Propping up the bar, as usual. Place would go down the crapper if it wasn't for ol' Rugbeard. Silly bleeding plonker: gets a sodding fortune for setting up trade between the guild and the *ocras* mines, then hands all the dosh back to us in return for drink."

"The guild runs this establishment?"

Buck put a finger to the side of his nose and winked. "So, my ol' mate, you handle the veg and I'll wait for Magwitch." He set the peeler on the chopping board and went to peer out the dirty window at the back of the kitchen.

Albrec sliced up the veg with practiced ease. It had been a long time since he'd performed such menial tasks, but he was actually finding it quite relaxing. "What about the tomatoes? What does Chef want done with them?"

Before Buck could answer, the back door opened and a boy of maybe twelve or thirteen stepped through. He had your typical peasant face, broad and flat, crooked lower teeth, thick eyebrows that nearly met above his stubby nose, and a shock of greasy hair that had probably never seen a brush. His cheeks were ruddy and he was out of breath.

"What are you doing here?" Buck rolled his eyes in Albrec's direction and gave an exasperated shrug.

"Look, Dad, I got the bread, like you said." The boy produced a stale-looking loaf from his coat pocket. "And some plonk." He pulled a bottle of wine from the other side.

Buck clipped him round the ear. "Ain't I told you not to come here?" He raised his hand for a more substantial blow, and the boy ducked down, shielding his head with the bread and wine. Buck seemed to remember Albrec was watching and turned it into a playful ruffle of the boy's hair. He gave one of those irritating false laughs and snatched the wine. "Good boy, Nils. Good boy. See that, Albrec? Chip off the ol' block. We'll make a guildsman out of him yet, eh?"

The boy shoved the bread back in his pocket and puffed out his pigeon chest. "So, I did good, Dad?"

"Yeah, son, you did fine. Now sod off. I got a customer

coming."

A huge grin cut the boy's face in two. He punched the air with delight and then slipped out the way he'd come. As the door slammed shut, the connecting door to the restaurant burst open and a fat slob in a stained apron and lopsided chef's hat lumbered through. Greasy ringlets curled down from beneath the hat, and the man's face was a piebald of angry sores and scaly flakes.

"Fargin, you little shit, I got Senator Rollingfield in tonight, so you better get a bloody move on with my…" His rheumy eyes alighted on the perfectly cubed carrots on the chopping board, then lifted to stare Albrec straight in the face. "…veg. Who's this?"

Albrec gave his most sheepish smile, but he was already trying to process what he'd just heard. Whatever would possess a senator eat in a dump like this? Silly he should need to ask, he realized. The guild. Crime and politics had ever been bedfellows. It was a gratifying thought. This place Shadrak's strange craft had landed him in was just the same as home: ladder-climbing crooks and bent politicians. He mentally rubbed his hands together. He was going to like it here, once he'd done a bit of ladder-climbing of his own, of course.

"His name's Albrec, Chef," Buck said, tearing himself away from the door, but still straining to see out the window. "He's our new kitchen hand."

"Oh, so you're doing the hiring now are you?" The chef snatched up a pan and flung it at Buck with such force it would have brained him, if he'd not squealed and ducked out of the way. "And why ain't you diced my tomatoes? What the shog do I pay you for, you useless clump of dung?"

"There's a deal going down, Chef." Buck jabbed a finger towards the back door. "Big Jake set it up. Put me in charge. That's why I brought Albrec in, to make sure everything got done right. I thought you'd be pleased."

The chef advanced on him a step then whirled on Albrec. "You worked kitchens before?"

"The finest in all Vanatus."

Chef scowled. "Vanatus! A likely story. Look, you got your secrets same as we all have—except for Fargin here: everyone knows he's a weaselly little pillock. So, if Vanatus is your story, that's fine by me, just as long as you work your balls off and do what I tell you. We've got an important guest tonight. You do good, and I'll treat you fair and square. Screw things up, though, and you'll be floating down the canal, got it? Now peel some spuds."

Albrec forced a smile so false it nearly split his cheeks. As he set about the potatoes, the chef stirred the muck bubbling in the cauldron and dipped his finger in to taste it. "You want to get on in the world, fat boy, then pay close attention to everything I do."

Oh, I will, Albrec thought, feigning interest as the chef slurped the gruel off his fingertip and rubbed his chin as if considering how to improve its near perfect flavor.

"Of course, I got it," Buck's voice came from outside. Presumably Magwitch the Meddler had arrived. "Here, have a gander."

"Know what a terrine is, fat boy?" Chef asked.

Nothing like that stinking pot of diarrhea.

"I don't, Chef," Albrec said. "Is that one?"

"Leave the spuds," Chef said. "Idiot boy can do them when he's finished his business." Buck could still be heard talking outside. Haggling, by the sound of it, and he seemed to be coming off worst. "Chop them tomatoes and sling 'em in. See, we don't need no fancy recipes here. It's all about taste and experience. Punters love it."

Buck's muffled voice grew momentarily louder. "Take it or leave it! See if I care."

The chef frowned towards the back door and shook his head.

"*Solanum lycopersicum,*" Albrec said, picking up a string of tomatoes on the vine.

"What?"

Buck's voice cut across their conversation once more. "All right, all right, I didn't mean it. Take the sodding *ocras*, but the Night Hawks ain't gonna be happy. Daylight bleeding robbery is what it is."

"Tomatoes," Albrec said. "From the nightshade family." *With stems and leaves that contain enough tomatine to keep you on the latrine for a week, or even kill you if you boil enough of them up into a tisane.* "Curative," he muttered, stroking a stem. "Quite the miracle plant."

"Just get on with the chopping, right?"

"Certainly, Chef." Albrec set about dicing the tomatoes with his usual efficiency.

Chef's mouth dropped open. "You know a thing or two about cooking?"

"I've picked up a little from some of the greats," Albrec said. "But no one who'd hold a candle to you, Chef…"

"Dougan," Chef said. "Faryll Dougan."

"Provincial cooks, all of them," Albrec went on. "Whereas the standards of a big city like this are somewhat more exacting."

Dougan nodded and narrowed his eyes. "Aye, that's right. Still, you can lean from anyone, I always say. We'll have to talk, you know, share secrets."

"Sounds fabulous," Albrec said, chopping away with abandon.

Dougan watched, scratching at his face, flakes drifting down like snow and settling on top of his broth.

"Nasty sores you've got there."

"What's it to you?"

"I know a remedy that can sort that out, if you're interested." Albrec held up the discarded leafy greens from the tomatoes. "My little gift to you."

"Oh, aye?"

"Tea of tomato leaves and stems," Albrec said. "Tastes awful, but you'll have the skin of a sixteen-year-old-virgin in no time at all."

"I will?"

"Change your life."

Dougan smiled, a big, brown stub-toothed smile. "You and me are gonna get along just fine, fat… what did Fargin say your name was again?"

"Albrec."

"Well, Albrec, you scratch my back…"

"Indeed," Albrec said.

"So, what are you waiting for?" Dougan snapped. "Let's be

33

having it, then."

Albrec gathered up all the greens and looked about for a pan to boil them in. "Trust me, Chef, after this, you'll never be the same again."

The back door opened and Buck came in holding up a drawstring purse. "Now that's how to do business," he said with a grin. "Put him in his place, I did. Wanker."

"Oh," Albrec said. "So, he paid up, did he?"

"Too bloody right, he did. Fleeced the shogger good an' proper."

"Well, I suppose you won't be peeling my spuds now that you're a made man," Dougan said.

Buck's mouth was working but no sounds came out. Finally, he thrust the purse in his pocket and grabbed the peeler. "Don't worry, I'll do the spuds, Chef. I ain't proud or nothing. And anyhow, we got appearances to keep up, ain't we? Don't wanna blow our cover just because I'm minted."

"You keep telling yourself that, Fargin," Dougan said. "But you don't get them spuds ready for Rollingfield's dinner, the only appearance you'll be keeping up is that of a bloated water-corpse, got it?"

"Yeah, right."

Chef grabbed a hefty iron pan, and Buck instinctively threw his hands up.

"All right, I got it. I don't never get no bleeding respect in this dump. Just you wait and see," he mumbled. "Buck Fargin's going places, then you'll get what's coming to you." He picked up a potato and pressed the blade to it. "Shit!" he yelled, putting his finger to his mouth and sucking on it. "Bleeding cut myself!"

FOUR

Two Red Cloaks surged into the cell, spears leveled. For a split second, the Nameless Dwarf thought they were demons, but it was a memory, a fleeting glimpse of horror. They were dwarves sure enough.

He turned the eye-slit of the great helm on them and they both took a step back. Three more dwarves slipped through the doorway and moved to his flanks.

Outside in the corridor, voices were raised, in among them Thumil's. "It's all right, Captain. He's all right. No, that won't be necessary. Did you hear me? I said no."

A burly dwarf with a salt-and-pepper beard and a horned helm pushed his way inside, a double-bladed axe over one shoulder. The Nameless Dwarf knew him: Captain Stolhok, a decent enough dwarf by any standard. Stolhok would have made a much better choice for Thumil's replacement as marshal than that pervert Mordin. More memories, knitting together, weaving the texture of his life. But there were patches of nothingness, and none so void as the memory of his name.

"Captain Stolhok!" Thumil yelled, but his voice was cut off by the slamming of the cell door.

Stolhok looked different: There was a grim set to his jaw, and his eyes conveyed nothing but loathing. That should have come as no surprise. Stolhok commanded a platoon of Red Cloaks. He would have lived through the massacre in the ravine.

Guilt and shame rose up to engulf the Nameless Dwarf, and he turned his back on the captain.

"What'f up, fogger," Stolhok said with his appalling lisp, "fcared to fafe a real dwarf?"

Boots scuffed on stone behind the Nameless Dwarf. A rush of air. Instinctively, he spun round and crashed an elbow into Stolhok's nose. The captain had swung for him with his axe.

Stolhok's knees buckled, and he went down. Blood spurted from his ruined nose. The Nameless Dwarf's hand snaked out to catch the axe before it hit the ground. He turned it over as he appraised it, while Zaylus watched him, open-mouthed. A fair weapon, nicely balanced. But it was no substitute for the Axe of the Dwarf Lords he'd once possessed—if, indeed, that's what it had been.

He recognized the pull of desire. It was the same as when he craved a flagon of mead at the end of the day. But in this case, it wasn't a healthy need for the *Paxa Boraga*: it was a compulsion, and it sent shivers beneath his skin.

The semicircle of spears shook, and worried looks passed between the Red Cloaks.

"Now look here," one of them said. "We don't want no trouble."

"Just put the axe down and move to the bench," another said. "No one needs to get hurt."

The Nameless Dwarf slapped the haft of the axe into his palm, and the Red Cloaks backed away against the walls.

"Don't know about you, laddie," he said to Zaylus, "but I'm parched as a parrot. Quick flagon down at Bucknard's Beer Hall, then I'll take you over to the *ocras* mines. How's that sound?"

He strode toward the door, but a guard darted in and took a jab at him.

The Nameless Dwarf swept the axe down, and the spear tip clattered to the floor. The Red Cloak was left staring at the splintered shaft in his hands.

The other Red Cloaks started to edge forward, thought better of it, and stayed where they were.

"Shog," the Nameless Dwarf said, pounding the side of the

ocras helm with his fist. "How am I going to drink in this bucket?" He turned on the Red Cloaks. "Any of you lads know a good blacksmith?"

They all exchanged looks.

"That won't help," Zaylus said. "The helm is fused to your skin."

The Nameless Dwarf ran his fingers along the seam connecting the helm to the base of his neck. Course it was. "Bloody shogging bastard philosopher," he said, shoving the door open and stepping out into the corridor. "I'll rip his girlie beard off when I get my hands on him."

A dozen spears thrust at him. He twisted past two, batted a third aside with Stolhok's axe, and hacked down. Someone screamed, and a hand flopped to the floor, fingers still wriggling.

"Sorry," the Nameless Dwarf said, wincing. He hadn't meant to do that.

A spear glanced off his chainmail. Another grazed his shoulder. He roared and swung with the flat of the axe, and the Red Cloaks scurried back.

Someone sounded a trumpet—short, desperate blasts.

Movement from behind caused him to pivot. Through the eye-slit of the helm, he could see the Red Cloaks in the cell were creeping closer with leveled spears. Zaylus stepped in front of them, manacled hands raised.

"Out of the way," one of them snarled, "or we'll gut you like a hog."

Seeing their opportunity, the Red Cloaks in the corridor surged forward, and the Nameless Dwarf spun back to face them.

Four guards went down to the flat of his axe, but a spear broke a link on his chainmail, and another glanced off the helm. Beyond his attackers, he caught sight of Thumil's white robe.

He hammered the flat of the axe into a horned helm, and the Red Cloak wearing it crumpled. A bristling wall of spears came at him. It was too close to what had happened before, he realized, when he'd thought he was facing wave after wave of red-winged demons and he'd plowed through them like a reaper with a scythe.

"Don't hurt him," Thumil cried. "He's using the flat."

D.P. PRIOR

"Not on my shogging wrist, he didn't!"

Zaylus backed into the doorway, dragging a Red Cloak with him. He had the chain connecting his stone manacles around the dwarf's neck and was using him as a shield. He shoved the Red Cloak back into the cell then slammed the door shut and slid a bolt across.

Heavy footfalls pounded down the corridor to the left, and that seemed to give the other Red Cloaks renewed courage.

"Come on, lads, we can take him," one yelled, and lunged with his spear. It struck the Nameless Dwarf in the guts but lacked the force to penetrate his armor.

"Laddie, I'm trying to give you a chance," the Nameless Dwarf said. He took hold of the spear shaft and yanked the Red Cloak forward so he could butt him in the face with the great helm.

"Stop!" Thumil cried, waving his arms from behind the dozen standing spearmen. "Please stop!"

The spearmen started to pull back.

"You'll do no such thing!"

Another white-robed councilor came into view at the head of a column of Red Cloaks with shields and swords.

"Kill him, and anyone who gets in the way."

"Grago," Thumil said. "You don't have the authority."

At a nod from Grago, a couple of Black-Cloaked Svarks emerged from the pack and escorted Thumil to one side.

The Nameless Dwarf backed up against the door beside Zaylus. "Crouch down and put your hands on the ground."

He raised the axe and brought it down, shearing straight through the chains.

Zaylus reached for a spear, changed his mind and took a dagger from the belt of an unconscious Red Cloak.

"Ready?" The Nameless Dwarf stepped away from the door.

Chainmail jingled and swords glinted in the dim light coming off the dust-covered glowstones set into the ceiling. The newly arrived Red Cloaks were packed four abreast, with shields locked, and shog only knew how many ranks deep.

"Ready," Zaylus said, turning the dagger over and over in his hand.

The Red Cloaks' shield wall retained its cohesion as they surged forward, absorbing the spearmen into their ranks.

"One…" The Nameless Dwarf rolled his shoulders.

The Red Cloaks roared, hammering swords against shields.

"Two…"

Thunder boomed, flames flashed, and smoke billowed.

A dark-haired woman—a human—stepped out of the churning brume. She wore a dirty white robe with the same red symbol as on Zaylus's surcoat.

"Rutha!" Zaylus cried.

A tiny man appeared behind her, delivering concussive blasts with some sort of wand. He had to be a faen; he was no taller than a dwarf child, and like a ghost he was part in, part out of reality. All the Nameless Dwarf could see were his pale hands and face, his pink eyes. The faen was wearing a concealer cloak.

The woman—Rutha—grabbed Zaylus's arm. "Let's go," she said

Whatever it was that shot from the faen's wand pinged from shields and sent up shards of stone from the floor. A few blasts got through, and blood sprayed.

Red Cloaks shouted and screamed, and then they started to scatter.

"Friends," Zaylus told the Nameless Dwarf. "Come with us."

They ran back the way Rutha and the faen had come, which took them deeper into the ravine. The only way out down there was the portal beneath the Sag-Urda, the lake at the foot of the ravine, and that was one place the Nameless Dwarf didn't ever want to see again.

"Back the other way," he said. "There are only fifty Red Cloaks, give or take. We can handle them."

"Someone shut scuttle-head up," the faen said. "I'm trying to concentrate." He ran his hands over the wall, muttering and cursing. "It was here. I bloody know it was here."

"After them!" Grago's voice rolled down the corridor, and it was followed by the tramp of boots on stone.

"Sure that's only fifty?" Rutha asked, casting a worried look over her shoulder.

The Nameless Dwarf saw what the faen was looking for, pushed past him, and stepped right through the wall.

He found himself in an entirely different corridor that wound its way up. It was a part of the ravine he'd not had access to before, but it was starting to become clear. The sense that told a dwarf where he was underground, where the air came from, and where the nearest point of egress was, told him they were inside the walls of the ravine, and not as far down as he had assumed—perhaps only a level or two below the Dokon.

He popped his head back through the wall.

"How the pissing Abyss did you—?" the faen started.

"Old miner's trick my pa taught me. Coming?"

His pa had told him how the dwarves had inherited a handful of ghost walls, if not the lore to create them, from the faen back in the distant past. You'd have thought this pale-faced midget would have seen it a mile off.

They followed him through the ghost wall, and Rutha led them along a maze of twists and turns and up a steepening incline. When they arrived at a door of rough-hewn rock, the faen produced a sliver of stone and broke it into two halves. It was one of the keys the Svarks used to access their secret places. More faen lore that was denied to the regular citizens of Arx Gravis.

The door began to grind its way upward, letting in a blast of fresh air from the walkway. The faen ducked into the widening gap and stepped over a black bundle as the others followed him outside.

They were on the top tier of the city, with nothing overhead save for clear blue sky. Beneath them were twenty-one more levels of platforms and intersecting walkways surrounding the great tower of the Aorta that rose from the foot of the ravine. The twin suns were at their zenith, causing the Nameless Dwarf to shield his eyes and blink. When he could see again, he was staring at the black bundle on the ground.

It was a cloak, small enough for a dwarf child. Or a faen. And it was covering something.

He reached down and pulled away an edge of the fabric.

Dead eyes stared up at him from a bearded face.

"Nice," Rutha said. "That your handiwork, Shadrak?"

The faen scowled.

"Laddie?"

The concealer cloak whipped up behind the faen in the gusting wind, taking on the blue of the sky, the grey of the ravine wall. He had to have taken it from the dead dwarf and left his own cloak to cover the body. Sunlight glinted from the blades nestled in his baldrics, and a pallid hand crept toward one.

The Nameless Dwarf set his axe head on the walkway and folded his hands atop the haft. "I can't blame you for not knowing, laddie, but this city's seen more than its fair share of blood."

"Not my problem," the faen said. "You don't like it, then sod off. I didn't ask you to tag along."

"I did," Zaylus said. "He can help us get into the tunnels from the mines."

The Nameless Dwarf swung his axe up onto his shoulder. "But no more killing, agreed?"

"You telling me how to do my job?" the faen said.

Zaylus glanced back at the entranceway. "Were you planning on closing that?"

"Bollocks," the faen said. He fumbled his two pieces of stone back together, and the door started to descend.

"So, who are you?" Rutha asked the Nameless Dwarf.

"Good question, lassie."

"They call him the Nameless Dwarf," Zaylus said.

"Sounds like one of the poxy monikers the journeymen are always coming up with," the faen said. "Twats."

"It's no worse than Shadrak the Unseen," Rutha said.

Now there was a shifty name for a shifty shogger. Presumably being unseen was an asset in the faen's line of work, which all the evidence indicated wasn't likely an honest trade.

As they reached the hub of four intersecting walkways, the grind of stone on stone caused them to look behind. The door they had come out of was once again rising, and booted feet could be seen in the widening gap at the bottom.

"Here," Shadrak said to Zaylus, unbuckling one of his baldrics. It slid free—in reality a sword belt, with a scabbarded shortsword that had been concealed on the faen's back, beneath his cloak. "Thought you might want it back."

"You found it?" Zaylus asked.

"Locked in a storeroom outside Rutha's cell."

"I should never have let the dwarves take it from me," Zaylus said, accepting the sword belt reverently and buckling it around his waste.

"Right," Shadrak said, "which way, Nameless?" There was scorn in his voice, but nevertheless…

"Nameless?" the Nameless Dwarf said. "I like it."

"I haven't got all bleeding day," the faen said.

Nameless pointed toward the archway on a plaza near the center of the tier. "Past the bald bastard and keep going till we reach the ravine wall."

"Bald bastard?" Zaylus said.

All eyes turned to look where Nameless was pointing. Judging by their sour expressions, they recognized the philosopher standing there just as much as he did.

Aristodeus.

FIVE

Finally!
After all these centuries, it was happening. The Unweaving was well and truly underway.

Sektis Gandaw felt the resistance in his taut face relent. He'd grown so used to its mask-like rigor as to not notice, but now he felt a tug on his cheeks, the curling of his shriveled lips. He imagined warmth suffusing his desiccated flesh like he was sure it once had. Useless sensation, useless emotional response. The sort of thing he had no time for. The sort of thing that would have no place in *his* universe. But he couldn't deny it; despite centuries of unrelenting discipline, damping down the slightest surge of passion, he was satisfied, content, a little elated even.

No doubt deserved, he acknowledged, as he shut the feeling down with a mental command that triggered the release of equilibrating potions via a hundred pinpricks that barely registered, so scarred up and hardened were the injection sites. There was an entire apothecary built into the *ocras* armor he wore like a second skeleton. Indeed, it had become his only skeleton—the only thing holding him together—given that the original had long since crumbled into dust.

"Finally," he said out loud, wholly approving of the detached monotone that emerged. It had begun. Endless series of meticulous calculations, hundreds of years of hunting for the Statue of Etala that had been craftily hidden from him since his last attempt at the

Unweaving had been thwarted by the turncoat dwarf, Maldark and his allies. Only he could have done it. Only he had the patience, the fortitude, the scrupulous attention to detail that could deconstruct the entire chaotic cosmos save for his mountain base. Sparing this island of imperfection irked him somewhat, but it was a necessary flaw that would be remedied once his creation had taken root. As soon as all else was stable, running smoothly according to his own faultless laws, he planned to move beyond the Mountain of Ocras and watch as it was the last thing to be unwoven.

He steepled his fingers in front of his mouth, eyes glancing over the symbols dancing across the dark mirror on his desktop. This time when he smiled, he did nothing to check it.

The patterns flickering before him on the mirror were old friends, his children, his collaborators in dismantling and rebuilding. He knew each of them intimately. He'd pared them down, permutated them, checked and revised them every day, every week, every month, year after year after year. No one else could say they had done that. No alchemist, no philosopher, no other sorcerer could ever say that each and every single element of their work was absolutely perfect, absolutely necessary and fit for purpose. Seeing the patterns of the Unweaving running like this, active and fulfilling their function, was as satisfying as it could get. The figures had moved beyond what they symbolized and now actualized what they stood for, all because he had unraveled the secrets of the goddess Etala, worked out how to harness her power.

He tensed at the renewed attack of the nagging thought that he hadn't created the serpent goddess, so his cosmos wouldn't really be created out of nothing, would it? And, of course, he wouldn't be his own creation either, would he?

He thumped down on the desk and then leaned back in his chair as more injected potions restored his equilibrium. The patterns continued their procession across the mirror. All perfect. So absolutely...

Wait, is that an ellipsis out of place?

It couldn't be. Impossible. He had scoured the patterns with infinitesimal scrutiny, again and again and again. There was no error. Inconceivable. That was the problem with smiling, with giving an inch to the slightest shred of emotion: it opened a crack on imperfection, on self-doubt. This time, when he smiled, it was willed entirely, a sardonic smirk that put such human thinking back in its place.

Nevertheless, he had to see.

He knew the patterns so well that they played through his mind as he left the room and took the elevator down to the hollowed-out core of the mountain. Stepping through the sliding doors, he expected to see the banks of mirrors that wound their way to the summit of the conical chamber ablaze with images. His jaw may have actually dropped, and for an instant his mind went blank, scattering the numbers and symbols into confused streams of verbiage.

"Mephesch!" he yelled into the dark. "Put the mirrors on!"

In the poor light, he could just make out the motionless forms of meldings bent over their inert mirrors, bat-wings cloaking them, and then the diminutive shapes of faen scurrying about the walkways.

A hum and a sparkle of amber, and there hung the serpent statue from the array of pulsing tendrils that connected it to the heart of the Mountain of Ocras. There was a sound like a roaring wind, and the statue swelled to ten times its size, its eyes flaring red, its fangs jags of lightning. Just as quickly, there was a hiss like a sigh, and the statue contracted to its normal dimensions, scarcely more than a foot in height. A crackle of amber burst along the tendrils and then all went dead.

"It's a bit glitchy," Mephesch said. The faen slunk away from the wall and strolled up to the statue.

Sektis gasped, then winced as a thousand needles jabbed him to restore his poise.

"Glitchy?"

"Nothing to worry about." Mephesch gave the serpent statue a slap, and its eyes flared once more as the tendrils festooning it flickered with amber light. "Not quite perfect, but it'll do."

"Not quite what?" Sektis said.

"What I mean is—"

"Then make it perfect! I haven't labored all these centuries to have some ignorant bloody faen botch my power source."

Mephesch grimaced and gave a slight bow. "I think she's putting up a fight."

"Impossible!"

The faen looked from Sektis to the serpent statue. "I agree. Theoretically impossible, but sometimes things just can't be explained."

"Rubbish! You merely ascribe to mystery that which you have not investigated thoroughly enough." Sektis jabbed a finger at Mephesch. "There is an error in the patterns, an error that can only have been introduced by one of your people."

"But we followed your instructions to the—"

"Find it, Mephesch. Find it now."

Mephesch turned to look at the radiant statue. "Seems to be fine now. Like I said, just a glitch."

Sektis narrowed his eyes, but he had to admit, it did seem to be working again. Did it really matter if there had been a mishap? Surely, if everything was working as it should now, it could still be perfect.

"What happened to the mirrors?" He switched his gaze to the walkways, where the bat-meldings stared at blackness. "Why aren't they working?"

"Not enough power," Mephesch said. "Virtually everything we have is being routed through the statue. We were certain you'd want to hit critical mass as soon as possible."

Sektis let out a hissing sigh. "Is that what I said?"

The faen's shoulders rose to cover his ears, giving the impression his head was sinking into his torso. "I assumed the mirrors were now redundant, what with the patterns being so infallible."

"Are you trying to be funny?"

"No, I merely thought that—"

"Turn them on, Mephesch. Now."

"Even if we have to slow things down?"

"Even if," Sektis said. "I've waited thousands of years, and I'm not about to rush things now. Come on, I want to see this."

Mephesch leaned over to the nearest desk and ran his hand

over a bank of crystals. The amber net holding the statue flickered and then stabilized. Red lights blinked into being, bathing the batmeldings in a hellish glow. The mirror to the left on the bottom level flashed on, showing the contents of its scrying: a panoramic view of arctic wastes. The mirrors to the right followed in rapid succession all around the circumference of the chamber. The awakening continued on the other tiers, each lightening mirror displaying a different location on the surface of Aosia, until finally the single overhead mirror 55 flickered to life and the Void yawned its terrible mysteries straight at Sektis. He looked away, feeling suddenly weak and foolish. When the pinpricks failed to activate, he asserted his will, ordered the potions to release. The *ocras* armor emitted a whir and a sputter, but nothing happened.

Empty!

"I don't believe it!" Sektis whined, spinning on his heels. He pulled open his coat, revealing the bandolier of empty vials crossing the front of his armor. "Piece of shit! I need my potions, Mephesch. I need them right now."

Mephesch snapped his fingers and one of the other faen melded with the wall. Quick as a flash, the faen walked back through the wall clutching a box of refills. Sektis spread his arms so that the creature could discard the old vials and fit the new. Within seconds a wave of calm washed over him. He was so relieved he almost thanked the faen.

Almost, but not quite.

SIX

The philosopher stood on the far side of the arch, toga flapping in the wind, a leather satchel on one shoulder. He was turning a sword with a curved blade over and over in his hands.

A shudder ripped through Nameless. He wanted nothing more than to hurl the bald bastard from the walkway. The violence of his reaction shocked him.

Shadrak pulled his concealer cloak tight until only his hands and eyes were visible. The rest of him was like the blurring of the sky, an undulation of the walkway.

"Now this I wasn't expecting," Aristodeus said as they approached. "The Nameless Dwarf. You weren't supposed to awaken without…" His eyes flitted to Zaylus. "Ah, of course. Well, this changes things," he said to Nameless. "A moment, please!" he yelled over their heads.

Nameless turned to see Grago emerge from the ravine wall at the front of the Red Cloaks. Thumil pushed through beside him.

More doors were opening all around the level, and from one came a group of white-robed councilors. Cordy was with them, her blond hair and beard making her stick out like gold in gravel. She flicked an anxious look Nameless's way, but it was to Thumil she ran.

"What do you mean, 'of course'?" Zaylus said. "He wasn't meant to awaken without what?"

"The philosopher's voice," Thumil said, as he drew near, hand in hand with Cordy. "Only Aristodeus's voice could break the spell."

"Must be the accent," Aristodeus said. "No other explanation for it. Dear old Vanatus, eh, Zaylus? Starting to miss the Empire yet?"

Zaylus frowned.

"Accent or no accent," Nameless said, "I've a bone to pick with you, laddie."

He took a step toward Aristodeus, but Rutha barged past him. "That's mine," she said.

The philosopher raised an eyebrow, an enigmatic smile tugging at the corner of his mouth. Then he reversed the curved sword and handed it to her. "You should be more careful where you leave it. Standard issue Vanatusian cavalry saber. Shouldn't you have handed it in when they discharged you?"

With a sullen scowl, Rutha slid the saber into the scabbard hanging from her belt.

"Now what was it about a bone you had to pick?" Aristodeus said.

Nameless tapped the side of his helm. "It's taking things a bit far when I can't get this shogging thing off, even for a beer."

"I'm sorry," Aristodeus said, producing a pipe and popping the stem in his mouth. "But you're not out of the woods yet. If we remove the helm prematurely, you might still be vulnerable to the axe."

"Do you still have it, or did you give it to the faen?" Nameless asked.

"Don't worry yourself about that. I'm sure you have enough on your plate right now." The philosopher patted his toga. "Anyone have a light? No, of course not." He sighed and thrust his pipe away.

"What about eating?" Nameless said. "A dwarf needs meat and bread and steaming bowls of salty broth. I'm already losing muscle!"

"I'll come up with something," Aristodeus said. "I hadn't expected you to be awake just yet."

Councilor Grago pushed his way past and jabbed a finger at Aristodeus. He was flanked by a pair of Black Cloaks. "You, sir, have some explaining to do."

"I do?"

"You gave us reassurances that this… butcher would never awaken, and yet here he is. You have placed us all at risk."

"What do you propose to do about that, Grago?" Thumil asked.

"Arrest Aristodeus?"

"I hadn't thought of that," Grago said with a sly grin. He waved the two Svarks forward, but Thumil stopped them with a raised hand.

"Then you will have to arrest me too," Thumil said. "Because I agreed with Aristodeus's plan to put the Nameless Dwarf into an unnatural slumber rather than kill him."

"There was a vote!" Cordy said. "It wasn't just you that agreed."

"Aye, lass, but as Voice I could have used my veto. Well, Grago?"

All around the connecting walkways, Red Cloaks were forming up into tightly packed shield walls, the odd Black Cloak among them.

The two Svarks with Grago exchanged nervous looks, and behind them the Red Cloaks had come to a halt twenty paces away. Marshal Mordin stood in the front rank, watching Thumil, waiting for the word. If it came to a showdown, the Svarks would support Grago, but the Ravine Guard would be loyal to Thumil, who had led them for so long.

Grago probably realized as much and backed down. "The Black Cloaks stand ready to follow your lead, my Lord Voice."

Thumil gave him a curt nod.

"Are you…?" Cordy started, edging nearer to Nameless. "How do you feel?"

"Lassie," Nameless acknowledged her, feeling suddenly self-conscious in the great helm. "Back to my old self."

"Really?" Cordy's eyes glistened with moisture.

"No," Nameless said. "No, I'm not. But I'm starting to remember things. I remember you, Cordana Kilderkin."

MOUNTAIN OF MADNESS

"That's good," Cordy said, and tears were tracking down her cheeks now.

"I trusted you, lassie. Trusted you enough to let Baldilocks here put the helm on me. I think I wanted to be stopped. For good."

"And so you damned well should be," Grago said.

Weapons clashed against shields in affirmation, and Thumil's eyes widened in shock. It was the Red Cloaks showing that they agreed with Grago on this. The Red Cloaks Nameless had once served with. The Red Cloaks he had later killed in their hundreds.

"Hear, hear," someone cried. It came from among the white-robed members of the Council of Twelve.

Nameless recognized Old Moary, the very definition of indecisiveness. He saw Castail, Tor Garnil, bespectacled Dorley, and they all looked like grim, unforgiving judges.

Grago beckoned to a Black Cloak in among the reds, and within moments, a knot of Ravine Guard started to advance. This time when Thumil held up his hand, they paid him no heed.

Shadrak pointed his wand at the sky. There was a crack of thunder, and smoke plumed from the tip. The Red Cloaks stopped dead in their tracks.

"Calm," Aristodeus said. "For goodness' sake let calm prevail. You're supposed to be dwarves. You're supposed to be indecisive, afraid to act, and yet here you all are acting like a lynch mob. Now listen. All of you, just settle down and listen. I set wards about the Nameless Dwarf so that I would be alerted if anything went wrong and he awakened. That is why I am here, and you'll note I did not delay."

That was the thing about Aristodeus, Nameless thought: always popping up all over the place, but never showing any sign of fatigue from his journey, and no wear or tear on his toga or sandals.

"Everything is under control," the philosopher said. "There is no need for concern."

"No need for concern?" Grago said. "The Ravine Butcher is awake and you said he wouldn't be. Now you expect us to believe that you have control over him?"

"I do not," Aristodeus said. "He is his own dwarf."

51

"He's a criminal, a murderer!" someone among the Red Cloaks yelled. Marshal Mordin spun round to see who it was.

"He massacred his own kind," Grago said. "And that cannot go unpunished."

"And he has been punished," Thumil said. "I mean, is being punished."

"Not if he's awake," Grago said. "Not if he's roaming free. And if you ask me, not if he's still breathing."

"Councilors," Aristodeus said, "this is not the time."

"Not the time?" Grago said. "Not the time?"

"What I mean is," Aristodeus said tightly, "there is a more pressing matter."

"More pressing?"

"Are you going to repeat everything I say, Councilor Grago?" Aristodeus said. "I do hope not. That kind of thing I find quite tedious. Already we have wasted enough time, and time is not something any of us have much left of. If you don't let these people go"—he indicated Zaylus, Rutha and the faen, Shadrak—"the worlds will be unmade, and if there is anyone left to tell the tale, which I sincerely doubt, your names will be cursed for all eternity. Rather than getting in the way, you should be doing all you can to prevent the Unweaving of all things."

"That, sir, is heresy, and you know it," Council Garnil said. "It was acting that brought us to the brink of doom before. That is why we can do nothing. Every step we take into the affairs of the world may be a snare of Mananoc."

"Yes, yes, yes," Aristodeus said. "So, you don't even ask someone to pass the mustard in case it's a trap. I thought Lukar was getting through to you, but then you went and had him killed."

Lukar! That was it: Nameless's brother. At least the helm hadn't stripped Lukar's name from existence. And then he remembered Lukar's screams, his flesh flayed from the bone as he was consumed by the seethers of Aranuin.

"It was Lukar's action that led to the finding of the black axe," Grago said.

Nameless lurched into motion, and every dwarf in the ravine seemed to flinch. More memories bloomed from Grago's accusation, and he said, "Lukar found mention of the *Pax Boraga* in the *Chronicles*, in a passage he thought was historical."

"And he was duped," Aristodeus said sadly. "I tried to warn him."

"Which is why we have the code of non-action," Old Moary said. "Even our histories cannot be trusted. The theory, as I understand it, is that a faen planted reference to the axe in the *Chronicles*, hoping that someone would be foolish enough to go looking for it."

"Lukar was no fool," Nameless growled. "Or if he was, he was a fool for hope. Hope that the axe was a link to a glorious past, something we could take pride in so that we might once more move beyond the ravine."

Through my boys, his pa had said, *the dwarves would become like the dwarf lords of legend.*

"Tell that to the families of those you slaughtered, Butcher," Grago said. "I think we can all see where this is leading."

"I haven't finished," Nameless said. "Lukar only sought the Axe of the Dwarf Lords, but you actually did something, Grago. You sent assassins, who fed him to the seethers. Besides leaving the city, Lukar didn't get to act. You got there first. If you hadn't killed my brother, I would never have completed his work for him. There's no telling how differently things would have worked out then. Lukar was no warrior, so I doubt he'd have made much of a butcher. My point is, you were prepared to act then, but what about now?" He turned the helm's eye-slit on the rest of the Council. "What are you willing to do?"

"Oh, we need to start acting all right," Grago said, "but in accord with our own reasoning. Our own agenda. I've been saying this for years, and yet it's fallen on deaf ears. Certainty of purpose, a clear vision of who we are and what we want is long overdue."

Aristodeus took his pipe back out and rapped the bowl against the stone of the archway until he had everyone's attention. "Whether any of you accept it or not, the mad sorcerer, Sektis Gandaw, has in his possession the Statue of Etala. Even as we speak, he is commencing the Unweaving."

All eyes looked to the sky. Besides a few soaring buzzards,

there was nothing but an expanse of blue and the glaring orbs of Aosia's two suns.

"Then why are we still here?" Grago asked. "What's taking so long?"

"It is not a fast process," Aristodeus said, "unpicking every thread of Creation. And besides, I am reliably informed that Gandaw's plans have been set back. My guess is we have a few days, a week at most, and then a great big nothing. When the lights come back on, assuming they do, Gandaw will be at the center of his own universe, and I doubt very much any of us will be perfect enough to feature in it."

"So, what are we expected to do?" Councilor Castail asked. "Trust you again, even after you told us the Ravine Butcher could only be awakened by your voice?"

"Do nothing," Zaylus said. "Just keep out of our way. Is it not action to prevent our going?"

The councilors turned to each other, clearly confounded.

"We only need to enter the mines," Zaylus said, "so that we can travel to the roots of the Mad Sorcerer's mountain. All action will be ours, not yours."

Aristodeus was grinning from ear to ear.

Grago took a stranglehold on his beard and shook his head. "Clever. Very clever. But is it not the case that willful non-action is itself still an action, albeit a negative one? No, my brother councilors, we cannot let them go, for in doing so, we may still be found culpable."

"That's illogical, incoherent, and idiotic, Grago," Aristodeus said.

"You're wasting your breath, laddie," Nameless said.

"I agree with Councilor Grago," Councilor Bley said, jowls wobbling. "But it's more than a case of willful non-action. If we allow these people to enter the mines, we are, in effect, opening the mines to them. We need no more complicated argument. We are prohibited by our own laws from granting outsiders admittance, are we not?"

"Balderdash!" Aristodeus said.

Thumil shrugged. "An excellent point, Councilor Bley, which

leaves us with only one solution."

Expectant eyes turned on him, and Thumil seemed to grow in stature.

"If we prevent them from leaving, we are guilty of the act of preventing."

Begrudging nods of agreement.

"If we admit them to the mines, we are guilty of the act of admittance."

Vigorous nodding this time.

"So, what are you going to do if we ignore you and enter the mines anyway?" Shadrak said, a wicked smirk on his face.

"Then you would be forcing us to act in preservation of the law," Thumil said. "And if we are forced, we cannot be held culpable. Marshal Mordin."

"My Lord Voice?" The hard-faced pervert stepped forward and saluted.

"Send two platoons to see no one enters the *ocras* mines."

Zaylus shook his head as the marshal issued commands and a ripple of troop movement ran across the walkways. "And I thought you had a modicum of common—"

Thumil held up a finger. "You are free to go, so long as you steer clear of the mines."

"Are you an imbecile, Thumil?" Aristodeus said. "Don't think you dwarves are safe from the Unweaving. It affects everyone. Everything!"

"Sod him," Shadrak said. "Let's go it alone."

"But you saw those silver spheres patrolling Gandaw's mountain," Zaylus said. "How are we going to get inside?"

"Buggered if I know," Shadrak said. "Raise an army?"

"You could always try Jeridium," Nameless said. Everyone knew it was the biggest city in Medryn-Tha. "They must have a fair few legions."

"Actually," Aristodeus said, "that's not such a bad idea. Take an army. Storm the mountain. So long as there's time."

Zaylus said, "It's quicker if you go. Magic yourself there, or whatever it is you do."

Aristodeus shook his head. "Can't do that. I need to prepare for other contingencies. And besides, the Senate of Jeridium and I don't exactly see eye to eye."

"What contingencies?" Rutha said. "The way I see it, we're running out of options."

"There are always options, my dear," Aristodeus said. "And this business goes much deeper than our current threat from Sektis Gandaw. We must stay one step ahead of the enemy at all times."

Zaylus sucked in a breath through clenched teeth. "All right," he said. "How far to Jeridium?"

"A couple of days?" Aristodeus said.

Zaylus caught Rutha's eye, but she scowled and looked away.

Aristodeus arched an eyebrow. "Why don't you come with me, Rutha?"

"And why would I do that?"

"If our nameless friend here is traveling to Jeridium, he's going to need feeding—he can't eat in the normal way, not with that helm on. I could use some help gathering my apparatus and taking them on ahead to the city."

"Screw you."

"And there are other matters—these contingencies I mentioned. Indulge me."

Rutha shot a venomous look at Zaylus. "Fine. Anything's got to be better than this."

Aristodeus held out his arm and she took it. Then the philosopher produced a drawstring purse from his toga and passed it to Nameless. "In case you need money. I assume they still use the same coinage. When you get to Jeridium, go to the Academy. Ask for Master Quilth."

"Quilth?"

"Just ask for him. I'll meet you there and make sure you don't starve. Mark my words," he said loud enough for the councilors to hear. "The day is coming when you will thank me for preserving this kinsman of yours. He's special, this one, and if I can only set him on the right track, he could yet prove our greatest weapon."

"Never been called a weapon before," Nameless said. "Except maybe once, but she was a feral lassie from the Sag-Urda wharfs."

Without warning, green light swirled about Aristodeus and

Rutha, and they vanished.

A confusion of emotions played across Zaylus's face.

Thumil gestured toward the top of the ravine. "Go now, before they come up with another objection."

Zaylus and Shadrak started along the walkway, as if they expected the dwarves to change their mind. Nameless hefted the axe he'd taken from Captain Stolhok and made to follow.

"This is exile, Butcher," Grago said. "Are we at least agreed on that, my Lord Voice?" He turned to gauge the reaction of the other councilors, and they all nodded. "Well?"

Thumil glanced at Cordy, and she closed her eyes as she bobbed her head. Nameless couldn't blame them. What choice did they have?

"Agreed," Thumil said.

Nameless put a hand on Thumil's shoulder. "Thank you, laddie," he said.

Thumil frowned in confusion.

"For being my friend," Nameless said. "You, too, lassie," he told Cordy.

And then he turned his back on them, on Arx Gravis, and the only life he had ever known.

SEVEN

The clangor of a kitchen at full tilt, the odor of hard labor, the aroma of cooking! It was enough to bring tears to a grown man's eyes. Yes, the sous-chef was more suited to bricklaying, the washer-upper needed a rough mama to scrub behind his ears, and the waiter was... well, the waiter was the greasiest toe-rag of the lot.

Right on cue, Buck Fargin shouldered his way through the swinging doors, plates and bowls stacked high in his hands, held steady by his chin.

"All pucker out there," he said, depositing the crockery on the side. "Ol' Rollypolly's slurping it up like there's no tomorrow."

"Rollingfield," Albrec said, wiping his hands on his apron. "Senator Rollingfield. So, he likes my terrine?"

"*Your* terrine?" Buck said. "Chef Dougan's, you mean."

Albrec didn't know how to break it to him, but what they'd served the senator was as far removed from Dougan's rancid concoction as a lace hanky from a snot rag.

"After taking my tincture, Chef went for a little lie down, and during the hiatus I took it upon myself to—"

"Farryl!" a booming voice sounded from the restaurant. "Farryl Dougan, you steaming offal of a man." The doors swung open and in burst the senator, capacious toga speckled with tomato sauce. "I don't know how you've done it, but you've excelled yourself." Rollingfield's gelatinous jowls wobbled as he turned his piggy

MOUNTAIN OF MADNESS

eyes on Albrec. "Where's that arse Dougan?"

"Having a lie down, Senator," Buck said with a nauseatingly obsequious bow.

"Tell him he deserves it," the senator said. "Sterling meal. Bloody sterling. Can't believe it's the same chef."

Albrec coughed delicately into his fist. "I'm afraid it was more than a lie down, Senator. Chef Dougan was taken unexpectedly ill."

Buck took on the semblance of a startled hare. "But you said—"

Albrec threw an arm around his neck, pulled him into a fierce hug. "I wanted to tell you, Buck, truly I did, but I knew how devastated you would be."

Rollingfield's shoulders slumped, and all the pomposity went out of him. "Is he going to be all right?"

"Alas, no, Senator. He has gone ahead of us on the road to eternity. So sad. So very sad."

Buck tried to say something, but Albrec squeezed him tighter.

"Dead?" Rollingfield looked genuinely shocked.

"Which is why I had to complete the meal with my own humble hands. My tribute to an unsurpassable god of the kitchen. I trust it was tolerable."

Rollingfield looked at him closely out of one eye. It was a calculating look, shrewd. The look of a man who had played the game of politics for a very long time and could read you like a menu. When his other eye opened, there was a glint of recognition in it.

"More than tolerable... uh..."

"Albrec, Senator."

"Albrec. It's a rare talent you have there."

Something told Albrec the senator wasn't just talking about the terrine.

"Join me at my table, Albrec. We should talk. Just you, mind. And, waiter," he said to Buck, "another carafe of red."

Albrec watched the senator's cumbrous buttocks roll beneath his toga as he waddled back through to the restaurant.

"Shog," Buck said, extricating himself from Albrec's embrace, "you're in there."

"Yes," Albrec said, "I believe I am."

"But you're dead meat, all the same."

"I am?"

Buck leaned himself against the counter and puffed out his cheeks. "Chef was well liked by the guild. Right up Dozier's arse, he was."

"Dozier?"

"Guildmaster of the Night Hawks. Top dogs around here, except maybe for the Dybbuks, and they don't play fair."

Albrec chuckled at that. What a concept! "No honor among thieves, eh?"

Buck scoffed. "They ain't thieves. They're more like merchants, only they ain't exactly got the blessing of the Senate."

"With one or two exceptions, no doubt. Like our friend Rollingfield?"

"I don't know all the ins and outs of it," Buck said, "but they dine together, him and Dozier. Reckon they talk more'n they eat. That's the thing of it. They always moan about Chef's cooking, but they keep coming back."

Albrec put a hand on Buck's shoulder and injected as much sincerity as he could into his voice. "You're a shrewd man, Buck Fargin. Thank goodness I ran into you when I did." He started towards the swinging doors and cast over his shoulder, "Time for a few changes around here, don't you think?" When Buck frowned, Albrec added, "Just remember, anything that happens, anything you see me doing, is for our mutual benefit. I haven't forgotten I owe you a back-scratching. When it comes to maneuvering, I've a lifetime of practice. Keep your wits about you, Buck; be patient, and question nothing. Do that, and in a few short months, there'll be a new king on the throne."

"King? Throne?"

"You, Buck. How do you think this Dozier rose to become guildmaster? Hard work and fair play?"

Before Buck could answer, Albrec pushed through the doors into the restaurant.

Rugbeard was still there, propping up the bar. Actually, he

seemed to be sleeping, drool soaking into his beard, a half-empty flagon clutched in a limp hand.

The restaurant area was growing emptier by the second as a handful of soldiers muscled the clientele outside. The soldiers wore leather kilts, bronze cuirasses, greaves and vambraces, akin to the classical style of Vanatus several hundred years ago. They each had a shortsword hanging from a belt with a golden eagle buckle.

Complaints about unfinished meals fell on deaf ears, and Albrec couldn't help feeling somewhat aggrieved that his cooking was being discarded in the name of this thuggery. Worse still, considering his plans to run the place, these were patrons who were unlikely to come back. Rollingfield was eyeing him above the rim of a wine glass.

"Forgive my legionaries," the senator said, running his wine-stained tongue around his plump lips. "They are somewhat unimaginative in carrying out my orders. I thought it best, however, that we talked alone." He gestured for Albrec to take the seat opposite.

A soldier tapped Rugbeard on the shoulder, eliciting a loud snore.

"Leave him," Rollingfield said. "Even if he heard anything over his own din, his booze-sozzled brain would forget it in an instant." He rolled his eyes at Albrec. "Odious heap of dung. Still, he has his uses. It's a rare man who has access to the *ocras* mines above Arx Gravis."

The last of the customers was slung unceremoniously out into the street and the soldiers locked the doors and shut the blinds. Albrec's hand strayed to his pocket, seeking the reassurance of his cheese-cutter and finding only fluff.

Rollingfield guzzled down the dregs of his wine and slid the glass onto the table. He plumped up his belly and wriggled back in his chair, one eyelid drooping, the other hanging half-open like a sagging curtain. The exposed bloodshot eye roved around the tomato-smeared bread crusts he'd used to mop up the sauce on his plate. Of the terrine, there was nothing left, which Albrec took as a compliment.

"And what about me, Albrec?" the senator said, glancing at the snoring Rugbeard. "Are they going to find me face down on the table, drowned in my own vomit?" He shook his head and gave a low, gurgling chuckle.

"Senator?"

Rollingfield's eyes snapped fully open and a thin smile slashed through his puffed pillow-cheeks. "Don't worry, my friend, I feel quite safe with you. Quite safe. At least for the time being." He leaned forward, nudging the table with his belly. "I've been in this game a long time, Albrec, and I'm sure you have too. These kinds of meetings, between people such as you and I, are not uncommon now, are they?"

Straight to the point, then. Well, if that's how he wanted to play it. Albrec interlaced his fingers and pursed his lips. "No, Senator, they are not."

"I knew it!" Rollingfield clapped his pudgy hands. "Good man, Albrec. Good man. No mincing." He raised an eyebrow at that, and Albrec felt as though someone had just bathed him in sewage. "No beating around the bush."

"Perish the thought, Senator."

"So, who are you with, then?" Rollingfield asked. "The Dybbuks? The Catterwauls? No, no, let me guess. Man with your culinary skills, your bearing, your evident education… has to be with…"

"The Street-Creepers, Senator?" one of the soldiers ventured.

"Thank you, Corporal, I can finish my own sentences." Rollingfield sighed and narrowed his eyes. "Well, Albrec?"

"A small outfit, Senator. You've probably never heard of us. Not from Jeridium. Long way off."

"I see. Brink? Portis? Surely not Malfen?"

Albrec decided to say no more. He relaxed back in his chair and gave a sheepish smile.

Rollingfield tapped the side of his nose. "Say no more, my friend. Now, no one can blame you for not knowing, seeing as you're from out of town, but Dwan Dozier is not going to be happy about this. You see, Albrec, the Night Hawks have their territory, as do the Dybbuks and the smaller guilds. Chef Dougan might have been a turgid little fart serving swill to clients who wouldn't

MOUNTAIN OF MADNESS

know a ratatouille from a rat's arse, but he paid his dues."

"Protection?"

Rollingfield refilled his wine glass and proffered the carafe to Albrec. Albrec hesitated for a second then took it. "It's the way of the world," Rollingfield said. "You know that. Dougan paid the Night Hawks to keep the Dybbuks away. Nasty crew, the Dybbuks, not the sort you'd want to be dealing with. Leader's some kind of sorcerer, and his second's a shapeshifting bitch who's a devil in a knife fight. Dozier likes this place for meetings, too. Probably because no one of any note would be seen dead here."

"Surely not?" Albrec said.

"It wouldn't be good for me to be observed meeting with the guilds," Rollingfield said, "so what better place to come? Anonymity is everything in the subtler aspects of my profession."

"Quite so, Senator. Quite so."

"Every profession has its subtler regions, Albrec. Am I right?"

Albrec said nothing, happy to let the senator lay it all out for him.

"I for one would rather this establishment served decent food if I'm to be forced to meet here," Rollingfield said. "I'm something of a gastronome." He jiggled his gut for emphasis. "And I know talent when I see it. But let's come clean, Albrec, shall we? I've exposed myself to you,"—that eyebrow raise again—"now you do the same for me. Let me make it easy for you. You dabble in herbs and the like—"

"It's more than that, Senator."

"Yes, yes. You have, shall we say, expertise in the pharmaceutical arts?"

"Poisons, Senator. It's something of a passion."

Rollingfield's smile was broad, wet, and full of unsavory promise. "Excellent. You are exactly the man I hoped you were, Albrec. You'll appreciate, in my trade, from time to time it is necessary for truculent politicians to take a turn for the worse."

"It's the way of the world, Senator."

Rollingfield's laugh was coupled with a release of gas that caused him to shift his weight onto one buttock. "Pardon me. Must have been the terrine."

"My apologies, Senator."

"The way I see it, Albrec," Rollingfield said, "meetings at Dougan's Diner would be far more bearable if the food was edible. You pick up here and I'll see to it that the guild leaves you alone. I'll have my legal man switch the deeds. I don't think Dougan had any living relatives, and even if he did, leave it to me. We'll take care of that. For your part, just keep paying Dozier and you'll have no trouble. Play your cards right, and keep serving this quality of food, and I'll consider moving my offices here. Just joshing, of course, but you get my meaning. And from time to time I may have special work for you. How does that sound?"

Like a dream come true.

"Can I change the name?"

"Please do." Rollingfield stood and dusted the crumbs from his toga. "How's the weather now?"

The corporal peeked through the blinds. "Sky's turned mauve, Senator. Must be a storm coming. Twister, I'd say."

"Maybe," Rollingfield said. "All the same, best be off. I'll be seeing you, Albrec. Oh, and congratulations on becoming the new owner of… what are you going to call it?"

"Queenie's, Senator. After my dear old mama."

"Queenie's? Like it! Very good."

A soldier unlocked the door and held it open for Rollingfield to squeeze through, and the others filed out after him.

Buck slid out from the kitchen, absently wiping at a glass with a dish towel. "That seemed to go well."

Eavesdropping little dog turd. "Ah, Buck. Glad you were listening in. This Dozier you mentioned: can you set up a meeting?"

"Uh, well…"

"I thought you were a big man in the guild. Shouldn't be too much trouble for you."

Buck's face took on the semblance of a constipated donkey. "Well, you see, I'm kind of freelance. I do a bit of this, bit of that."

Thought as much. "You don't really know Dozier, do you?"

"Yeah, I do. I see him when he comes in here."

"But you don't actually know him."

Buck dropped his chin to his chest and shook his head.

"You might at least recall what he likes to eat."

"Pie and mash, but he never eats more'n a bite. Says it tastes like shite."

"Well," Albrec said, surveying his new acquisition and already planning the wall coverings, "that's all about to change."

EIGHT

Shadrak led the way up the switchback pathway cut into the ravine wall. When he reached the final incline, he sprinted the last few strides, leapt, and kicked off the rock face to land lithely at the top. With a swirl of his concealer cloak, he vanished into the brilliant blue of the noonday sky.

"That's Shadrak for you," Zaylus said, taking a breather by the high step leading up from the penultimate level. "Everyone else is an amateur to his mind. Still, given what happened down there, when Rutha and I got ourselves captured,"—he angled a nod below at the receding walkways and plazas of Arx Gravis—"he might have a point."

Nameless thought he detected a certain reluctance in Zaylus moving onwards and upwards. Shadrak had ascended the steps and inclines like a ravine goat, but Zaylus had wavered on the way up. Once or twice, he'd leaned against the ravine wall, sucking in shallow gasps of air.

"Worried about what's waiting for you up top, laddie?"

Zaylus glanced above then shook his head. "You ever feel like you're galloping on horseback and you can't get off? The horse is taking you someplace you don't want to go, but it doesn't respond when you try to make it stop?"

"I'm a dwarf," Nameless said. "I live in a ravine. A horse to me may as well be a fairy or a unicorn."

"You scuts coming, or what?" Shadrak called down from

above. His pallid face and pink eyes were there one second, gone the next.

"The little fellow's in a hurry," Nameless said.

Zaylus sighed as he turned to take the step up to the last sloping pathway. Worrying about the course of action they were taking, worrying about the Unweaving, was natural enough, but it struck Nameless that Zaylus's foot-dragging came from another cause. The knight did his best to disguise it as he climbed up, but it was starting to become obvious: Zaylus was scared of heights.

"Come on, laddie," Nameless said, following him up. "Just this last incline and we're there."

Zaylus looked green. He swayed and threw an arm out to clutch at the wall.

"I'll be right behind you," Nameless said. "You'll be in good hands. I've yet to hear of a dwarf losing his footing—except after one too many."

One careful step after the next, they inched their way to the top. And to be honest, Nameless was glad of the slow pace. Having fantasies about leaving the ravine and actually doing it were two different things. He felt the lure of the taverns, of the Slean, of home calling him back down. And he would have heeded their pull, but no matter how much he wanted his old life back, it was as gone as the name he had been stripped of.

He hadn't noticed when Zaylus climbed over the lip of the ravine without his help or support, and it startled him when the knight reached down to offer him a hand up.

Nameless felt himself teetering on the brink, literally as well as figuratively. All he had ever known, everything that defined him, lay in the city below. How could he expect to cope in the world above? How could any dwarf? The thought flitted across his mind that he should simply back to the edge of the incline and step off into the chasm. There would be a moment's terror as he plummeted toward an upper-tier walkway, maybe a split-second's pain, and then it would all be over.

"Nameless," Zaylus said. "Are you all right?"

Nameless peered through the narrow slit in his great helm, and the world came slowly into focus around the knight's piercing blue eyes—it hadn't just been the voice that had reminded him of Aristodeus: Zaylus also had the same eyes.

"Aye, I'm fine," he said, though that was far from the truth. "Tell me, Zaylus," he asked, continuing up the last stretch of the ravine pathway behind the knight, "are you and old Baldilocks related?"

"Aristodeus?" Zaylus said over his shoulder as he climbed the last step. "I certainly hope not."

And then Nameless was standing beside the knight on the grass above the ravine.

He felt vulnerable. Exposed. Zaylus must have sensed his discomfort, because he placed a steadying hand on Nameless's shoulder, then gave him the time to drink it all in.

Nameless panned the great helm left and right, piecing together the view one strip at a time through the eye-slit. Ahead, the rock-strewn ground rose in steps and ledges that burgeoned into a low range of hills. They looked like nothing so much as a cluster of tuberous growths above the *ocras* mines.

Zaylus followed his gaze and said, "The road we came by skirts those hills."

"Aye, that'll be the one the Founders built. Follow it east, and we'll reach Jeridium." With the suns directly overhead, he wasn't sure which way that was, and he said as much.

Zaylus seemed as clueless as Nameless. He looked to the left. "That's the way we came, the way to the Sour Marsh and the Mountain of Ocras."

"So, we go right, then," Nameless said, turning to face that way.

A dense mountain range rolled away toward the horizon. At the near end, it came close to the hills above the mines, and the Founders' Road entered a pass between them.

He turned again, this time to look back out across the ravine. In the far distance, he could make out what had to be the peak of Mount Sartis, the volcano his people had once tried to engineer.

"Found us some eggs," Shadrak said, startling Nameless and causing him to turn around.

The faen was a blur of movement coming from the direction of the hills. His hood was down, revealing close-cropped white hair and clipped box beard. Black rings surrounded his pink eyes, and his lips were thin, set in a permanent scowl.

Shadrak held out a pouch he had crammed full with speckled quail's eggs. The birds were regular visitors to the ravine, and their eggs made for a hearty breakfast, along with a few rinds of bacon and doorstops of toasted bread. And kaffa, of course.

Just the thought of all those succulent smells, and the bitter yet invigorating taste of freshly roasted kaffa, made Nameless's stomach rumble. And then he remembered: he couldn't take the helm off to eat.

"Not hungry, laddie. But thanks anyway."

Shadrak reattached the pouch to his belt, where half a dozen smaller pouches hung.

"Your loss." To Zaylus the faen said, "We should save them, in case there's no hunting to be had this side of Jeridium."

Zaylus nodded his agreement, and then they were off, making a beeline for the road.

Despite the patches of overgrowth, there was evidence the road was still in use. A few hours out of Arx Gravis, they took a short break beside a broken wagon wheel. There was fresh dung close by, which Zaylus identified as coming from horses.

When they passed the shoulder of the hills above the mines and entered a plain, Nameless was stunned by the wide-open spaces, and began to realize just how shut away from the world he'd been in the ravine. Everything he'd taken for reality in Arx Gravis now seemed like moonlit shadows cast on the ravine walls.

At the end of the first day, the road brought them along the shore of an inland sea. Shadrak continued on, scouting out somewhere they could camp for the night.

All that water made Nameless nervous, but he was growing increasingly aware of the blood scabbing up his arms and coating his boots and britches. Not only did it serve as a constant reminder of the things he'd done, but it would probably not go down well when they reached Jeridium.

He asked Zaylus to help him out of his chainmail hauberk, then he walked into the water until it came up to his waist. He rubbed it into his forearms, and picked away at the worst of the scabs. After a while he grew more confident, and ducked down until the water came up to his neck. Finally, he came back to shore, stripped off his clothes, and plunged back in naked, save for the *ocras* helm and the manacles on his wrists trailing lengths of chain.

When he emerged, Zaylus was wringing out his clothes for him. Nameless put them back on, still wet.

Shadrak returned and led them to a copse of ash trees set back from the bank, where he said they should rest for the night.

Off in the distance, Shadrak claimed he could see the spires of a city. Try as they might, Zaylus and Nameless could see nothing but an endless expanse of scrubland. The faen must have had eyes as keen as an eagle's, because there seemed no possible reason for him to lie.

After they had gathered deadfall and kindling, Shadrak got a fire going with his tinderbox. Nameless leaned his axe against a tree, then pulled off his boots and his sodden socks so he could rub his aching feet.

Shadrak took a quail's egg from his pouch, cracked it open on a rock, and swallowed the contents raw. When he saw Zaylus's disgusted reaction, he said, "What? You expecting an omelet?" He cracked open and ate another.

"There's something I've been meaning to ask you," Nameless said.

Shadrak rolled his pink eyes and swallowed another egg. He wiped his mouth with the back of his hand and said, "What?"

"Are you a member of the Sedition?"

"What's that?"

"Something Aristodeus mentioned—a dissident group of faen."

"You calling me a scutting faen?"

"I just thought… your size…"

"Size ain't everything," Shadrak said, as if it were a challenge.

"To the ladies it is," Nameless said, but when Shadrak scowled and looked away, he added lamely, "At least in my experience."

"Are those squirrels in the treetops?" Zaylus asked, clearly seeking to break the tension. "We used to boil them up on campaign when I was with the Seventh Horse."

MOUNTAIN OF MADNESS

"I ain't eating squirrels," Shadrak said. "Wait here, and I'll see if there's something better." Wrapping his concealer cloak around him, he was lost in the foliage.

"You want to be careful around Shadrak," Zaylus said, wincing as he popped his back.

"Oh, don't worry about me, laddie. I can more than look after myself."

Zaylus drew the shortsword Shadrak had returned to him back at the ravine, turning it over to examine the blade. It looked perfect—not a nick or blemish, and it seemed to exude a faint golden glow.

Nameless's skin crawled, and he started to tug his socks and boots back on. Zaylus's sword reminded him too much of the axe he had found in Aranuin—one minute black, the next blazing like a small sun. "You sure you know what that is, laddie?"

Zaylus gave a solemn nod. "It is called the Sword of the Archon."

"The Archon? The shogger who wants me dead?"

"He does?"

"That's what he said. He was there, Zaylus, in the Dokon, after Aristodeus put this helm on my head."

"What else did he say?"

"That I was a pawn of Mananoc. That if I lived, thousands would die."

Zaylus looked away and pinched the bridge of his nose. When he turned back to Nameless, his eyes were more grey than blue. "Can you talk about it? What happened…?"

Nameless held up his hands, inspecting them for any lingering stains of blood that the water might not have washed away. "If you want me to leave," he said.

Zaylus said nothing for a long while, but when he spoke it was to change the subject. "I was entrusted with the Archon's sword," he said, "by the supreme head of my Order. We have kept it hidden from the world until such time as it would be needed."

"And where does Aristodeus come into this?" Nameless asked.

"You said he was your mentor. I told you, didn't I, that he mentored my brother?"

Zaylus frowned. "Aristodeus was instrumental in my joining the Order. He is thick as thieves with the elite of Vanatus. You have heard of the Empire?"

"Aye, I've heard of it, but other than Aristodeus, you and Rutha are the first humans I've seen."

"And Shadrak. He might be small, but he's a human like us."

"You're sure about that, are you, laddie?"

Zaylus sighed and, without looking, untied the cord from his belt and began to pick at the knots on it. Nameless was beginning to think the knight had chosen not to answer, but when one of the knots came undone, Zaylus said, "I don't know. All I know was that Aristodeus said Shadrak would prove useful, and thus far he has been right. But other than the fact that Shadrak's some kind of assassin, I know next to nothing about him. He brought us here, though, which is the main thing?"

"He's a sailor too?"

Zaylus shook his head. "Some kind ship that can cross vast distances in next to no time. I've never before seen the like. He calls it a lore craft."

"I bet he does," Nameless said. "Maybe he's a faen after all."

Thunder cracked from beyond the copse, and they looked at each other. Shadrak must have found supper.

"What is that wand thing of his?" Nameless asked.

"More lore. He calls it the Thundershot. Things like that are rare on Vanatus, but from time to time the secrets of the old world come to light."

"So, Vanatus has a mythical past, just like we do. Ours is full of dwarf lords, flying axes and sinking cities."

"Ours is…" Zaylus started, and then stopped to recollect himself. "Ours is divided into the times before and after a cataclysm known as the Reckoning. Our ancestors lived under the rule of Sektis Gandaw before he was driven out and fled here to Medryn-Tha."

"Lucky us," Nameless said. "And he's still here, causing strife, hundreds of years later. Sure you don't want him back?"

A tree trunk rippled and Shadrak emerged from it, the concealer cloak falling open as he walked. He held a dead

MOUNTAIN OF MADNESS

armadillo by the tail.

"Now that beats a squirrel any day," he said.

"Just make sure you cook it thoroughly," Nameless said. "Old Thom Larny caught one in the ravine and ate it half raw. He later lost the feeling in his hands, and his dwarfhood dropped off."

"Brought this, too," Shadrak said, tossing Nameless a waterskin. "Thought you might be able to pour some through the eye-slit, maybe get a drop or two in your mouth."

"Obliged to you, laddie." Nameless unstoppered the costrel and tipped his head back. The cold water splashing his face felt good, and some of it trickled to his lips.

Shadrak slung another waterskin to Zaylus. "Drink as much as you like. The inland sea's fresh water. We can refill before we set off in the morning."

An hour later, Shadrak and Zaylus tore off strips of char-blackened armadillo and chewed morosely. Nameless dropped a piece of meat through the eye-slit, but it fell to the bottom of the helm, and try as he might, he couldn't snag it with his tongue.

His rumbling tummy brought the black dog scampering from the recesses of his mind. If it had been a real dog, it might have wolfed down the meat he'd dropped through the eye-slit, rather than leaving it there to molder. Instead, it harried him with gloomy thoughts and a crushing sense of hopelessness.

Dimly, he became aware Shadrak was asking him a question, and was holding up a slender pick.

"Want me to get those manacles off you? You two go waltzing into a city with chains hanging from your wrists, they'll lock you up in no time. And while I'm about it, you can tell us what you know about Jeridium."

Nameless held out his wrists, and Shadrak began to poke about with his pick.

What he knew? Nameless didn't know much, save for what he'd heard from the *Chronicles*.

"All I can tell you is that it's said to be big. Very big. And it's governed by a senate. Of course, they probably stole the idea from our Council of Twelve."

"Fat lot of good you are, then," Shadrak said.

The first clasp clicked open and the manacle thudded to the floor trailed by a snaking length of chain.

"Thing that's been troubling me," Nameless said, "is why we can't go straight to the Mountain of Ocras. I know you said there were things outside, guarding it, but with that concealer cloak you stole and my axe…"

"Even with them," Zaylus said, "we'd last no more than seconds. We were lucky to get back to the Sour Marsh last time."

"But not lucky enough to find my scutting lore craft," Shadrak said, as he worked on the second manacle. "We landed in the marsh, but when we went back, the lore craft was gone."

"Sure you went back to the right place?" Nameless asked.

Another click, and another thud and rattle of chain. "Course I'm bloody sure." Shadrak tapped his temple. "Perfect memory. Never forget a place, a face, or a name."

"Wish I'd met you sooner, then," Nameless said. "So, what was the Sour Marsh like?"

"Shithole, is what it is," Shadrak said. He pointed with his pick at Zaylus's manacles.

"The place is alive," Zaylus said, holding out his wrists. "Sentient."

"That's what the stories say," Nameless said. "The Sour Marsh oozes beneath the Farfall Mountains, and it carries the taint of Cerreth, the land of nightmare. I envy you. I've always wanted to go there."

"Why?" Shadrak said, freeing Zaylus from one restraint, then setting to work on the other. "You got a thing for giant maggots and marsh lights that lead you into the mire to drown?"

"And lizard-men," Zaylus added, rubbing his wrists when Shadrak freed him of the other manacle. "Let's not forget the lizard-men."

"As if I could."

"We should get some sleep," Zaylus said, settling himself on the ground by the fire.

Nameless couldn't argue with that. He was bone weary. He lay down beneath his tree, wondering if it had been the philosopher who had sent Zaylus and the others to Arx Gravis. Surely

Aristodeus must have known what would happen.

And then it struck him: maybe he had known. Not only that the intruders would be imprisoned, but who they might find in the cells set back in the ravine walls. For there were so few of them—the dwarves had other ways of maintaining law and order, not least of which was the threat of banishment to the foot of the ravine where the baresarks lived. What if Aristodeus had known that Zaylus was likely to end up in the same cell as him? What if the philosopher had arranged it? And what if he'd known that Zaylus's voice would arouse Nameless from his slumber, as if it were Aristodeus's own?

Shadrak muttered something under his breath, but then it fell quiet.

Nameless rolled over onto his side. It was best not to think about it. Whatever the truth of what had happened, he was committed now. There was no going back.

Last thing he remembered was the gentle lapping of the waves from the inland sea, the chirping of cicadas, and the flutter of bats' wings overhead.

NINE

"Bit cramped, isn't it?" Rutha turned her nose up at the white-walled room, although white would have been stretching it. It had more the look of yellow-stained teeth about it, or old bones. "There's not enough room to swing a cat in here."

Aristodeus riffled through some papers on a desk, scribbled a note on one of them and reached for a chain hanging from the ceiling.

"Then it's a good job I don't have a cat." When he pulled the chain, a trapdoor opened and a ladder extended in sections.

It was a cat Rutha likened him to, though, when he lithely bounded up the rungs. For an old codger, he certainly was agile.

"And besides," Aristodeus called from above, "what it lacks in length and breadth, it more than makes up for in height."

"That's what they all say." Rutha heard him stomp around upstairs, dragging things across the floor, cursing and muttering. She took hold of the ladder and peered up, half inclined to go see for herself what he was up to, but something about the stark light lancing down the opening unsettled her. It didn't seem quite natural.

Same as how they had arrived here, quick as a flash. No bells and smells, no sparks, no nothing, save a gut-curdling feeling of wrongness. The mere recollection made her retch, and she fell back against the ladder in a swoon.

"I'll be right with you," Aristodeus said. "Soon as I find the…

MOUNTAIN OF MADNESS

Ah, there it is!"

Rutha pushed herself away from the ladder, blinking to clear her head as she took in the room. It must have been eight, maybe ten feet square, and most of that was taken up with clutter: stacks of ancient-looking books on the floor, wooden crates, a scatter of boxes. The desk was intricately fashioned from what looked like walnut, its top inlaid with leather and gold leaf. It was piled high with notebooks and loose sheets of parchment, but she couldn't make head nor tail of what was written on them. It looked like Ancient Vanatusian, but her Ancient Vanatusian was worse than useless.

Her eyes alighted on a wall chart. It depicted four interlocking circles, one atop the other, and within each was a diagram. She edged closer to see better: ten smaller circles arranged in a pattern of three columns, and there were connecting lines between them. Cursive lettering crowned the larger circles, and there were blockish symbols inside the smaller ones. Just looking at them made her head hurt, and she turned away, spotting a door on the adjacent wall. It was the same off-white as the walls, ceiling and floor, yet it had a gleaming brass doorknob that just begged to be opened.

She reached for it and drew back. She could swear there was heat—intense heat—coming from the other side of the door.

"Don't touch that!"

Rutha's heart bounced into her throat and she whirled around.

Aristodeus slung a knotted mess of tubes to the floor and clambered down the ladder with dozens of clear packets tucked under his arm.

"I'm feeling sick," she said. It wasn't exactly a lie. "Just needed to get some air."

"Nothing wrong with the air in here," Aristodeus said as he shot back up the ladder to grab a crate. It rattled as he once more descended. Catching her look, he set the crate down and squinted at some print on one of the slats. "Nutrition. Marvelous stuff and lasts forever. Now, where did I put the needles?" He rummaged around in some boxes beneath his desk.

The air felt stifling, and Rutha could have sworn the walls were closing in. "Don't you have a window or something? I can't breathe."

"Ah, here they are!" Aristodeus held up a see-through packet backed with white.

Rutha's vision blurred and a wave of nausea washed over her. She put out a hand to steady herself on the desk. "Door," she gasped. "Open the door."

Aristodeus set the packet down. He touched a palm to her forehead then pressed two fingers to her neck. "Febrile and fibrillating. Here, sit down." He pulled out the chair for her and she collapsed into it.

"I'm fine. I just need some air." Rutha put her head in her hands and leaned her elbows on the desk.

"Not pregnant, are you?"

"Get lost."

Aristodeus patted her on the shoulder, gave a gentle squeeze. "It's the effect of the transition. Don't worry, it'll wear off."

"Wear off a bloody sight sooner if I could just get some air and take a walk. Or am I a prisoner?"

"You wouldn't want to open that door," Aristodeus said. "Believe me."

"Why not? Where the Abyss are we?"

He gave a tight smile and rolled his eyes. "It's just not ready yet. I have a hard enough time maintaining the vertical, never mind the horizontal."

Rutha followed his gaze to the ceiling and the open trapdoor. "How many stories? How high's it go?"

"Last time I counted, seventy-two, but it's never enough. Now listen. I don't expect you to understand, but I do need you to obey a few simple rules. Go nowhere, touch nothing, without my express permission. Understood?"

Rutha wrinkled her nose at him. "How long are you planning on staying? I thought we were just grabbing some junk and heading for this Jeridium before the dwarf starves to death."

"We are, Rutha. We are. But first things first. There are matters I want to discuss with you."

"Let me guess. Zaylus?"

Aristodeus frowned and perched on the edge of the desk. "He's not quite what I'd hoped for."

"Tell me about it." She knew she was being unfair, but Zaylus had taken something from her, something she could never get back. Taken it and then turned cold on her, confessed his misdeed and gone on with his career in the Order. She ground her teeth and felt a rush of heat beneath her skin.

Aristodeus sighed, and for a moment looked almost guilty. "My relationship with Zaylus is, shall we say, complex. I had a vision for him that is not coming to fruition, and if things don't change very soon, the enemy will…" He licked his lips and sat perfectly still. Rutha could almost hear the cogs of his mind turning. "He will win."

"Sektis Gandaw?"

"Gandaw's the immediate threat, the first wave, if you like. Mind you, if he pulls off the Unweaving, it's game over. He almost succeeded before. I was part of the effort to stop him, but things didn't go quite to plan."

"Seems to happen to you a lot," Rutha said.

Aristodeus tutted and stood. "When you consider the infinitude of permutations, the sheer magnitude of the battlefield, the cunning of the adversary, I'd say I've been thwarted very few times. Very few indeed."

"Good on you. So, it's a long game, but you've got all the cards, right?"

"This is no game!" A fire came into Aristodeus's eyes, and Rutha shrank back in her chair.

"Shouldn't we get going?"

Aristodeus held up a hand and his face softened. "Time has no meaning here. We can take as long as we like, get acquainted, discuss strategy, and still arrive in Jeridium before Zaylus and the others."

"Strategy? Right."

Aristodeus leaned in close. Too close. "You sell yourself short, Rutha. It's not how the Order saw you."

"The Order asked me to leave."

"Because you wouldn't confess. Zaylus did, and purity was

restored. All you had to do was tell your superiors what they wanted to hear, and you would have received their blessing."

"And pretend it never happened?" Rutha said.

"It was a one-off failing in chastity," Aristodeus said.

"Was it?"

"You slipped up again? With Zaylus?" He looked worried—far more worried than he should have been.

Rutha let him stew a moment longer then shook her head. "Not with him." That was the thing about her: no half measures. She had fallen from grace, so she embraced the passions the Order had made her suppress for so long. And like with the booze, one drink, so to speak, had led to another.

"I see," Aristodeus said. "Now listen. I have a proposal for you."

Aristodeus reached for her breast.

Rutha swung for him, but he caught her wrist in an iron grip that hurt right down to the bone. She went for her saber with her free hand, and Aristodeus stepped back, releasing her.

"What's the matter with you, woman?"

"What's the matter with me? Pervert! That what you had in mind all this while? Bring me back to your squalid little shithole for a quick grope and a romp?"

The color drained from the philosopher's face. His lips worked silently for a moment before he said, "I was going for your shoulder."

"Never heard them called that before."

Aristodeus sighed and the color came back to his cheeks, red and fiery. "I said proposal, not proposition. For goodness' sake, if I wanted to cavort, I would already have done so."

"Over my dead body. Oh, don't tell me, that's the way you like it."

Aristodeus clutched at the air above his head, closed his eyes and took a long, slow breath. When he opened them again, he seemed tired, and the wind had gone out of his sails.

"I was merely trying to... oh, never mind." He whirled away from her, slinging out his arm as if he were throwing an invisible hat. The wall shimmered and vanished, and beyond it there was another room, this one lit by the orange glow of a crackling fire. Beside the fireplace were a couple of barrel chairs and a low table, atop which were two glasses and a bottle.

"Have you always been strung so taut?" Aristodeus said, leading her into the room and standing behind one of the chairs, indicating she should sit.

She lowered herself into the soft-cushioned chair and immediately felt the philosopher's fingers on her shoulders, his thumbs kneading the knots in her upper back. At first she flinched, then she stiffened, and finally, when he persisted, tears spilled onto her cheeks and she shook.

"Let it all out, Rutha. You are quite safe here. Let it all out."

He moved away to the table, popped the cork on the bottle and poured a golden liquid into both glasses. It fizzed and sparkled as he passed her one.

Scowling at him, Rutha took the glass and ran it under her nose.

"Pearlescent wine from Numosia. I've been saving it for something special." Aristodeus took a quaff of his and smacked his lips before seating himself in the other chair. Setting the glass down, he took out his pipe, tapped the bowl on the edge of the table, and proceeded to fill it.

The wine was bitter-sweet, with tangs of overripe pear and citrus, maybe a hint of musk. Rutha took another sip, then drained the glass. Aristodeus looked up, shook his head, and took a taper from beside the fire to light his pipe.

"Impressions?" he asked.

"Too early to say." She held out her glass for a refill and Aristodeus obliged.

She looked into his glinting blue eyes, seeing in them an easy familiarity she'd not noticed before. There was something about the shape of his face, too, the nose, his cheekbones. The barest hint of a smile curled one corner of his mouth, and he stroked his beard, watching her watching him. When he gave the subtlest of nods, she couldn't help herself; it all came pouring out, the tears, the self-hatred, her sense of betrayal and abandonment. As she told him everything—about her struggles in the Order, about Zaylus, about just how far she had fallen since—Aristodeus topped up her glass, barely touching his own drink. He chewed on his pipe stem, grunted attentively, occasionally asked her to clarify something.

"Life in a Wayist military Order can be so taxing," he said when she ran out of things to say. The philosopher's head bobbed, a new warmth exuding from his face. "Perhaps it was never the right life for you… the sacrifices… I know I would have struggled with the purity! Zaylus is different, though. He inherited his mother's piety."

"You knew her?"

"Knew both of them, his real mother and the woman who fostered him."

"Zaylus was fostered?"

"Most of us are thrust haphazardly into the care of those that sired us, and it's blind luck whether or not they are suitable. In Zaylus's case, a little more thought went into who should raise him. Please don't tell him, but Zaylus is not from Vanatus, as he believes. Oh, he was brought up there, but he and I share a common homeland—an arid country, steeped in history and culture. My point is that Zaylus was not simply the product of blind chance. He was plucked from his birth family and planted in the somewhat less salubrious soil of a far-flung province of Vanatus."

"You took Zaylus from his real parents? Did they agree? Does he have any idea?"

Aristodeus rapped his pipe against the side of the hearth, spilling burnt tobacco to the flames. "Zaylus must never know. But we are getting too far from the point. You do not have to remain as you are, bitter, angry, and powerless. If you wish it, I can offer you what I gave to Zaylus, albeit somewhat belatedly." He stooped to retrieve something from just inside the hearth. Rutha expected him to recoil from being burned, but the philosopher showed not the slightest discomfort, as if the hearth itself gave off no heat.

"Look." Aristodeus half drew a sword from a dark leather scabbard studded with dull red gems. The blade was black and etched with strange symbols. "I'll swap you this for your cavalry saber."

MOUNTAIN OF MADNESS

Rutha's skin crawled, yet she couldn't look away. Her heart pounded. Sweat broke out on her forehead, and she reached for the sword with a shaking hand.

"Like strong drink, am I right? You know you shouldn't, and yet still you crave it."

Rutha nodded.

"Like the Sword of the Archon, it is a Supernal weapon," Aristodeus said. "One I took great pains to find. There are three such weapons I have knowledge of, and there are legends of several more. Mananoc's agents sought the blade, but I got there first."

"Where did you get it?" Rutha said, eyeing the sword hungrily.

"That is irrelevant. The important thing is that it is a Supernal blade, and one that does not require purity in order to wield it. You are good with your saber, Rutha? With this sword and my training, I can make you better."

"I doubt that."

"You've seen Zaylus, how incomparable he is with a blade?"

She nodded. "He was the best of us in the Order."

"I trained him," Aristodeus said, "and it is a rare pupil who outgrows his master."

Rutha studied him with a new respect. "You're a swordsman?"

"I am many things, my dear, and I have lived long enough to excel in more than one discipline."

Her gaze returned to the black sword. "You can make me as good as Zaylus?"

Aristodeus reversed the sword and offered her the hilt. "Maybe better."

Rutha leaned forward, curled her fingers around the grip. Her skin prickled where it came into contact with the hilt, and a thrill shot along her arm. "Why?"

Aristodeus tucked his pipe away and steepled his fingers. "Because I am losing confidence in Zaylus. He has already lost his purity once"—he arched an eyebrow at Rutha—"and I'm not certain he will prove zealous enough to land the final blow."

"That's been your plan all along? Have Zaylus kill Sektis Gandaw with a magic sword?"

Aristodeus gave a tight smile. "Zaylus's sword is more than magical. It is intimately linked with the Archon himself; you could say it's a part of him. But it's not Gandaw we need it for. If it had just been the Mad Sorcerer we had to worry about, the Unweaving would not even be a possibility, and I would have ended this centuries ago." He closed his eyes and a tic started up beneath one of them. "Gandaw has the Archon's sister, the goddess Etala, and has found a way to harness her power against her will."

"The sword is for her?"

Aristodeus opened an eye and pursed his lips. "Seems logical, don't you think? A Supernal sword to slay a Supernal being? If Zaylus fails, there is no one with the necessary skill that the Archon's sword will accept: not the Nameless Dwarf, not me, and most certainly not you. But the black sword you are holding… now that's an altogether different matter."

Aristodeus squeezed her knee and she didn't even bat an eyelid. A warm tingle thrilled its way up her spine. He bade her stand and he unbuckled the saber's scabbard from her belt, replacing it with the one that held the black sword. Rutha just stood there, heart racing, and watched.

"Let us enjoy another bottle," Aristodeus said when he was done. He conjured one out of thin air and popped the cork. "There's no hurry. We'll begin your training slowly, then take the feeding apparatus to Jeridium and go from there. How does that sound?"

Rutha's eyes were rooted to her glass as Aristodeus refilled it. He shuffled his chair closer to hers so they could chink glasses. She laughed, feeling a rush of heat through her veins, but it was a shrill laugh, full of nerves.

And at her hip the black sword felt icy cold through its scabbard.

TEN

Nameless knew he was dreaming. He'd fallen asleep beneath a tree, but here he was in an immense cavern formed from coal, walking around a monolith of ice. There was a shape within the glistening block, much as the black axe had been encased in crystal. While it was no axe, it was formed from the same shadowy substance: a giant as tall as the Aorta. Nameless had to step away from it to see the head hundreds of feet above. The face was featureless, save for eyes of simmering violet. The figure didn't move, didn't speak, but somehow he heard it laughing inside his skull, a bubbling, malign mirth that burned him with shame and crippled him with despair. He was a disappointment, a failure. But above all else, he was a butcher.

Something roared.

The cavern shook under the impact of thunderous hooves. A rasping slither. A tortured flutter. A pounding, galloping wind, crashing toward him like a rockfall.

He snapped awake and rolled aside.

Something huge shot past him as he found his feet. Where had he left this axe?

Thunder boomed.

Shadrak.

Nameless panned the great helm, seeing only the denser black of the copse.

A flare of golden brilliance—Zaylus drawing his sword.

A horse galloped toward him out of the dark.

"Out of the way!" the rider cried. "Maresman business!"

Nameless stepped aside as horse and rider sped in pursuit of whatever it was they were chasing.

Shadrak dropped from a low branch and landed in a crouch, tracking the horseman with his Thundershot. "See that thing he was chasing? I tell you, you don't want to be sleeping on the ground no more."

Nameless saw the glint of his axe in the glow coming off Zaylus's sword and snatched it up. "What the shog was it?"

"Leave it," Shadrak said. "Not our problem."

A shrill scream split the night.

"The horse!" Zaylus said. He was already running toward the sound.

Nameless barreled after him, dimly aware of Shadrak slipping away to his flank.

They emerged from the other side of the copse into a chaos of limbs. The horse was on its back, kicking and whinnying. Something thick and scaly was coiled about its body. Swaying above the horse was the torso of a man, tapering away into a serpent's body. It had the head of a bull, and ruby eyes flashed in the moonlight. Feathered wings flapped furiously from its back. One of them was broken.

The rider must have been thrown. He was scrambling to his feet. Black coat, black hat, broad face, heavy with scars. He ran at the beast constricting his horse. He had no weapon, but his fist came up wreathed in flame.

The bull-head cannoned into him, butted him skyward. The man rolled as he hit the ground, came up in a crouch, then charged again.

Zaylus darted in and rammed his sword into the undulating body. A wing smacked him aside, leaving the shortsword buried to the hilt in scales.

As the bull-head veered toward Zaylus, blocking him from retrieving his blade, Nameless delivered a woodcutter's chop to its mannish torso. It reared up so fast, he struck the scales beneath its thorax, and the axe flew from his grasp.

MOUNTAIN OF MADNESS

Shadrak fired, and blood sprayed. The beast roared and launched itself at him, anchoring its tail on the weakening horse. Shadrak tumbled aside as the bull's head almost gored him, fired again, but the creature switched back with blistering speed and caught him by the cloak in one monstrous hand. Shadrak backflipped and kicked it in the snout. His cloak came unclasped, and he dropped lithely to the ground.

The black-coated man leapt onto the beast's back and slammed his flaming fist into its neck. It screeched and bucked, and flung him clear. This time, he hit the ground hard and struggled to rise.

The head came at him, but the man got his palm up in time. Flames burst from it, and the creature recoiled screaming. Its coils contracted with sudden force. There was an answering crack of bone, and the horse shuddered then stilled.

Shadrak came on, blasting with his Thundershot. The first two shots ricocheted off scales. The third punched a hole in the beast's torso. The tail whipped out from beneath the horse and lashed at him. He ducked beneath it, sprang atop a coil, and bounded off to one side, firing as he fell. The tip of a horn shattered, and Shadrak tumbled clear.

Nameless retrieved his axe, even as Zaylus darted in and yanked his sword free from the scales. As the head arced down, the knight slashed at it, but the tail whipped around his chest. He gasped and hacked at the coils.

Nameless bellowed and charged, and the head swung toward him. His axe thudded into fur and sinew, but the impact jolted his arm. Slinging blood in its wake, the head slammed into the *ocras* helm and the axe went flying. Nameless stood his ground—the *ocras* had absorbed all the force—and threw a right hook that connected. The beast snorted and hammered him with a punch of its own. His chainmail bore the brunt, but the force of the blow drove him to his knees.

The black-coated man was there then, flinging fire in its face. The beast howled and thrashed. The man bobbed and weaved between its flailing arms and flat-palmed it in the sternum. Fire lit its body from within, and it shrieked.

Zaylus groaned. His face was purple, his sword arm hanging

limp at his side, fingers loose about the hilt of his sword.

Shadrak stepped in, skimming silver stars that lodged in the creature's torso, head, and arms. The man in the black coat crumpled beneath a pounding fist. Zaylus began to gurgle.

Nameless pushed himself to his feet and hit the beast with an uppercut, rocking its head back. It chomped down on his shoulder, but the chainmail held.

Silver streaked across his vision. One of Shadrak's stars lodged in the creature's eye. It screamed and turned toward the assassin, and in that instant, Nameless grabbed it by the horns and twisted with everything he had. Massive fists pounded at him, but he refused to let go.

Shadrak ran in, stabbed at its heart with a dagger, but an arm came down to block, and the assassin swirled away. "Zaylus!" he cried.

"I know, laddie, I know!" Nameless grunted.

The beast bucked and flailed, reached behind to grab his forearm, started to squeeze. And then something ruptured deep within Nameless. Magma surged through his limbs, and he put everything he had into a last desperate heave.

The beast's neck snapped. At once, its coils grew flaccid, and Zaylus flopped on top of them.

Nameless released the monster's horns, and it slumped to the ground.

He lay there for a moment, catching his breath. Another second, and they would have lost Zaylus.

He heard the knight cough and splutter, then breathed a sigh of relief. A pallid hand clamped down on his shoulder, and then Shadrak reached down and helped him to sit.

"What did I tell you pair of scuts? Leave it, I said. Did you think I was joking? Does this look like a face that jokes?"

Nameless peered through the eye-slit at the assassin's pallid face, his unnerving pink eyes.

"Honest opinion, laddie? It's an ugly mug more suited to frightening children and slurping the rancid fluids from corpses than it is to a stand-up routine in Slim Shafty's House of Grog, home to the best comedians in Arx Gravis."

MOUNTAIN OF MADNESS

Shadrak helped him all the way to his feet. "They have comedy in Arx Gravis?"

"It's a city within a ravine. It gets frightfully boring at times."

Nameless went over to Zaylus and crouched down. "Are you all right, laddie?"

Zaylus's breaths came in tortured wheezes, but he held his hand up to forestall any more questions. Golden light flared along the blade of the Sword of the Archon and he stiffened, then let out a long, slow breath.

"Am now," Zaylus said, standing and rubbing his ribcage.

"You folks have some explaining to do." It was the man in the black coat. He'd found his feet and was stumbling over to them.

"Do we now?" Shadrak said, fastening his cloak around his neck.

"I told you," the man said, his fist starting to smolder, "this is Maresman business. That means stay the Abyss out of it."

"Laddie," Nameless said, "I don't mind a bit of bluster, but an ungrateful..." He flicked a look at Shadrak. "I was going to say 'ungrateful shogger,' but I feel the occasion warrants something stronger."

"Tosser?" Shadrak suggested.

"That works. An ungrateful tosser," Nameless said to the man in the black coat, "will never get to drink mead at my table."

"That so, stumpy?" the man said. "Then let me give you some advice."

"Not interested," Nameless said. "Are you, Shadrak?"

"Nope."

Zaylus came to stand at the assassin's side. "What you could do is give us some answers," he told the man. "What was that thing, and why were you chasing it?"

"It's my job, that's why. And as to what it was, I can't give particulars, because it's the first of its kind we've seen, but it's some kind of husk, like all the other husks that think they can come across the Farfall Mountains. Don't know what's gotten into them, but there's been more incursions these past few days than we usually get in a year. The Senate has every last Maresman out hunting. You two, though,"—his eyes flicked from Shadrak to

Nameless—"you two don't exactly look human."

"You think they're husks?" Zaylus said. "Don't be so ridiculous."

The Maresman's hand burst into flame. "I'll be the judge of that." To Nameless and Shadrak he said, "You want to tell me where you came from?"

"My mother's womb," Nameless said.

"Funny." The Maresman stepped up close to Nameless. "Take off that helm."

"If I could do that, I'd be chugging down roasted armadillo with a flagon of strong beer—assuming I could find some beer."

The flaming fist came up. "I told you to take off the—!"

The Maresman doubled over, then collapsed to his knees, trying to stem the flow of blood from his crotch.

"Oh, I'm sorry," Shadrak said, holding a gore-stained dagger in front of the Maresman's face. "I just figured if you had nothing to toss with, you'd be cured of being a tosser."

"Shadrak…" Zaylus warned.

But the assassin slashed the blade across the Maresman's throat then watched him pitch to the ground.

"This isn't what we came here for," Zaylus said, sheathing his shortsword.

"You want my help, then stop trying to tell me how to give it."

Zaylus narrowed his eyes, then crouched over the body of the Maresman. "He said there had been an unusual amount of incursions." He glanced over his shoulder at Nameless. "You think it has anything to do with the Unweaving?"

"Don't ask me, laddie. I'm new to all this."

"Well I, for one, ain't likely to sleep after this," Shadrak said. "I say we press on, see if we can make it to Jeridium by morning."

"Agreed," Nameless said. "Zaylus?"

"We can't just leave the body."

"Watch me," Shadrak said.

"We could find rocks for a cairn, I suppose," Nameless suggested.

"That isn't what I meant."

Zaylus knelt down beside the dead Maresman and fished a

leather-bound book from his coat pocket. Paying no heed to Shadrak's impatient pacing, he began to read aloud.

Nameless thought he'd heard the same words somewhere before. And then he remembered: Thumil had read them over the body of Nameless's pa when they'd brought him back from the mines.

At the same time, one of the names he'd feared lost along with his own seeped through the cracks in his mind.

His pa's name.

Droom.

And in the privacy afforded by the great helm, he started to weep.

ELEVEN

Something was wrong.
The patterns of the Unweaving and the Statue of Etala should have produced a perfect sphere of nothing by now.

Sektis Gandaw's eyes tracked the mirrors until he located the view of the top of the mountain. At first he thought the mirror was dirty, but then he realized that the summit was wreathed in filthy smoke.

"That is meant to be the Null Sphere, is it not?" He was dimly aware of the faen, Mephesch, nodding slowly. "So, where is it?"

"Well," Mephesch said, rubbing his chin. "Uhm…"

"Is it dispersing? It's meant to be compacting, increasing in mass. What is happening, Mephesch? It should be building towards critical. I need answers!"

"I'm sure it's nothing," the faen said.

"It's meant to be nothing, you imbecile!" Sektis yelled at the mirror. "A great ball of nothing getting denser and denser until it explodes with such infinite, perfect, omnipresent, cataclysmic, devastating, sublimely ordered—"

Mephesch gave a polite cough.

Sektis's whole body was corpse-rigid until the needles from his armor lanced into him, filling his veins with calming fluids.

"What?" he said. "What was so important that you had to interrupt me?"

"Forgive me for bringing this up," Mephesch said, "but do you recall the imperfection you mentioned in the patterns?"

The ellipsis!

The faen stepped back as if he expected to be hit. Sektis impressed himself, however, with how calm he remained. Of course, it was all down to the potions, but he had been the one to concoct them.

"Route the patterns back to my office, Mephesch. And shut the Unweaving down for now." He was a patient man. He could endure the delay. "I'll need at least two days to sift through all the symbol chains to make certain there wasn't more than one error."

Mephesch pulled the main power lever and the pulsing mesh around the serpent statue shut down. The goddess Etala's eyes went glassy and dull, and her fangs were once more amber shards. A crackle ran around the chamber and lights blinked on.

Sektis was about to head for the elevator when he thought he glimpsed movement—the slightest shift of Etala's jawline, a glint in one of her eyes. He glanced at Mephesch to see if he'd noticed too, but the faen met his gaze with a blank expression.

Not for the first time, Sektis wondered about the origin of the faen. How come of all the mysteries of the world, only the Abyss, the Void, and Mephesch's kin had continued to vex him? Everything had emerged from the same primal darkness, and so everything could be returned to it, and yet the Abyss, the faen, and the gaping emptiness of the Void all seemed to say he'd got it wrong, that he'd missed something. Something very, very important.

With the steely resolve that the potions provided, he shut out the voice of doubt. His theory was infallible. All that exists would cease to exist, save for the epicenter of the Unweaving, which was the Mountain of Ocras itself. That would have to include the Abyss, and if the Void really was nothing, then surely it would simply dissolve like a raindrop in the ocean of nothingness he was about to create. He emitted something like a sigh of relief. These little disparities could easily be accounted for, squeezed into the perfect circle of his logic.

For an instant, his thoughts took on a life of their own, bubbling and echoing with laughter from a dark space he didn't recognize. He clamped down control in an instant. He couldn't stop himself, though, from glancing up at mirror 55 and frowning at the taunting blackness of the Void.

As he peeled his eyes away, he saw Mephesch watching him, the remnants of a smirk melting from his face. Well, Sektis had a nasty surprise for him and the rest of the faen once this was over: They would be among the last victims of the Unweaving, along with all the aborted experiments still gurgling and shrieking in the roots of the Mountain of Ocras.

The smile that was curling his lips of its own accord froze in place. There was a shadow to his right, so close it chilled his skin.

A whispered voice spoke inside his head. "You wanted to see me?"

Sektis suppressed a sigh of relief. He'd forgotten, though, and that was not acceptable. "I did, indeed."

The harvester stepped back and gave a half-bow, and Sektis's eyes ran over it with begrudging admiration. Not one of his creations, but fit almost perfectly for purpose: gangly limbs for speed and reach; obsidian skin as tough as boiled leather; padded feet for silent stalking; hollow bones; fibrous membranes between the arms and torso that allowed it to glide; and an ovoid cranium packed with senses so enhanced it could scent, hear and see its prey from miles away. Sektis should know; mere hours ago he'd had the creature on his dissecting table, carved up into tiny pieces.

"You are recovered, I trust?" he said.

The harvester ran slender fingers down its body and inclined its featureless head. The blades that adorned its harness like splinted armor glinted, and one hand hovered above the handle of the lore weapon the faen had produced for Sektis: a hand-grip and a tube that spat thunder and sent a projectile hurtling forth, too fast to see. The faen had called it a gun.

"I am better than before."

That would be the effect of the sorcerous regeneration following vivisection. Before Sektis could find a use for the creature, he had needed to study it, inside and out. While not perfect, the harvester was a great improvement on anything Sektis had found on Aosia. Thanatos, the faen had called the dark world

MOUNTAIN OF MADNESS

they had snatched the creature from in one of their lore craft—a world of pure hostility. It hadn't figured on any of Sektis's astronomical charts, but it was undeniably there, once the faen had shown him where to look. He didn't like it. Didn't like it one little bit. Like the Abyss and the Void, the dark world of Thanatos couldn't be accounted for in his theories and observations, but it was of no consequence. If he was right about the Unweaving, and he undoubtedly was, the slate would be wiped entirely clean, ready for him to commence his own creation, and then there would be nothing he didn't know about in the most intimate, exacting detail.

He ran his hand over the crystals on his vambrace and a ghosting image appeared in the air: the knight Zaylus, the black-haired woman, and the albino midget. The three who had pursued his agents all the way from Vanatus.

"You told me yours is a planet of death," Sektis said.

The harvester was motionless. It had no eyes, but Sektis knew it was drinking in every detail of the three targets he had given it.

"Find them and kill them." Although nothing could penetrate the Mountain of Ocras's defenses, Sektis had learned long ago from Maldark never to underestimate his enemies. "Succeed, and I will return you to Thanatos."

The harvester gave an almost indiscernible bow.

"Be cautious," Sektis said. "The small one has a weapon like the one you carry."

Faster than thought, the harvester's gun was out of its holster, and a blast reverberated around the chamber, ever diminishing until it was swallowed by the darkness of mirror 55. There was a moment's silence and then a bat-melding on the second tier flopped backwards and pitched over the railing.

The harvester spun the gun on its finger and snapped it back into the holster.

Impressive. The weapon must have been totally unfamiliar, but already the speed, the accuracy... Sektis nodded his approval and then glared at the blood pooling from the bat-melding onto the burnished floor.

Mephesch clicked his fingers and a team of faen came running to clean it up.

TWELVE

Dawn light drenched Jeridium's battlements as one sun crested the horizon. The walls must have been close to five-hundred feet tall, and the sections stretching between the scores of cylindrical towers were heavily buttressed, and embrasured on dozens of levels. Hooded lanterns ghosted in between the merlons. A cluster of bronze-capped minarets peeked above the walls, and way off to their left, an immense chimney billowed smoke that swirled into a dirty canopy of smog.

Boggy ground squelched beneath their boots as the trio trudged the last few miles toward Jeridium. Eventually, the second sun rose to join its twin, and they both climbed at their usual hectic rate, setting the domes of the minarets aflame and limning the smog with gold.

Nameless angled the great helm back the way they had come, where the sky was blemished with a patch of mauve. It must have been way past Arx Gravis, perhaps as far as the Mountain of Ocras.

Zaylus, too, was looking back to the west, a frown on his face.

"Reckon it's started," Shadrak said.

Lightning flashed in the distance, forking and branching across the mauve stain like cracks in a mirror.

Shadrak shrunk into his concealer cloak, part-merging with the browns and greens of the fens that were beginning to cede ground to the freshly plowed fields skirting the city.

"There's something odd about that lightning," Nameless observed.

Zaylus nodded. "It's traveling upward."

Where the forks of lightning met the sky, specks of blackness were left in their wake, as if they scorched the very air and hardened it into scabs.

"We need to hurry," Zaylus said. "There's no telling how much time we have left."

The shadow cast by the walls fell over two or three acres of farmland. It smothered the blaze of the twin suns and sent a chill into Nameless's bones.

Zaylus tugged his coat tight about him and pressed on. Shadrak glanced at Nameless, pulled his hood up, and together they set off after the knight.

"What we gonna do, knock?" Shadrak said as they approached the barbican thrusting out from the curtain wall between two towers. It was big enough to be a castle in its own right. In place of gates, it had huge double-doors of stone etched with cursive script. The writing was Old Dwarven.

Nameless walked right up to the doors and scanned the letters through the eye-slit.

"Something from the time of Maldark," he said. "My Old Dwarven's not too good, I'm afraid. Dead language, if you ask me."

Zaylus squinted where Nameless pointed. He started to translate out loud: "'The last act of the dwarves of Medryn-Tha, a gift for the first of the free.'" He turned to Nameless for an explanation.

Nameless was momentarily stunned that the knight could read Old Dwarven, but then he recalled Aristodeus saying a similar language existed in Vanatus.

"According to the stories Rugbeard used to tell us kids, 'the first of the free' must refer to the humans Sektis Gandaw stole from their families in Vanatus and brought to Medryn-Tha in strange craft that were as big as villages and could travel great distances in the blink of an eye."

Zaylus glanced at Shadrak, who gave an almost indiscernible

shrug.

"They were slaves until Maldark and his allies liberated them when Sektis Gandaw's first attempt at the Unweaving was defeated," Nameless said. "What's the rest say?"

"'May this city vouchsafe the protection of these, our brothers, our fellow victims,'" Zaylus read. "'And may it serve as an acceptable penance for our sins.'"

"That'll be about Maldark's betrayal," Nameless said. "From then on my people mistrusted themselves so much, they withdrew from the world above."

"Think they've noticed we're here yet?" Shadrak looked up at the crenellations atop the barbican, where there appeared to be a change of guard taking place. "Want me to climb the walls, slit a few throats, and open the doors from the inside?"

"Can't been done, laddie," Nameless said. "That's dwarf stonework. Mortar's thinner than a gnat's hair."

A trumpet blast sounded from the barbican, and a soldier peered down at them through a crenel. His face was framed by a bronze helm with a white horsehair crest. "Stand clear," he called.

There was a heavy clunk, followed by squeaking and groaning as the stone doors opened outward.

Shadrak started forward, but Nameless put a restraining hand on his shoulder. The assassin's eyes flashed dangerously.

"You might want to take off the concealer cloak," Nameless said. "People see you blending with the surroundings, and they'll assume you're up to no good. Don't want to get off to a bad start now, do we?"

Shadrak scowled, but he went ahead and removed the cloak, bundling it under his arm. It looked like he was carrying a boulder the same color as the city walls.

"Give it here, laddie," Nameless said. He took the bundle and stuffed it up the front of his hauberk. "They'll either think I'm up the duff or a bit too friendly with the beer."

"Make sure I get it back when we leave," Shadrak said, starting through the doors. "After you've had it washed."

Nameless and Zaylus followed the assassin into the barbican, entering a long hallway lit by softly glowing crystals set into the vaulted ceiling. Fluted pillars ran in three evenly spaced rows, and polished wooden doors flanked both sides of the hall. Switchback railings formed a maze-like channel down the center, presumably for those times when long lines of people were entering and leaving the city.

Past that, the hall was dark and devoid of furnishings. The ceiling crystals there cast no light, and heavy cobwebs hung like drapes.

A guard stepped from the shadows to usher them into a featureless grey corridor that took them to a squat chamber. Barred windows looked out onto a gloomy street. A couple of soldiers with crossbows watched from each. Between the windows, a massive oak door was fastened shut by three thick bolts. A man in a wrinkled toga stood to the side of it next to a waist-high table, upon which were stacks of papers and crudely bound booklets. Apparently, Aristodeus wasn't the only one to wear such a ridiculous garment.

"Welcome to Jeridium," the man said. "Bastion of the free and first city of Medryn-Tha. My name is Lawson, your greeter today. Is this your first visit? Good, well, then you'll need one of our exquisite street maps and a guide book, which details places of interest such as the Capitol, the Old Mint, our incomparable restaurant strip, the…"

Shadrak sidled up to the table behind the greeter and pocketed something.

"… Cotze's Foundry," Lawson went on. "The Raymark Brewery—"

"Let me see," Nameless said, snatching the map from the greeter's hand.

"We have a special discount this week only," Lawson said. "A shekel for the book, same for the map; but if you take both, we'll work something out."

"Just the map, laddie," Nameless said, withdrawing the purse Aristodeus had given him and fishing out a silver coin. "Is that a shekel?"

Shadrak rolled his eyes. "I've already nabbed a map," he mouthed.

MOUNTAIN OF MADNESS

Lawson shot Nameless a beaming smile as he took the proffered coin. "That will do nicely, sir. Enjoy your visit. Uh, guard, would you be so kind…"

One of the soldiers sighed and set about pulling back the bolts so that he could open the door.

"Once again," Lawson said, "welcome to Jeridium."

In the street beyond the door, it could have been night, so dense were the shadows thrown by the city walls. Glowing crystals suspended from tall posts shed dirty yellow light in swaths upon market stalls already bustling with activity, despite the early hour. The bitter aroma of kaffa hung heavy in the air, and a brief gust of wind brought a whiff of pipe smoke through the slit of Nameless's great helm.

Shadrak slid in among the crowd and disappeared.

"There he goes again," Nameless said. "Slippery little shogger, that one."

Zaylus spun round as if he'd been stung.

"Sorry, mate," a stoat-faced man said, snatching his hand away from the knight's pocket. "Missed my footing."

Nameless took a step toward him, and the man slunk back into the throng. "Just like the Sag-Urda wharfs," he said, unfolding the map he'd bought. He tried scanning it through the eye-slit before giving up and handing it to Zaylus.

"The city's divided into a perfect grid," Zaylus said as he studied the map. "With some additions. The Academy is north-east of here." He glanced up, and Nameless followed his gaze to the smoking chimney they had seen from outside.

"That's Cotze's Foundry," Zaylus said. "Only a couple of blocks from where we need to be."

They set out onto the high street and followed it north through the shaded market stalls, making their way around the scattered pavement tables and chairs in front of a bewildering array of eateries. The smell of roasted meat and garlic was torture to

Nameless. He would have given his right arm for a hot stew and a hunk of freshly baked bread.

He led the way east down a side street that ran along the back of yet more restaurants. Crates were stacked outside weatherbeaten doors, and refuse spilled from overturned cans.

They turned north into a wide alley and left the shadows cast by the walls. The temperature went from cool and refreshing to muggy, and suddenly the stench of rotting food became overbearing.

They had gone barely twenty yards when three dark figures stepped from an alcove. One of them snapped his fingers, producing a tongue of flame, which he used to light a weedstick. It might even have been narcotic somnificus, same as everyone said Councilor Yuffie smuggled into Arx Gravis. The other two raised crossbows.

"Let me guess," the smoking man said. "You got lost and just happened to wander into our territory? No, don't tell me: you're a pair of Wayist priests looking for converts? You do know that's illegal, don't you?"

"I never knew that," one of the crossbowmen said with a smirk. "Did you know that?" he asked the other.

"Bloody hate Wayists," came the reply.

"Or how about: you're disgruntled Night Hawks," the smoking man said, narrowing his eyes at Nameless's dark helm, "wanting to jump ship now there's a new king on the dung-pile? See, the thing is, no one comes down here unless they're really stupid, or they've got business with—"

In one smooth motion, a shadow dropped down behind the trio, rolled left, lunged right, and the two crossbowmen crumpled into heaps.

"Thing is," Shadrak said, ramming a punch dagger into the smoking man's kidney, "you got a big gob that's just about starting to piss me off."

The man screamed, and his weedstick dropped to the ground. Shadrak kicked him in the back of the legs, sending him sliding off the dagger and onto his knees.

"Stop!" the man cried amid a spray of pinkish spittle. "Wait!"

MOUNTAIN OF MADNESS

Shadrak rammed an elbow into the man's nose. There was a sickening crunch and a gargled scream.

Nameless turned the great helm on Zaylus. "The little fellow's got the makings of a circle fighter, if you ask me."

"Enough, Shadrak," Zaylus said.

Shadrak picked up the still-burning weedstick. "No, it ain't." He jabbed the smoking end in the man's eye, and this time the scream seemed to go on forever. "Show this kind one jot of mercy, and they'll take it as weakness. Believe me, I know." He burned the other eye and stood back to watch the man thrashing and whimpering on the ground.

Nameless had half a mind to step in and put the fellow out of his misery. He glanced at Zaylus and saw he was thinking the same thing.

With a pathetic moan, the man curled himself into a fetal ball. Shadrak bent over him and punched the dagger repeatedly into his skull. There was a grunt, a few twitches, and then it was over.

"Shogging journeymen," Shadrak said. "Hate the scuts." He wiped his dagger on the man's clothes and straightened up. "Place ain't so bad," he said. He threw Zaylus a paper-wrapped package. "Good food, lame city watch, and now what sounds like rival guilds ripe for the picking. I tell you, after we've finished with Sektis Gandaw, I've a good mind to come back here."

The package contained a hunk of fresh bread and a slab of cheese. Zaylus glanced guiltily at Nameless and then tore into it.

"Sorry, dwarfy," Shadrak said to Nameless. "I had a turkey leg earmarked for you, and a flagon of ale, but then I remembered…"

Nameless growled.

THIRTEEN

By the time they reached the street at the far end of the alley, Zaylus had wolfed down his bread and cheese and looked better for it. Nameless, on the other hand, felt as though rats were gnawing on his innards, he was so hungry. He gritted his teeth, determined to bear it a while longer, and followed the knight and Shadrak through a bustling shopping district loud with the clatter of carts and the clip-clop of horses.

They found themselves walking behind a man in a wide-brimmed hat and drab grey robe. He was handing out slips of paper to anyone who would meet his eyes, weaving his way in and out of the central throng. As they passed a pavement restaurant sheltered by an awning, the man went from table to table leaving his slips for the diners. Some pocketed them surreptitiously, but others shook their heads or snapped their fingers at the waiters.

When they came out the other side of the awning, the man handed a slip of paper to Zaylus then entered a three-story house nestled between two shops. A balding man poked his head outside, checked the street both ways, then shut the door.

"What's that he gave you?" Nameless asked.

Zaylus passed the slip of paper to him. There was a drawing on one side of a bird stabbing itself in the breast with its beak. On the reverse was written something in Old Dwarven—or, rather, Ancient Vanatusian.

Nameless shook his head and handed it back.

"O Dayspring," Zaylus began to translate for Nameless, "brightness of the everlasting light, shine on those that sit in the chaos and darkness of Mananoc."

"That's the sort of thing Thumil used to spout," Nameless said, "when he was drowning in his own vomit in Bucknard's Beer Hall."

The memories were coming easier by the minute, but there were still great swaths of emptiness. He could recall all manner of inconsequential things: day-to-day life in the ravine, faces, places, customs. It was certain specifics that eluded him, things even closer to home; things that threw up an overwhelming wall of dread whenever he tried to think on them. Probably for his own good, he surmised, because they were memories drenched in blood, and his were the hands that held the axe.

Zaylus eyed the door the man who'd handed him the paper had entered through, took a step toward it.

At the same time, Nameless saw something far more appealing:

"Tavern!" he cried, setting off at a staggered run. He pulled up sharp and slapped the side of his helm. "Bloody shogging goat's nards! I forgot again."

Shadrak was on him like a shadow. "Outfitters," he said, pointing at the clothes store opposite. "My cloak, remember?"

"Ah, laddie," Nameless said. "You've a fine memory on you. Here, hold this." He handed Shadrak his axe, ambled over to the store, and went inside.

Tiny bells tinkled as the door closed behind him, and an elderly woman looked up from behind the counter.

"Oh my, a dwarf!" she said, coming round to get a closer look. "They said there was a dwarf in the city last year, but I never clapped eyes on him. And now I have. Do me a favor, darling, take your helm off."

"Last year?" Nameless said. "Madam, I've only just arrived."

"Then there must be two of you."

Another dwarf, leaving Arx Gravis to come to Jeridium? "Are you sure of your facts, madam? Where I come from, there are stories of a monster in the lake, but no one I know has ever seen it."

She circled him like a predator, lightly touched her fingers to his shoulder as she passed. "Not as short as I imagined," she said. "And such muscles."

"Always like to keep in shape," Nameless said. "As regards the helm, I'll have to disappoint you. It's stuck."

"I'll get some butter, see if that'll help."

"Really stuck," Nameless said. "Utterly and completely."

"Oh dear. But do tell me you have a beard under there."

"A big one, lassie. Thick and bushy."

That seemed to please her. "So, tell me, sir dwarf, how can I be of assistance?"

"I'm looking for a cloak for my runty little friend outside." He held his hand out level with his chest. "He's so tall, and built like a half-starved fairy."

The shopkeeper gestured toward the far end of the store. "Have a look in our children's section. There's lots of bright colors, and some with embroidered patterns and sequins."

A few minutes later, Nameless stepped outside with a sturdy backpack and a sky-blue cape trimmed with gold.

"You're having a laugh," Shadrak said.

"It has a hood," Nameless explained helpfully. "All you need now's a shiny bell and you could earn a living as a prancing pixie."

Shadrak snatched the cape from him and stormed into the shop.

Nameless chuckled and pulled out the concealer cloak from under his chainmail so he could stuff it into the backpack.

"I think he likes you," Zaylus said.

"Oh? And why's that then?"

"Because you're still alive."

Shadrak eventually came out, fastening a black cloak around his neck. "Now, why was that so hard?" he said, accepting the backpack from Nameless.

"It'll draw the heat," Nameless chided, as the trio set off again.

The street opened onto a crowded plaza, which was dominated by a three-tiered fountain sending up sparkling arcs of crystal-clear water. Sunshades had been set up all around the perimeter, where market stalls were bustling with trade and thick with the smells of fish, roasting meat, and fresh-baked bread.

MOUNTAIN OF MADNESS

Zaylus studied the map and lifted his eyes to the broad avenue leaving the plaza on the far side. "Come on. It's just off that road."

People were stopping to look up at the sky. Nameless angled the helm so he could see. Wispy fingers of mauve seemed to be clawing their way toward the city walls, but when he blinked, he realized it was a matter of perspective. The discoloration was still some way off.

Zaylus had noticed it, too.

"Don't look good, mister," an old woman said. "Enjoy the sunshine while it lasts."

Zaylus nodded and forced a smile. He started to say something, but an earsplitting boom rocked the plaza.

Nameless instinctively ducked. All about the plaza, people were running and screaming. He turned a circle, trying to locate the source of the blast, but there was nothing to be seen.

"Why all the panic?" Shadrak said. "It was just a bleeding clap of thunder."

There was a second boom, and this time the assassin swore and covered his ears.

Out of nowhere, rain sheeted across the plaza. Zaylus ran for the shelter of a doorway at the edge of the square. Shadrak was close on his tail, but Nameless merely ambled after them at his own pace. He'd heard worse during the storms at Arx Gravis, where the thunder would reverberate from the ravine walls, amplified tenfold by the time it hit the bottom.

Stalls were swiftly covered, and within minutes the square was empty.

"Funny thing about this rain..." Nameless said catching up with the others.

"What?" Shadrak grumbled from beneath his hood. "It's sodding wet?"

"It's falling sideways."

Lightning flashed, and a second or two later there was another thunderclap. A dust devil stirred up the center of the plaza, spun into a covered stall and dispersed.

Leaving the shelter of the doorway, Zaylus led the way down the avenue. Fierce winds were gusting, and he gave up trying to look at the map.

"Cotze's Foundry." He pointed above the rooftops at the smoke-spewing chimney. "The Academy must be near."

"Want my advice?" Shadrak said. "Follow the geezer in the hat."

A man in a dark green coat and a chimney-stack hat was picking his way along the sidewalk, completely unfazed by the weather. It was as though he were in a bubble of sunshine and calm.

They followed the man down a series of backstreets. The architecture started to change in subtle ways the farther they got from the plaza, but after a while the difference was startling. Twisty narrow buildings leaned precariously over cobbled streets. Flying buttresses and arched walkways crossed overhead, and many of the buildings had turrets with burnished copper roofs, atop which flew flags of various designs: horse heads, skulls, green garlands, frogs, snakes, geometric shapes, pyramids of numbers.

The man in the tall hat was at the far end of a narrow lane when they entered it.

Even through the great helm, Nameless wasn't spared the stench rising from the cobblestones. Rats scampered out of their way, burying themselves in moldering piles of refuse, or splashing through the dank water spilling from the gutters.

The lane ended at a wrought-iron gate flowing with intricate whorls and vine-work. The hinges squeaked as Zaylus pushed it open and went through ahead of the others.

The cobbles of the lane gave way to a mosaic pathway between banks of trellises interwoven with ivy and dotted with violet petals. After a stretch, the pathway opened onto an ornamental garden skirting a towering edifice. Harmonious pairings of rockeries and fountains, flowerbeds and herb gardens did their best to soften the looming grey facade of the Academy.

Flying buttresses splayed from the sides of the building, like the legs of an enormous spider. Each story—there were seven in all—was surrounded by a stone balustrade, upon which sat gargoyles in various lewd poses. The windows were of stained glass, depicting men with the heads of beasts, retorts, crucibles, patterns of fire, water, air, and earth. Passing beneath the shade of the portico's vaulted ceiling, Nameless approached twin doors of polished oak, which Zaylus had already passed through.

Shadrak followed, turning this way and that, pink eyes glittering scarlet in the sunlight. And that was when it struck Nameless: The storm still raged beyond the garden, but here, all was tranquil, calm as a perfect summer's day.

Inside, he was greeted by the smell of must and sulfur. To the right, the antechamber opened onto an enormous circular room with balconied levels rising all the way to the ceiling. Each level was crammed with bookshelves, and the floor space of the lower level accommodated dozens of desks. Shining crystal globes were suspended from silver chains. There were people browsing the book cases, and still more bent over the desks, with stacks of books and papers before them. Lukar would have loved it.

The man with the tall hat was leaning on a counter, sharing a joke with the librarian.

On the opposite side of the antechamber, there was an impossibly vast hall dominated by displays of skeletons, some human, but most of giant beasts. Some were four-legged, with long sinuous necks, while others stood upright and had cavernous maws lined with sword-like teeth.

The antechamber continued past both rooms to a reception area. A young girl with pigtails looked up from the desk as Nameless and Shadrak caught up with Zaylus.

"We're here to see Master Quilth," Zaylus said.

"Straight ahead, second door on the left," the girl said. She sounded bored. "They're expecting you."

Zaylus led the way along a carpeted corridor, where raised voices spilled from an open door.

"You're missing the point."—Aristodeus.

"No, it is you who are missing the point: the point of your swollen-headed hubris!" The second voice was a lilting bass, stressing the consonants like a declaiming actor.

"Have you no logic, Quilth?" Aristodeus's voice again. "If your so-called magic is drawn from the dreams of the Daeg…" He trailed off as Zaylus moved to the doorway. "Oh, you're here."

The other man in the room—presumably Master Quilth—was half a head taller than Aristodeus, broad-shouldered and barrel-chested. His black hair was streaked with white and twisted into spikes, and his beard was a braided trident. He threw out an arm in an expansive gesture, spreading his crimson cloak like the wings of a bat. The air about his hand shimmered, and a staff appeared in his grip.

"The Unweaving has started," Zaylus said.

"Yes, I saw the storm," Aristodeus said. "We were just debating it. Master Quilth and his sorcerers think a bit of psychic self-defense will see it off!"

"That is not what I said," Quilth objected.

Aristodeus wagged a finger at him. "Call it a semantic quibble, if you must," the philosopher said, "but it makes no difference. You draw power from the dreams of the Daeg, do you not? The so-called god that sleeps at the core of Aosia."

Quilth sighed through clenched teeth.

"Well, let me tell you, Quilth, the Unweaving will pull the rug out from under you. Everything will be undone. Nothing will be left—no Daeg, no magic, not even your precious Academy."

"And where's your evidence?" Quilth said, punctuating the words by rapping the heel of his staff against the polished floorboards.

"Look," Aristodeus said, "why not turn your sorcery against the Mountain of Ocras? At least it might create a distraction and keep Sektis Gandaw's eyes off Zaylus long enough for him to get inside."

"Impeccable logic!" Quilth said. "Even if we could penetrate the *ocras*, which we could not, Gandaw has harnessed the power of the goddess Etala, if you are to be believed. What chance do you think magic drawn from the Daeg would have against the poor wretch's own mother? No, if you are right about the Unweaving, defense is our best chance."

"Balderdash!" Aristodeus said.

Quilth raised a placating hand. "Then we must agree to disagree. I'll not hinder your efforts, so long as you don't hinder mine."

MOUNTAIN OF MADNESS

"Fine," Aristodeus said. "I take it I can still use your room, as we agreed?"

"How long will this feeding take?" Quilth cast a leery eye over the tubes and packages heaped on the desk.

Sight of them turned Nameless's stomach.

"A few hours at most."

"Just today," Quilth said, "and then you can find somewhere else. Clear my desk and shut the door on your way out. Gentlemen." He gave a stiff bow and left.

"Typical," Aristodeus said as he pushed the door to. "They plan to expand the Academy's magical shielding over the entire city, as if that will do a damned thing. And I can tell you now, the Senate will be just as bad. This idea of yours," he said to Nameless, "getting the Senate to send their legions against the Mountain of Ocras—they're going to take some persuading. According to Quilth, the senators are convinced they've appeased Sektis Gandaw over the years by suppressing the Wayists, same as Gandaw once persecuted them in Vanatus. What the Senate fail to realize, though, is that Gandaw is way beyond his hatred of religion now. And even if he doesn't spare Jeridium, as far as the Senate is concerned, nothing can get past the city walls. Why is it so difficult to understand that there won't be any walls if everything's unwoven? If I thought it would do any good, I'd speak with them myself, but I have more than enough on my plate with that bloody woman of yours."

"Rutha?" Zaylus said. "She's her own woman, not mine. Where is she?"

Aristodeus closed his eyes and drew in a long, slow breath. "I left her propping up a bar. She certainly knows how to drink."

Rutha liked to drink? That was a sorely needed point in her favor, Nameless thought.

"Which bar?" Zaylus said. "Where?"

"Place called Dougan's Diner, a roach-infested cesspit on Seventy-First Street, but also a mine of contacts and information. I've frequented the place for years."

Zaylus started for the door.

"No, Hale," Aristodeus said. "You must try talking sense to the

Senate. I've never had good relations with them—there's a lot of history between us—but you may have a chance. Tell them what you've seen, what's coming. Reason with them."

"Don't worry, Zaylus," Shadrak said. "I'll go find Rutha. I ain't got the patience to come with you and argue with politicians." Before anyone could stop him, the assassin was out the door.

"Wait for us there," Aristodeus called after him. "And whatever you do, don't eat the food. After I've finished with Nameless," he told Zaylus, "we should rendezvous at the diner. Do you need me to tell you how to find the Senate Building?"

"I have a map," Zaylus said.

"Good. At least that's one less thing for me to do." The philosopher ushered Zaylus out of the door and slammed it behind him.

Nameless felt the loss of his new companions almost as much as the loss of home.

When Aristodeus came round to peer in through the eye-slit of the great helm and tried to smile reassuringly, it only made matters worse.

FOURTEEN

Fist-sized hail hammered against the rooftop, and sleet spewed across the purple stain spreading above Jeridium. Shadrak pressed his back against the chimney breast, making a tent of his cloak so he could study the map he'd stolen when they entered the city.

Jeridium was designed along a simple grid, and it didn't take a genius to find Seventy-First Street. Shadrak scrunched up the map and threw it to the street below. No need for it now; he only had to look at something once to have its image burned into his mind. After navigating the maze of passageways that made up the lore craft, Jeridium was going to be a doddle.

His face tightened at thought of the lore craft, and his eyes narrowed as he ran through the possibilities for the thousandth time. He couldn't have just lost it, not with his memory. Either the Sour Marsh had swallowed it, or someone had found it.

A flash erupted in the sky. Shadrak stood, holding onto the chimney so the gusting winds didn't fling him after the map. Where the light had flared, the purple smudge was speckled with black. It was impossible to tell how big the spots were from so far away, but whatever was happening above the Mountain of Ocras, it wasn't good.

He slid to the edge of the roof on his backside and was reaching for the drainpipe when he saw a dark shape out of the corner of his eye. It was on an adjacent rooftop.

Shadrak rolled from the roof, caught hold of the guttering, and shimmied along till he'd put the building between him and whatever was watching him. Because it was watching, he was sure of that.

He dropped to a window ledge, found fingerholds in the wall beside it, and climbed down.

The street was deserted. Water spilled from overflowing gutters, and swirls of wind sent leaves and dust dancing into the air.

Something leapt from the rooftop and glided down to the pavement farther along the street. It was black, save for the shimmer of silver on its torso, with slender limbs and a long head. Shadrak caught himself staring, momentarily frozen. It had no eyes, no facial features at all. Quick as a flash, its hand went to its hip and came up firing.

Shadrak dived and rolled and ran. Air whistled past his ear, and then he flung himself headfirst through a window. Glass shattered, and he tumbled into a room, cuts stinging his face and arms.

Scanning the room, he took the stairs up two at a time, barged through a door, and ran across a bed. A woman screamed and a man swore. The whole place stank of sweat and musk, but Shadrak went straight for the sash window, lifted it, and climbed out onto the sill.

He saw everything larger than life now, slow and easy, like he always did when his blood was up. He jumped for the drainpipe and shimmied up to the roof.

More screams from below, and two booms.

It had a weapon like his Thundershot.

He sprinted, threw himself to the next roof, rolled and ran without breaking his stride. He kept on leaping from rooftop to rooftop until he was sure nothing could have kept up with him.

Collapsing against an ornate balustrade, he focused on slowing his ragged breaths.

He'd panicked, he knew that; but he also knew that if he hadn't panicked, he'd most likely be dead. Whatever that thing was, it was fast. Faster than should have been possible. Question was, why had it come after him? Chance? Bad luck? Or was it

MOUNTAIN OF MADNESS

something else?

He looked up at the roiling skies, half-expecting the creature to glide down out of the clouds. A few more deep breaths, and his heart stopped its flapping. He was seeing shadows everywhere, but that only told him he was still spooked.

He made a couple of practice draws, spinning the Thundershot before holstering it each time. With one last look around, he decided there was nothing more he could do. Death, when it came, was as swift and as sudden as a knife in the back. All you could do was stay sharp and be ready to do whatever it took to survive. He'd been cheating death most of his life; no reason this should be any different.

He made his way to Seventy-First Street, and besides the odd patrol of bedraggled and miserable-looking militiamen, he didn't see a thing.

The sign above the door used to read "Dougan's Diner", but some scut had half-painted out "Dougan's" and put "Queenie's" there instead. And they'd added "Fine" in between. It couldn't have been long ago, either, because the paint was still running from the base of the letters.

Whatever Aristodeus had said about the food, it sure smelled good from outside, and it set his stomach rumbling. Garlic, if he wasn't mistaken, and the yeasty smell of fresh-baked bread.

Bells tinkled as he pushed through the door. The place was a mess—tables stacked with dirty crockery.

The waiter was over by the bar, between a short, bearded punter with mottled cheeks and Rutha, who was out cold, a flagon of beer clutched in her hand.

The waiter jumped as though he'd just stuck his hand in boiling water. Shadrak narrowed his eyes. The waiter was a weedy looking beggar in outsized clothes, and he was starting to lose his hair. The only thing that set him out as staff was the neat black apron tied round his waist. What he was doing up so close to the bitch was anyone's guess.

"We're closed," the whelp said.

Shadrak's eyes moved pointedly to Rutha and back.

"I was checking her pulse," the waiter said. "Too much to

drink, silly cow."

"Strange place to look for a pulse."

"Yeah, well I ain't no doctor, am I?" The waiter's eyes widened, and he guffawed. "What the frig are you, a dwarf to a dwarf?" He patted the bearded man on the back. "Eh, Rugbeard, you didn't tell me you had a kid."

The bearded man seemed oblivious. He downed his drink, belched, and then tugged Rutha's flagon out of her grasp. He must have been roughly the same height as Nameless, though skinny and knotted up with arthritis.

"Spirit of a dwarf," Rugbeard said with a pitying look at Rutha, "but not the constitution." He took a long pull on Rutha's drink, swayed in his seat, and then his head hit the bar. Within moments, he was snoring.

"Get me a bucket of water," Shadrak said.

"Bucket?" the waiter said. "Don't you mean glass? Mind you, a little geezer like you might be better off with a wooden cup, so you don't cut yourself. Looks like you've already got more than your share of nicks. What happened? Someone drag you through a bramble bush?"

Shadrak growled and whipped out a knife. "I'll give you worse, if you don't shut your trap and do as I told you."

"Yeah?"

"Yes." Shadrak advanced on him, pressed the tip of his blade against the idiot's nuts.

The waiter's lips trembled, and a tic started up under his eye. He gulped and tried to back away, but Shadrak went with him.

"Water, you cretin. In a bucket. Understand?"

The waiter nodded and cocked a thumb over his shoulder toward the kitchen. Shadrak turned him around and booted him up the arse, sending him sprawling through the louvered doors. Someone yelled, and the waiter started blubbing.

Shadrak lifted Rutha's head by the hair. Her face was smeared with puke. The sight of it nearly made him gag, and he dumped her head back down with a thud. It was going to take more than a bucket of water to rouse her, that was for sure.

The kitchen doors flew open. "Knife or no knife, I'm not

having that kind of carry on in my... Oh, my shitting... Shadrak!"

Shadrak gasped, then frowned, then scowled. "Albrec."

Same as ever, the poisoner was dressed in a charcoal jacket and britches with hairline stripes, but he wore a stained white apron over the top. His bald head was covered by a chef's toque, which he removed and clutched to his breast.

"I..." Albrec started, chewing his bottom lip. "I suppose you're wondering how I came to be here?"

"Where's my scutting lore craft?"

Albrec waved his hat around, the same way he used to flap his papa's hanky when he was nervous. "I can explain, but just look at this place, this city. Me coming here has done us both an enormous favor."

"I asked you where my craft is."

Albrec gave a delicate cough. "Safe. I had a little accident, but it's fine. I left it a few miles outside the city and hitched myself a lift here."

The waiter peered out from behind one of the kitchen doors. "Safe, my nut-sack. I picked him up near some boreworm holes. Stupid plonker nearly got himself ate."

"Eaten," Albrec said. "And you're exaggerating, Buck. Haven't you got something useful to do, like fetch that bucket of water?"

"But you said—"

Albrec slammed the door in his face.

"Twat," Shadrak said.

"That, old friend, is Buck Fargin, soon to be guildmaster of the Night Hawks."

"What's that, flower arrangers' guild?"

"Entrepreneurs," Albrec said.

"Thieves, then."

"And assassins. This city, Shadrak, is incredible. It makes Vanatus look like a village in comparison. I've already made a contact in the Senate, and plans are afoot to raise our friend here to the top of the most powerful guild."

"With you pulling his strings," Shadrak said. He knew the poisoner of old, and besides, it's what he'd have done himself. Had done, back in Vanatus, with Albrec by his side.

Buck shouldered his way through the kitchen doors, sloshing water from a bucket all over the floor. He swore and set the bucket down.

"Mop, cretin. Mop," Albrec said.

"I know, I know!"

Shadrak looked around at the diner. "You've got a nice place here, Albrec. Didn't exactly waste much time."

"None at all. The owner was an oaf, more suited to bricklaying than cooking. He fell ill, and so I stepped into his shoes, with the blessing of my senator friend, I might add. Come on, Shadrak, what do you say? You and me, taking over the guilds one by one, like we did in Vanatus."

Until it had all gone wrong, and they'd both been lucky to survive the resultant backlash.

Shadrak smiled and shook his head. It was tempting, but what good would it do if the world was about to end?

"Any other time, but you seen the storm outside?"

"So?"

"It's the Unweaving, Albrec. The end of all things. It's started. If we don't find a way to stop Sektis Gandaw, there won't be no guilds for us to run."

"We? Surely you're not suggesting—"

"There's three of us." Shadrak picked up the bucket. "And her." With a heave, he upended it over Rutha's head.

"Shit!" Rutha shot upright, as if she'd been struck by lightning. She tried to stand, but the stool tipped over and she fell sprawling to the floor.

Shadrak toed her in the ribs, but she just grunted and rolled onto her side. Within moments she was snoring as loudly as the dwarf.

"What the heck?" Buck said, bashing his way through the doors with a mop. "All I spilled's a little trickle. What did you have to go and flood the place for?" He tried to hand Shadrak the mop. "You clean it up."

"Careful, Buck," Albrec said. "This is Shadrak the Unseen, probably the nastiest bastard I've had the pleasure of working with.

He must be in a rare good mood. The way you've been carrying on, you should be floating down the sewers by now."

"Still time for that," Shadrak said.

Buck paled and set about mopping up the water with vigor.

"Don't worry about her," Albrec said, stepping over Rutha on his way back to the kitchen. "I have the perfect remedy for drunkenness. She'll be right as rain in a couple of hours. Well, not quite right, but she'll be conscious."

"I can hardly wait," Shadrak said. "And Albrec..."

The poisoner paused in the doorway. "Dearest?"

"I haven't forgotten about the lore craft."

FIFTEEN

Nameless watched numbly as Aristodeus took three metal rods from Master Quilth's desk and screwed them together. Within minutes, the philosopher had assembled a stand with a hook at the top. From that, he hung a pliant silver bag that bulged at one end when he squeezed it. To the bottom of the bag he attached a length of clear tubing, and then he selected locking forceps, which he used to clamp the tube.

Next, he ripped open a packet and took out a broad needle.

"You might want to look away," the philosopher said. "Actually, you might want to remove your chainmail first."

When Nameless didn't move, Aristodeus asked, "What's the matter?" A flash of impatience passed across his eyes, swiftly masked with a good impression of genuine concern. "Let me guess: grief? You didn't have time to mourn your pa, let alone Lukar, before I put you to sleep, is that it? Or is it guilt for the massacre? Let me put that particular misapprehension to rest: it was not your fault. You understand me? We are all deception's prey."

"I dreamed," Nameless said. "On the way here, I slept beneath a tree, and I dreamed."

"Of what?"

Nameless thought back to the cavern of coal and its stench of sulfur.

"A gigantic figure. A man of shadows, encased in ice."

Aristodeus flinched. "Mananoc," he breathed. "The deceiver who feeds on chaos and destruction."

"Violet eyes," Nameless went on, "and mocking laughter."

"Pay him no heed," Aristodeus said.

"Easy for you to say. You didn't see it."

Aristodeus stooped before him, gazed in at the eye-slit. "But I have seen him. I feel him every day, hear his insidious whisperings in here." He tapped his head. "But I am a wolf, not a sheep. I choose to fight back."

"How?" Nameless asked. "How do you fight such a thing?"

"With cunning," Aristodeus said. "With guile. By using his own tools against him."

"You think you can outwit a god?"

"Mananoc is just a being, like the rest of us," Aristodeus said. "Powerful beyond measure, but a being nonetheless. A creature from the Supernal Realm, just like his brother, the Archon, and his sister, Etala. The Supernal Triad, they are called in Zaylus's insipid scriptures, but that's as good a title as any. The three who fell through the Void.

"Why they fell is anybody's guess. A conflict, from what I can gather from the Archon: Mananoc's challenge to the Supernal Father, Witandos. But when they arrived in our cosmos, Mananoc raped his sister. The Archon drove him off using the very sword Zaylus now wields. Drove him back to the Void, where nothing can exist. But the will of Mananoc is without peer. He threw up his own realm about him, preserved his essence on the cusp of the Void, and in so doing created the Abyss. That's what you saw: Mananoc frozen within his own creation, powerless to act save by an extension of his mind, and by the generation of offspring to do his bidding."

"The faen?" Nameless asked.

"And demons."

"But why me? Not just the dream, but the black axe. Mananoc intended it for me, I feel that now."

"Because you are special, and he wanted to pervert that. Mananoc craves only conflict and ruin. He hates all that is not himself—something he has in common with Sektis Gandaw."

Aristodeus turned away. "I saw the ploy, but too late. Too late to prevent Lukar from going into Aranuin."

"And yet you still aided me in following him."

Aristodeus whirled round. For an instant his eyes seemed to plead for understanding, for forgiveness, but they swiftly hardened over with icy blue.

"What would you have had me do? Abandon Lukar? He was my friend, not just my pupil. And he was your brother. Would you seriously have left him to his fate?"

Nameless's legs buckled, and he stumbled. Strength was no longer bleeding from him, it was pouring away in torrents. "But it made no difference. They killed him. They threw my brother to the seethers."

Aristodeus steepled his fingers beneath his nose. He sighed, and for a moment closed his eyes. "I know."

He looked away, a forlorn figure on the cusp of despair.

"I once told you that the future is not written in stone," the philosopher said. "And though Lukar's death plunged me into doubt, it is a truth I will defend till my dying breath. I cannot accept a world without the will to act freely. We must fight, Nameless—me, you, Zaylus—and keep on fighting, until we have exhausted every option. If we are but puppets, then we can at least be puppets that bite the hand of the puppetmaster."

"But what is the point," Nameless said, "if we can never win?"

"Do not believe that," Aristodeus said. "Not even for a moment, because once you do, then all is lost. Let me ask you this: Do you believe in good and evil? In right and wrong?"

Nameless gave a slow nod of the great helm.

"Well, I never did," Aristodeus said. "Not until I met Sektis Gandaw. It was in Vanatus, centuries ago, when his blend of lore and sorcery first posed a threat to the world."

"Centuries?" Nameless said. "You met him centuries ago?"

Aristodeus waved off the question as if it weren't important. "I was sent to meet with him, reason him on to a different path, a path of concession and peace. I failed. For all my skill with logic, my reputation for never losing an argument, he just sat there and observed me like a specimen on the dissecting table. You see,

Sektis Gandaw didn't believe in evil, either. But during that meeting, to my mind, he came to embody it. Don't you see? Sektis Gandaw is as deceived as Lukar—as you were when under the sway of the black axe. He's just another tool of Mananoc.

"The things that man did in the name of knowledge—to animals, to people, to children... I am not squeamish by nature, but somewhere, in some hidden strata of my being, I knew that everything about Sektis Gandaw was wrong. And then he let slip his dirty little secret: his plan to harness the energy of a Supernal being, so he could unweave all of Creation. I thought him mad at first, but then he showed me the schematics, and a millennia's worth of algorithms he had meticulously worked out from the unimaginable amounts of information he had collated during his long and unnatural life. He found patterns in the cosmos, connections between all things that he traced to a singular starting point: the moment that imperfection first arose; what was for him the generative act of an imperfect god."

"The Supernal Father, Witandos?"

Aristodeus shrugged. "One would assume so, though I'd never say it to his face. Witandos, in Sektis Gandaw's mind, was unfit to be a creator, which accounts for all that is wrong with the world."

"And Gandaw thinks he could do a better job?" Nameless said.

"That's about the sum of it. When Gandaw commenced the Unweaving before, your ancestor, Maldark the Fallen, aided him at first, swallowed his lies. But Maldark was no one's fool. He saw through Gandaw in time. Maldark and I joined forces, along with the Wayists who had driven Gandaw from Vanatus, and we confronted Gandaw within the Mountain of Ocras."

"And Maldark retrieved the Statue of Etala," Nameless said. That much he knew from the stories in the *Chronicles* Rugbeard used to read to the children of Arx Gravis. "And he hid it from the world."

Aristodeus sighed as he nodded. "But there was collateral damage. To me. Damage that to this day is still being worked out."

"What kind of—?"

Aristodeus silenced him with a raised hand. "Chainmail. If you're going to emulate Maldark and help put a stop to the end of all things, you need to be fed."

Nameless tugged the hauberk over his head and removed his padded gambeson.

Aristodeus pulled out a chair from Quilth's desk and bade him sit. "Now, this is going to hurt."

The philosopher pressed the needle to Nameless's belly and pushed. Nameless winced and bit his lip, but he refused to let a sound escape his lips.

"All the way into the stomach," Aristodeus said. "Now, I just need to attach the tube and we're away."

Blood seeped around the needle, but Aristodeus ripped open another packet and stuck a patch of something glossy over the site. Then, with the tube from the bag connected to the needle embedded in Nameless's stomach, the philosopher released the clamp, and whatever was in the bag began to flow.

"It'll take a while," Aristodeus said. "But look at it this way: you'll not need another feed for a few days. And if we are successful, if Gandaw is stopped, I'll put together a denser, slow-release formula that should keep you going for a month or so. Call it a miracle of the Ancients who founded Vanatus, if you like. You might even want to thank Sektis Gandaw for his part in its development."

"And the helm?" Nameless asked. "Because I'll not spend the rest of my days without feeling the wind on my face, or a lassie's bristles pressed up against mine. And the beer: no amount of gunk in a tube can make up for Ballbreakers' Black Ale." He would have said Cordy's Arnochian brew, but the memory was too painful. A lost friend. A love that might have been. Gone, along with Thumil and everyone else he'd known in Arx Gravis.

"You must have patience," Aristodeus said. "I am following up on leads that may yet see you out of that helm, and the black axe destroyed."

"Does it involve your dissident faen?"

"The Sedition, yes."

"How did that work out for you last time?"

"These are complex issues. So many variables. So many interconnected patterns. By the time my contacts in the Sedition confirmed my suspicions about the inserted passages in the *Chronicles* that spoke of the Axe of the Dwarf Lords, Lukar had already gone off to look for it. The last thing I'd have expected from dwarves was a loose cannon. Always so staid and predictable. But apparently not you and your brother."

Aristodeus crossed to the window and peered outside. Nameless had the impression the philosopher wasn't really looking; he was masking his need to think, to check he was making the right decisions.

Nameless glanced through the eye-slit at the slowly emptying bag that was feeding him.

"A little longer," Aristodeus said, turning away from the window. "And then we'll join the others at Dougan's Diner. Hopefully, Zaylus will have some good news."

"You think the Senate will listen to him?"

"More than they ever listened to me." Aristodeus's eyes widened with sudden realization. He slapped himself on the forehead three times in quick succession. "You stupid idiot, Aristodeus! Zaylus is a Wayist!"

"Something you want to share, laddie?" Nameless said.

"Oh, it's probably nothing. The Senate of Jeridium are paranoid about Sektis Gandaw. Years ago, they thought they could appease him by outlawing religion: specifically, the followers of the Way."

"So, Zaylus is in trouble?"

"Not necessarily," Aristodeus said. "Though the symbol on his surcoat, the Wayist Monas, will give him away."

"Maybe he'll keep his coat done up?" Nameless suggested.

Aristodeus scowled.

"Do you want me to go after him?" Nameless asked.

"No, that might make matters worse. Zaylus has been in tight spots before. He can handle himself."

"So I've seen," Nameless said, "but who is he exactly?" He meant, "Why was his voice able to awaken me?" but assumed he would get no answer to that particular question, and so he added, "And who is Rutha? I've worked out for myself that Shadrak's a nasty piece of work, though I think he's warming to my humor, but

Rutha… Is there bad blood between her and Zaylus?"

"Rutha is a nobody," Aristodeus said. "There was once something between her and Zaylus, but that relationship was… discouraged. Between you and me, she's got issues."

"That's more than I need to know," Nameless said. "But how does she fit into this plan of yours? Can she fight?"

"Oh, she can fight all right. Rutha is my back-up plan. Or rather, my second back-up. You are my first. Zaylus is our best hope, of that I am certain; but if he fails, I need you to step in. What can't be achieved by painstaking preparation might yet be achieved through brute force. And if not, then I've started to plan for other contingencies."

"Which is why you asked Rutha to go with you."

"Indeed."

"Go where?"

"That would be beyond even my ability to explain."

"So, she's your last resort, eh?" Nameless said. "That's a lot of trust you're putting in a nobody. Or is there more to this than you're saying?" Which would be nothing unusual.

"Rutha has been prepared the best she can be," Aristodeus said. "Only, there are matters beyond my control. She has a dreadful temper for one thing, and worse than that, she drinks. A lot."

"Laddie, she sounds like a dwarf."

SIXTEEN

Zaylus's eyes drank in the view, but he couldn't believe what he was seeing.
   The avenue he'd been following opened onto a vast piazza flanked by colonnaded walkways that formed two halves of a broken circle. A slender obelisk stood at the hub, and at the far end, broad steps led up to the portico of a domed basilica that bore an uncanny resemblance to Luminary Trajen's Basilica, where he had been consecrated as a knight. Even the gigantic statues of the luminaries atop the colonnades looked the same, except many had been damaged at some time or another and were missing arms or heads. If not for the city walls looming in the distance, and the red-plumed and kilted soldiers stationed at intervals around the piazza, he would have thought he was back home in Vanatus, and that these past few days had been no more than a waking nightmare.
   Darkening skies swirled above the city, a maelstrom of purple clouds fractured by jags of unnatural lightning. Far to the west, the black spots he'd seen earlier had coalesced into a pool of inky blackness that looked for all the world like a dead or dying sun.
   Tugging down his hat against the sheeting rain, he cut a path across the center of the piazza. Soldiers stationed around pillars glanced at him, but for the most part their eyes were on the sky. He splashed through the puddles threatening to flood the mosaic floor and took a moment's shelter at the base of the obelisk. The basilica dome loomed above him like the head of a curious god, just the

same as in Vanatus, and the curving colonnades created the impression of all-embracing arms.

When he reached the steps, a soldier moved to intercept him.

"Business?" The man looked miserable, water cascading from his bronze helm, running in rivulets down his spear shaft and spattering his shield.

"I need to speak with the Senate."

"Don't we all?"

"It's urgent."

The guard puffed out his cheeks, eyes focused beyond Zaylus's shoulder on the chaotic skies. "Always is, sir. Always is. Desk on the left as you go in."

What should have been the narthex was a reception area with a long counter closing off the entrance to the nave. Behind it were a pair of ornate doors and a couple of guards with crossed spears. A sign hanging by chains from the ceiling marked it as the "Senate Chamber." In front of the counter, smaller signs pointed to a dozen or so doorways, each with its own guard. A rope railing sectioned off the right side of the chamber, beyond which men and women in white togas mingled. Just inside the entrance, a drenched crowd had gathered, looking out at the rain, mumbling and pointing.

To the left, there was a disinterested soldier behind a leather-topped desk. His helmet sat atop a stack of papers, and a scabbarded sword hung from the back of his chair.

"Name?" the soldier said, shutting the book he was reading and taking up a quill. He dipped it in an inkwell and looked up expectantly.

"Zaylus. Hale Zaylus. I need to—"

"Keep hold of this." The soldier scrawled on a slip of paper, tore it in half, and gave one piece to Zaylus. "Hand it in at the main counter, and they'll be only too glad to help."

The queue at the counter was short but slow moving. Those being attended to asked the most inane questions, and the receptionist listened with practiced interest before hunting through drawers of paperwork, as if there were some kind of virtue in being slow.

Zaylus drummed his fingertips against the *Lek Vae* in his

pocket, fiddled with his prayer cord, all the while stretching up on tiptoe to see what the hold up was. Last time he'd been in line for any length of time was for confession, and the Way alone knew how long ago that was.

Maybe that was what was wrong with him, he thought: a soul like a drain badly in need of unclogging. So many of his thoughts, words and actions had heaped sin upon sin, and yet here he was carrying on like the last great hope of all creation and putting the Way to one side to be picked up when he'd set the world to rights. Not him, he thought bitterly: Aristodeus.

He stepped to the side of the queue so he could get a better look at what the receptionist was doing.

"Is there a problem, sir?"

Zaylus started. A soldier stood at his shoulder, peering at him through narrowed eyes.

"This is taking too long," Zaylus said. "I need to see a senator urgently. You've noticed the weather outside? Is that normal?"

The soldier puffed his cheeks out and looked about till he caught the attention of one of his colleagues, who stepped towards them. "Keep your voice down, sir. Don't want to start a panic now, do we?"

"I know what it is," Zaylus said.

The other soldier took hold of him by the arm. "Step this way please, sir."

Zaylus complied and was escorted to a door with a soldier on each arm. The guard on the door moved aside and let them into a waiting room.

A woman with long mousy hair looked up from a row of chairs. She was scantily clad in the most gaudy colors, and her face was rouged and streaked with tear tracks.

"What you done?" she asked Zaylus.

"Done?"

But before she could respond, Zaylus was whisked off down a corridor and into a windowless room with a desk and two chairs.

"Sword belt," one of the soldiers said.

When Zaylus hesitated, the other man glared and gripped the hilt of the sword at his hip.

"Standard precaution," the first soldier explained. "You'll get it back when you leave."

Zaylus shook his head but did as he was asked. Last thing he needed was a fight, not if he wanted to elicit the Senate's help.

"Wait here, sir," the first soldier said as he accepted Zaylus's scabbarded sword and trailing belt. "Someone will be with you shortly."

The soldiers left, shutting the door with a clang, which was when Zaylus noticed it was iron. Then he saw the reddish stains on the whitewashed walls. The desktop was dappled with dark splotches.

To his relief, the door opened almost immediately, and a hawkish man in a grey tunic came in with both guards in tow. With a curt nod to Zaylus, he seated himself at the desk and gestured for Zaylus to take the chair opposite.

"I am Darylius Mesqui, clerk to the Senatorial Prefecture for Civic Rectitude. I will take some details and ask some questions; after which, you will have the opportunity to ask questions of your own." He held out a hand, and one of the soldiers passed him a clipboard. The other soldier set an inkwell and quill on the desk, and then both retreated to the door and stood in front of it, arms folded across their chests.

Zaylus leaned towards Mesqui. "Are you a senator?"

"No, which is why I introduced myself as a clerk."

"I need to speak with—"

Mesqui held up a finger. "Details first. My questions. Then yours." He dipped the quill in the inkwell and scratched away at the parchment on the clipboard. "Name?"

"I've already given my name to the guard on my way in. Can we please—?"

Mesqui sighed and scratched his forehead. "Must I repeat the question?"

Zaylus gritted his teeth. "Look, there isn't time for this. I came here to speak with a senator, not a clerk." He started to stand, but strong hands pressed down on his shoulders.

"Make it easy on yourself, sir," the soldier said. "Just answer the questions."

"Zaylus. Hale Zaylus, as I already told the man on the desk. Don't you people talk?"

Mesqui rolled his eyes. "May I continue, or would you prefer to tell me how to do my job?"

"Just get on with it," Zaylus said.

The soldiers stepped away behind him once more.

"Now, Mr. Zaylus," Mesqui said, "empty your pockets."

With a shake of his head, Zaylus tugged the *Lek Vae* from his coat pocket and slid it onto the table.

Mesqui leaned forward and squinted at the title. His eyes widened, and he looked past Zaylus to the guards, before riffling through the pages, pausing now and then to skim over a passage, all the time shaking his head. "This is yours? You read it? You pray?"

Zaylus sat back and looked up at the ceiling. What could he say? No matter how tenuous his faith in the Way had become, he couldn't lie about it. "Yes."

Mesqui sat perfectly still for a long moment, his eyelids drooping almost shut. Finally, he pinched the bridge of his nose and sucked in a whistling breath through his teeth. "I think it's best you see the Prefect."

Zaylus took back the *Lek Vae* and slipped it in his pocket. "Is he a senator?"

Mesqui stood and picked up the inkwell, balancing it on his clipboard. "Yes, he's a senator. Thank you for your time. The Prefect will be with you presently."

The guards parted for Mesqui to exit then shut the door and stood either side of it, one tapping out a rhythm on the pommel of his sword, the other clenching and unclenching his fingers.

Zaylus didn't have long to wait. Within minutes, the door was slung open and a pot-bellied man in a toga flounced in.

"Mr. Zaylus." He held out a hand, eyes twinkling, a perfect smile cutting a white line across his box beard. "Senator Whittler. I'm the Prefect here. Mr. Mesqui has given me the bare essentials, but you'll have to fill in the blanks." He came round the table and grunted as he lowered himself into the chair Mesqui had used earlier. "I'm sorry you've had all this trouble getting to see me."

He threw up his hands and rolled his eyes. "That's bureaucracy for you. Now, Mr. Mesqui was concerned about a book in your possession. May I see it?"

"Senator," Zaylus said, "This storm—"

"Oh, really, Mr. Zaylus. A little inclement weather and everyone's talking about the end of the world."

"It's the start of the Unweaving," Zaylus said.

"Of course it is," Whittler said. "Either that or Mananoc the Deceiver ate an overly spicy meal and as a consequence has a bad case of wind."

Whittler's eyes flicked between the two guards before he leaned across the desk. This time when he spoke, there was no pretense of amiability. "The book."

Zaylus passed him the *Lek Vae*, and Whittler flicked through the pages, muttering to himself. Finally, he handed it back and gave a resolved nod.

"What's that beneath your coat?" the Prefect asked.

Zaylus's hand flew to his collar, where the white of his surcoat was plainly visible.

"Remove it."

The guards stepped in close, giving Zaylus no choice but to take off his coat.

Whittler peered at the red Monas on the surcoat—the symbol of the Way. "Just like those underground Wayists who prowl the markets, handing out their nauseating little slips of paper. This city was built by dwarves," Whittler said, "on the orders of Maldark the Fallen, a devotee of the Wayist religion. You know, of course, that Sektis Gandaw hates Wayists, not just because they were the ones to exile him from Vanatus, but because Maldark, once his ally, betrayed him.

"Odd, don't you think, that your arrival coincides with the storms coming from the Mountain of Ocras? Coincidence? I think not. Sektis Gandaw sees everything, Zaylus, which is why we work so assiduously to root the Wayists from our city."

"You seek to appease him?" Zaylus said.

"And why wouldn't we? We've not heard a peep from the Mountain of Ocras all the years we've done our best to eradicate the Wayists, but recently they've grown emboldened, and now you just happen to show up, wearing that accursed Monas symbol and shamelessly carrying a copy of the *Lek Vae*."

"I came here to warn you about the Unweaving," Zaylus said, "and to ask your help."

"You want Jeridium to oppose Sektis Gandaw?"

"It's the only way."

Whittler ran his hand over his mouth, considering. "No," he said at last. "I can think of another." The Prefect stood and headed for the door, but turned back to Zaylus as a soldier opened it for him. "I think, by the morning, we should see some big improvements in the weather." Then, to the soldiers, he said, "I trust you men haven't forgotten how we deal with Wayists."

The soldiers smiled at each other.

As Whittler left the room, they both turned to face Zaylus. One of them took off his studded belt and wound it around his fist.

Zaylus cursed and ran at him, meaning to barrel past and through the door, but the other soldier moved quickly, and smashed the pommel of his sword into his head. As Zaylus's knees buckled, the first soldier's belt-wrapped fist struck him in the face. Metal studs smashed into his lips, and he tasted blood. He tried to rise, but blow after blow pummeled him to the ground. He curled his legs up to his chest and covered his head with his arms as the soldiers stomped on him. He cried out as a rib cracked and pain lanced through his chest. And then it was all a hazy blur accompanied by the muffled thuds of boots and fists.

SEVENTEEN

"I thought you said it was called Dougan's Diner," Nameless said.

"Well, that's new." Aristodeus wrinkled his nose at the sign. "The paint's still wet. And who, I might add, is Queenie? Dougan's owned this dump for years. Everybody who's anybody eats here. Well, everybody who's anybody in Jeridium's underworld."

"And yet you told Shadrak not to eat the food."

"When I said everybody eats here, I should perhaps have said 'meets.' Chef Dougan is a man of many talents, but cooking isn't one of them."

Nameless had the sudden feeling of being watched. He turned and looked up at the rooftops behind. Was that a shadow crouched beside a chimney?

The tinkling of bells distracted him, and Aristodeus entered the diner. At the same instant, a scrawny-looking man in clothes a couple of sizes too big came flying out head first. He hit the road, tumbled badly, then picked himself up and set off down the street, mustering as much dignity as he could.

Nameless glanced back at the rooftop, but the shadow was gone.

"Nameless," Shadrak said as he stepped across the threshold and shut the door behind him. The assassin's new cloak was ragged and frayed, and his face and hands were cut in a score of places. "About bloody time."

"These things can't be hurried," Aristodeus said. "But he is now fed, and that is the important thing."

The scent of garlic and fresh-baked bread wafted through the eye-slit of the great helm. It didn't matter that Nameless had just been fed through a tube, he was instantly hungry.

A dozen or so tables were stacked with smeared plates and half-empty glasses, but no one seemed to be clearing up. Toward the rear of the diner there were louvered swing doors, from beyond which came the clatter of pots and pans.

Shadrak grabbed Nameless by the arm and took him to one side. "You see anything out there?"

"How did you know?"

"Because it damned near killed me, that's how. Up on the rooftops. A creature, all black and featureless. Glided down on some sort of membranes beneath its arms."

"There was a shadow," Nameless said. "On one of the roofs opposite."

Shadrak started toward the door, but Nameless held him back. "Gone now. When the scruffy ragamuffin was slung out onto the street. Must have scared it off."

"Buck Fargin?" Shadrak said. He shared a look with a fat man in a jacket and trousers, both of which were charcoal grey with hair-thin lines in a lighter shade. "Least he was good for something."

"And he'll be good for a whole lot more, if he just does as he's told," the fat man said. He was bald, save for a strip of hair that ran around the base of his skull. He puckered his lips when he spoke, and he had roving eyes that seemed to take in everyone and everything in the diner.

"This is Albrec," Shadrak said. "An old colleague of mine."

"And he came with you from Vanatus?"

Albrec winced, but before either he or Shadrak could answer, an interior door slapped open, and out staggered Rutha. Judging by the stench that followed her, it must have been the latrine. She looked green as a corpse, her eyes bloodshot and sunken. "Look what the cat dragged in," she growled at Aristodeus. "What do you want now?"

The philosopher looked down his nose at her. "From you, nothing more at this juncture. But when you are recovered, we should talk."

"What's there to talk about?" she said, propping herself on a stool at the diner's bar and reaching for a bottle.

On the stool next to her, one of the punters was slouched over the counter with his head in his beer. He looked a shambles, all matted grey hair and beard, and clothes that were coming apart at the seams.

Albrec stepped across Nameless's field of vision to confront Rutha. "I wouldn't," he warned her. "The tisane I gave you doesn't mix well with alcohol."

"Great," Rutha said, then held her head in her hands.

"Albrec's the new owner of this shithole," Shadrak explained.

"Oh?" Aristodeus said. "What happened to Chef Dougan?"

"He ate something that didn't agree with him," Albrec said.

"It was Albrec that moved my lore craft," Shadrak said to Nameless. "The fat scut stowed away when we left Vanatus."

"An old colleague, you say?" Nameless said. "You mean an assassin?"

"Poisoner," Shadrak said. "Best I've worked with."

"Where's Zaylus?" Aristodeus said. "He should have been finished with the Senate by now."

"It's not been that long, surely," Nameless said.

Aristodeus grimaced. "I was an idiot to send him dressed as he was."

Albrec raised an eyebrow. "I once turned up at a function dressed as a harlot—some joker gave me the wrong address."

"Bet you made a fat lot of coin, though," Shadrak said.

Albrec looked hurt. "A shekel or two," he mumbled. "Hardly worth the effort."

Aristodeus gestured toward Rutha in her once-white robe with the red symbol on the front. "He was wearing his Wayist surcoat."

"So?" Albrec said.

"The Senate have made following the Way a crime punishable by death."

"Can't say I blame them," Albrec said. "Pious little hypocrites. Do you know I once laced a bottle of peach brandy for a bishop who was hoping to get lucky at a seminary bash."

"So, why didn't they arrest me?" Rutha said.

"Presumably because your robe looks like a used arse-rag that someone puked on," Shadrak said, "and doesn't have a thread of white left."

"Hilarious," Rutha said, then to Aristodeus, "What are you going to do about Zaylus?"

"Me?" the philosopher said. "Nothing. There's nothing I can do." Aristodeus looked haunted, and something fiery flashed across his eyes, but he swiftly regained his composure. "I am already overstretched, and even if I appealed to the Senate, they wouldn't listen."

"You mean you can't be bothered," Rutha said. "So, the great Aristodeus is a coward as well as a creep."

"The way I see it, laddie," Nameless said to Aristodeus, "if you won't or can't do anything to help Zaylus, you should go pour yourself a drink and let the grown-ups do the thinking."

Aristodeus started to scowl, but then he nodded. "Perhaps you're right. Maybe this is something you could do. Think of it as reparation."

"That was uncalled for," Nameless said.

Aristodeus went to hover over Rutha at the bar. The sleeping man next to her sputtered and shook, turned his head the other way, then resumed his snoring.

Shadrak gestured to a table, and Nameless and Albrec joined him there. "So, what are the options?" Shadrak said.

"We pay the Senate a visit." Nameless patted the haft of his axe.

Shadrak gave a thin smile. "Exactly what I was thinking."

"Isn't that a bit reckless?" Albrec said. "Quite out of character for you, Shadrak."

"It ain't exactly like we have a bunch of time," Shadrak said.

"But we have a little, surely. Personally, I'd find out where they're holding him and break him out."

"And how are you going to do that?" Shadrak asked. "You've

hardly been in Jeridium any longer than we have."

"A day or two more," Albrec said, leaning back in his chair and clasping his hands in his lap. "Enough time to make a powerful connection."

EIGHTEEN

Sektis Gandaw stepped onto the silver disk and allowed the potions to do their work as he descended into the roots of his *ocras* mountain.

He shouldn't have been concerned, but you could never be one-hundred percent certain something was working as it was supposed to until you saw it with your own eyes.

Sektis allowed himself a wry chuckle at that, for his own eyes had long since rotted away to nothing and been replaced by eyes of brilliant violet grown by the lore of the faen.

The disk touched down, reoriented itself, and skimmed along one of the metal tubes that formed a labyrinth beneath the mountain. It slowed to a stop beneath a vertical tube before starting to rise. A circle of *ocras* set into the rock of the ceiling parted like the petals of a flower, and the disk wobbled as it passed through the opening—it wasn't meant to do that.

Sektis stepped off, onto the bleached dust of the Dead Lands. Wind buffeted him and sent strands of hair across his vision. He swept it out of his face with a surge of irritation. The hair wasn't meant to do that, either. He wondered when it had lost its hold.

Three silver ward-spheres shot toward him from the mountain—a little tardily. Even they were no longer living up to his expectations. They stopped abruptly and then began to circle him, each in its own orbit. Anything could have happened in the seconds he'd been left unguarded.

The sky was the color of off-meat, and the bone-dust that formed an island around the Mountain of Ocras was shifting and swirling into jagged monoliths that disintegrated and reformed like waves of wrongness. Even the mangroves at the edge of the Sour Marsh were in upheaval, a writhing, undulating mass. The *ocras* mountain itself was the only stationary point, an anchor amid the chaos, just as it should be. And, of course, it wasn't really chaos if it was planned for, was it? These were expected side effects, the grumblings of nature as it prepared to be unwoven.

High above the Mountain of Ocras, the Null Sphere glistened blackly, gyring and pulsing as it grew fat on the substance of a world.

Sektis sent a mental command to the silver disk. He'd seen enough. Everything was going to plan. He really didn't need to waste his time and energy worrying about—

What about the Void?

He started to descend, patting down his errant hair now that the tube shielded him from the wind.

And the Abyss... You know they exist, and yet you have studiously ignored them.

He wanted to retort that the Abyss was an absurdity, someone else's fantasy. Wanted to say that the Void was just absence, not a thing in itself, and so no part of his patterns. But was that true? He had believed it was, but what if he'd overlooked something? What if he'd been blindsided?

Too late to worry about that, he told himself, and besides, how could he examine and codify emptiness itself? Furthermore, was it even possible to make a reliable study of the Abyss, the realm of Mananoc, a being whose essence was purportedly the very stuff of lies?

As needles pricked him and the potion took effect, Sektis's rational mind reasserted itself. It was nerves, that was all. He was succumbing to phantasms, to irrational fears, to superstition.

Without even noticing the intervening journey, he found himself back in the conical chamber at the heart of the mountain.

Mephesch greeted him with glittery eyes and flicked a look at the winking crystals on his vambrace. "Not long to go now."

All Sektis could manage was a nod.

He strode past the faen and craned his neck to look up at mirror 55 and the inky image of the Void. Gaseous strands crisscrossed its face like a taunt. He was about to turn away when a flicker of flame limned the entire web. He glanced at Mephesch, who merely shrugged, and when he looked again, the flames had gone.

"Problem, Sektis?" Mephesch said.

"No problem." Perhaps he should cut back on the potions—he was starting to see things, and he had to wonder if he was growing paranoid.

Mephesch stuck out his bottom lip and nodded, then he turned his attention to the tiers of mirrors.

The bat-meldings remained hunched over their desks, poised to cry out the instant their respective mirror went blank—when there was nothing left in that part of the world for their scrying to convey.

All going to plan. All going perfectly to plan.

If Sektis repeated the mantra enough, he'd start to believe it. Had it really come to this? Endless years of rigorous planning only to rely at the last on self-deception. Maybe the Unweaving would work despite the omissions. How much difference could it make, not factoring in two things that couldn't possibly fit with the pattern of the rest of creation?

But there it was again: that gulf between "good enough" and perfection. Only, he was starting to get the inkling this was about more than being blindsided by irrational fear; more than a simple case of negligence.

He was starting to feel like he'd been duped.

NINETEEN

My, a senator in my bed. Aren't I the lucky one! Except it was Senator Rollingfield, drugged to the eyeballs and corpulently naked. His discarded toga was a sorry heap on the floor. It didn't seem possible it could fit Rollingfield's lily-white mountains of blubber.

Albrec screwed his face up as he touched two fingers to the senator's throat and raised an eyebrow at the half-empty cocktail glass on the nightstand. Just the memory of Rollingfield tonguing the cherry and guzzling the sugared egg-brandy was enough to give him a case of the shivery jingles.

Albrec let out a hissing sigh of relief. Rollingfield's pulse was down to a trickle, which is just where he needed it.

"You may enter," he called out as he stepped back from the bed and straightened his shirt.

The door opened a crack, and Shadrak slipped in. "Well?" His pink eyes widened at the semi-conscious whale on the mattress.

"Lovely, isn't it?" Albrec said, sweeping up his jacket from the back of the chair and shrugging it on.

"Tell me you didn't."

Albrec rolled his eyes. "Oh, the idea! Mammaries as pendulous as Mama's, and peccadilloes that would make even that old witch turn in her grave. Well, river. Estuary, even."

Buck Fargin burst into the room just as Albrec was situating himself on the edge of the bed once more.

MOUNTAIN OF MADNESS

"Any word on the streets about Zaylus?" Shadrak asked.

Buck puffed out his chest. "Nothing." He gave an uncertain look at the senator sprawled atop the bed. "But I've got my best man on the job."

Albrec scoffed at that. "Are you saying there's been some kind of miracle and your son's not inherited a single one of your defining traits?" He leaned over Rollingfield and pried open an eyelid.

The senator smacked his chops and muttered something incomprehensible. His liver-spotted hand groped around the blubber burying his crotch. "Where is it, my boy? Find it for Rolly."

Albrec held either side of Rollingfield's face. "Look into my eyes, Senator."

"Oh, yes!" Rollingfield's chins quivered, and his tongue darted between his lips. "What else would you like?"

"Just listen."

"I'm listening, dear boy. But first, tell me you like what you see." He jiggled his belly fat.

Behind Albrec, Shadrak sniggered.

"Think I'm gonna throw," Buck said.

The door opened and closed, and Buck's footfalls sounded like a herd of cattle stampeding down the stairs.

"Future guildmaster, you say?" Shadrak said.

"It's how you like them, dearest: dumb and malleable. Now, can we get this over with?"

"My way's better." Shadrak patted the knives in his baldric.

"I didn't cultivate" —Albrec clamped his hands over Rollingfield's ears and hissed—"such a high-up political ally just to have you send him bobbing down the river."

He removed his hands from the senator's ears, eliciting a jowl-wobbling, overly moist smile.

"You're so naughty," Rollingfield said. "Whispering your salacious secrets and not letting me hear because I'm such a bad boy." He rolled onto his side and slapped himself repeatedly on the buttock. "Bad Rolly. Bad, bad, bad Rolly."

Albrec looked at Shadrak, who merely shrugged and mouthed,

"Should've given him more."

"Senator," Albrec said above the spanking. "Senator!"

Rollingfield flopped onto his back and lifted the apron of flab that had been covering his nethers.

Oh, Mother!

Albrec shifted his gaze to the senator's glazed eyes. "Before we... Before we get down to business, uh... Rolly, I wanted to ask you to do something for me."

Rollingfield propped himself up on one elbow. "Anything you like, dear boy."

"It's about the Senate."

"Rut first, politics later."

"But you said anything, Rolly, remember?"

Rollingfield sighed and fell back on the bed. "One of those, are you? Little tease! Very well, what is it you wish to know?"

"A friend of a friend went to the Senate Building earlier today, and he's not been seen since."

"Tall fellow in a brown hat and a white thingymawhatsit over his armor?"

"Surcoat, Senator?"

Shadrak's breath was hot on Albrec's ear as he whispered, "That's him. Ask where he is."

"Yes, yes, thank you," Albrec hissed back, swatting the midget away. *Because I obviously wouldn't have thought of that myself.*

Rollingfield pushed himself into a sitting position and gawped at Shadrak. "You brought a friend?" He patted the mattress. "Come on, sonny, don't be shy."

"Senator," Albrec said, "I need to know what happened to this man. His name is—"

"Zaylus," Rollingfield said. "The Prefect told me when I went to see the prisoner and sign off on his execution. Good-looking fellow. Such a waste, come the morrow, but it's the only way to deal with these holy types."

"You're going to execute him?"

"Enough," Rollingfield said. "I don't know what was in that cocktail, but I'm going to explode if I don't have you right this instant; and then I mean to have your little friend, too. I've not felt so vigorous in years."

"A moment more, Senator." Albrec frowned at the glass on the nightstand. For whatever reason, the powder seemed to be having a paradoxical effect—probably due to the absorbency of the blubber. "Where are you holding Zaylus before the execution?"

"The jail, of course. Now do be a good chap and—"

"Which jail?" Shadrak demanded.

"Small one," Rollingfield said. "Just like you. A teensy-weensy jaily waily."

"Street," Shadrak said. "What street's it in?"

A thick rope of slobber ran from the corner of Rollingfield's mouth. "Ooh, I feel... sleepy." He flopped over onto his side.

"Street!" Shadrak said, drawing a dagger.

Albrec grabbed his wrist and held up a staying finger. "The jail, Senator. We could all go together. You said you liked the look of Zaylus, remember?"

"Ooooooh, yessssss," Rollingfield slobbered. "101st Street. Arse-end of the Senate Buildingy-thingy."

Rollingfield's mouth hung open, and drool trickled down his chin onto the sheets. Within moments he was snoring like a pig with a bad cold.

"I do hope I didn't accidentally overdose him," Albrec said. "Could be catastrophic for his liver."

"How you gonna explain him waking up here?" Shadrak said.

"That's Fargin's job," Albrec said as he opened the door and gestured for Shadrak to go first.

Buck was loitering on the stairwell, arms folded across his chest.

"I thought you were coughing your guts up," Albrec said.

"Yeah, well, I got better."

"You swallowed it, didn't you?"

Buck gave a sheepish grin.

"Are we gonna stand about nattering all day, or do I have to sling you head first down the stairs?" Shadrak said as he pushed past Buck.

"Oi, watch it!" Buck said.

Albrec put a warning hand on his shoulder. "Come on, don't

upset the poison pixie."

They followed Shadrak into the diner, where Nameless was sitting morosely at a corner table fingering a knife and fork and looking out of place in his dark helm. Aristodeus was over by the bar next to the unconscious Rugbeard, smoking a pipe. "Well?" the philosopher said as they entered.

"Thought you wanted nothing to do with it," Shadrak said, as he reversed a chair and sat on it. "Now, this jail on 101st Street, Fargin: what do you know about it?"

"No way," Buck said, taking the chair opposite. "That's only the most heavily guarded place in Jeridium. No one gets in or out. Not never."

"Zaylus is in jail?" Aristodeus said.

Shadrak glanced at Albrec. "Don't think you're staying out of this. We might need your expertise."

"Anything I can do to help," Albrec said as sincerely as he could manage.

"Let me put it another way," Shadrak said. "I ain't letting you out of my sight till I get my lore craft back. Got it?"

Just then, Rutha came stumbling out of the latrine. "I'm coming with you." She promptly belched, clutched her guts, and went back in.

Albrec winced and looked away. Still, he'd told her not to drink on top of the tisane he'd given her.

"No," Shadrak called after her. "You're staying here."

"Yeah," Buck said, as if he was suddenly someone important.

"You, too," Shadrak said. "You might shit the locals, but I know a pillock when I see one. Now, tell me what you know about this jail."

"Impregnated, it is," Buck said. "There's no way you'll get your mate out."

Albrec slapped a palm to his forehead as he joined them at the table.

"What?" Buck said. "I ain't kidding."

"I know," Albrec said. "That's what worries me, but the word you're looking for is 'impregnable.'"

"That's what I said."

Shadrak clicked his fingers. "You two finished? So, what makes it impregnable? Locks? Traps? The number of guards?"

Buck shrugged at each suggestion.

"All of the above?" Shadrak said.

Another shrug.

"So, you don't know the first thing about it, right?"

Buck grimaced. "I hear things."

"Who from?" Shadrak slid off his chair and stalked towards him.

"Well, people say things—"

"The guilds?"

"Maybe."

Shadrak grabbed him by the collar. "Maybe?"

Buck shook his head, his eyes welling up. "I've told you all I know."

Rugbeard sputtered and shook, his face pressed against the bar, buried beneath a mass of unruly grey hair. He coughed and grumbled something, then resumed his snoring.

Aristodeus glanced at Nameless, who didn't see. The dwarf was still sat alone at his table, though the eye-slit of his dark helm was angled toward Shadrak now, as if he were paying close attention. The philosopher gave a pitying shake of his head and proceeded to tap out the bowl of his pipe on the countertop, much to Albrec's chagrin.

"Look," Shadrak said, "all we know is Zaylus is being held in a jail at the back of the Senate Building. Now, usually, I'd stake it out, see all the comings and goings, work out the locks and all that, but we don't have the time. The way I see it, if we can't prepare for the specifics, we prepare for everything. That's why I need you," he said to Albrec. "And you, my friend,"—he finally acknowledged Nameless—"are there for if it goes tits up."

"Sounds like a plan to me," Nameless said from across the room.

Albrec scratched his head and wondered how his skills could be of any use when they knew so little about the target. If it was a matter of killing a few guards by poisoning their grub, then he was the man for the job, but when they had no idea how many guards there were or what they liked to eat… What was it Shadrak had said? Prepare for everything? What they needed was a one-fit solution, and with a flash of inspiration, he thought he knew what it was.

"Buck," he said, "where's the nearest blacksmith's? I need a bellows and a—bugger, where are we going to get some tubing?"

Nameless coughed and stood, lifting the front of his chainmail hauberk as he approached. There was a coil of clear tubing taped to his belly, one end terminating in a blue cap, the other penetrating the skin.

"Feeding tube," Nameless said with a nod to Aristodeus. "I'm sure old Baldilocks has plenty more where this came from." With a grunt, he yanked it out and stemmed the flow of blood with his free hand.

"Yes," Albrec said, taking the tube between thumb and forefinger. "That will do nicely."

TWENTY

The rising suns cast the Senate Building in a battlefield hue, but the brightening sky was the color of bruises as sickness spread across it from the Mountain of Ocras.

The jail behind the building was a squat brick and mortar construction with just the one way in and out: an iron-bound hardwood door. The soft glow of lantern light spilled over from the far side, where workmen were hard at it putting the finishing touches to a guillotine.

Nameless staggered past Albrec under the weight of the beer keg he'd lugged all the way from Queenie's Fine Diner. Tankards clattered inside the bag slung over his shoulder.

Albrec was already in position, kneeling beneath the nearside window of the jail and running the tubing Nameless had yanked from his guts up through the bars. The other end was attached to the hand bellows Buck Fargin had come back from the blacksmith's with, which in turn was connected to the bell jar containing the evil-stinking gas the poisoner had concocted.

The guard on the front entrance started awake as Nameless passed him and set the barrel down. Before the fellow could say anything, Nameless cried out in a booming voice, "Beer for the workers! Come and get it, lads!"

A chorus of exclamations erupted from the platform the guillotine stood upon, and a big man approached—presumably the foreman.

"Beer? Who sent it? Not the Senate, surely?"

Nameless didn't reply. He simply tapped the barrel and filled one of the tankards. The big man took it from him, had a taste, then called his workers over.

"Sir?" the door guard said, as he approached. "Excuse me, sir…"

Nameless handed him a beer. "I won't say anything if you don't, laddie. Go on, get that down you."

Desire was written all over the guard's ruddy face. Judging by his bulbous nose and the veins webbing it, he was as likely to refuse a drink as any self-respecting dwarf.

Taking his cue from the workmen bustling over to line up at the barrel, the guard took a sip that became a swig, and then he necked the tankard in a long, glugging pull.

All the while, around the side of the jail, Albrec was pumping furiously on the bellows, and the job was as good as done.

One by one, the workmen took to the beer as if it were Cordy's Arnochian Ale. Nameless could tell from its watery appearance that it wasn't. Even a drinker of Ironbelly's would have been hard-pressed to swallow such goat's piss, but Albrec had augmented it with something from a glass vial, and the workmen were buying it.

By the time Shadrak came jogging down the cobbled road, from where he'd been on rooftop lookout, everyone but the guard was out cold. The assassin had a bloodstained dagger in either hand.

Nameless perched on the edge of the barrel and held a tankard up before the eye-slit. Goat's piss or not, poisoned or otherwise, he would have given his right arm for a swill of cold beer in his mouth.

"What do you think you're doing?" Shadrak said, striding straight past.

Nameless swiveled round to see what he was talking about.

The guard had his sword out and was stumbling toward Albrec, who was reeling in the tubing with a smug grin on his fat face.

Albrec hadn't seen the danger, and as he bent down to disconnect the tubing from the bellows, the guard raised his sword and half-tripped, half-ran in a swaying zigzag toward him. Shadrak ran, as well, but he was too far off to use a dagger. He stopped for a moment to sheathe one of the knives and grab a razor star.

In that moment, Albrec lunged for the guard and got a garrote around his throat.

Nameless let out a booming laugh. He'd not expected that. The poisoner was full of surprises.

The guard's sword clanged to the cobbles. The poor man was arched back at an unnatural angle, arms thrashing, legs twitching, and Albrec was grinning like a baresark with a pitcher of mead. A couple more shakes and shudders, and the guard sank to the ground.

"Credit where credit's due, eh, Shadrak?" Albrec said, straightening up and picking bits of flesh from the garrote. "Chef Dougan might have been a lousy cook, but he had great taste in cheese-cutters."

"Good job, Albrec," Shadrak said. "That all of them?"

"Unless there's a change of guard on the way."

"There was," Shadrak said, slipping the razor star back in his baldric and sheathing his other dagger. "But not anymore. Key?"

Albrec rifled through the dead guard's pockets, checked his belt, and came up shrugging. "It's all yours, then."

Shadrak slipped out his tool-pack and unrolled it. He put a hook pick between his teeth and selected a torsion wrench. The lock was at eye-level for him; anyone else would have had to bend down. Without looking, he wagged his fingers over his shoulder. "Light," he hissed.

Nameless slid from the barrel, set down his untouched beer, and grabbed one of the workmen's lanterns. He ambled over to stand behind Shadrak and illuminate the lock.

"What you need is a hammer and chisel," he said. "It doesn't look a sturdy lock. One good whack—"

"Do I tell you how to lop heads off with an axe?" Shadrak said. "No? Then shut up and let me concentrate."

The assassin placed the torsion wrench in the lower part of the keyhole and applied torque to the cylinder, turning it the merest fraction of an inch. Taking the pick from his teeth, he poked it into the upper part of the lock and felt around.

"My way's quicker," Nameless grumbled.

Shadrak turned the wrench. The lock clicked, and he pushed with his shoulder, but the door didn't budge.

"Don't tell me…" Albrec said.

Shadrak stepped back from the door and gave it a kick. "Barred from the inside. This is why I don't like rushing. Everything needs to be planned out in advance."

"Here," Albrec said, removing the pick and wrench from the lock and passing them back to Shadrak. "Can't say we didn't try."

"Stand back," Nameless said. He handed Albrec the lantern then hefted his axe.

"No," Shadrak said. "We'll use this." He took a glass globe from one of his belt pouches. "I was saving it."

He moved back, gesturing for the others to follow, then gave the globe a good shake and threw it at the door.

There was a blinding flash, a concussive boom, and Nameless was flung onto his back. Sulfurous fumes filled the great helm and made him cough.

"Well, no one would have heard that," Albrec said in a voice dripping with sarcasm. He made a show of dusting himself down as he stood.

Black smoke billowed away on the wind as Shadrak led them through the wreckage of the doorway.

There was a door with a grille opposite, and off to one side there was a heavy wooden chest. Two guards were slumped over a table, greenish drool oozing from their mouths.

Albrec lifted one's head and used his thumb to raise an eyelid, then let the head drop with a thud onto the table.

"Zaylus…" Nameless said, starting toward the cell door.

"Oh, he'll be fine. I dare say only a trickle made it through to the cell. Here." Albrec unclipped some keys from a guard's belt and flung them to him.

Nameless rattled through the bunch till he found the one that fit the lock. There was a healthy clunk as he turned it, and he pushed the door open.

Zaylus was face down on the floor. His hair was matted and caked with filth, and his surcoat was a shredded mess, soaked in blood. A pair of bunks was the only furniture in the whitewashed room. Bloodstained sheets draped down from the top one, and on the bottom lay a scrawny corpse with a face so bruised and bloodied it didn't seem human.

Nameless crossed to the bunks and knelt beside Zaylus, turning him onto his back. The knight had taken one shog of a beating, by the looks of him: split lip, puffy black eyes, streaks of dried blood from dozens of cuts.

"Help me," Zaylus groaned. "Help me up."

Albrec looked at Nameless and stuck out his bottom lip. Together, they supported Zaylus as he stood, coughing and wincing, clutching his side.

"Where's your gear?" Shadrak asked.

Zaylus shrugged, then lurched toward the man lying on the bottom bunk.

"Dead," Shadrak said.

Zaylus lowered himself to one knee beside the bunk and bowed his head. In spite of his injuries—and they looked severe—he was tight as a spring, and tension rolled off him in murderous waves.

Albrec gave a delicate cough and nodded that they should go. He crossed to the doorway and peered out across the guards' room they had entered by.

Nameless put a hand on Zaylus's shoulder. "Laddie, we need to get you out of here."

Zaylus pulled a bloodstained sheet over the corpse's face. "They tortured him," the knight said. "His name was Tovin. He was one of those people handing out slips of paper we saw when we arrived. You know what they were? Invitations to secret prayer meetings. He was a Wayist, Nameless. Like me. Like Thumil back at Arx Gravis."

"Thumil? He read that weird old book, but I wouldn't have said—"

"The *Lek Vae*. The holy word of the Way."

"And that's why they killed him?" Nameless said.

"I don't think they meant to. They were softening him up for execution, but he was too frail, and they went too far."

"Looks like they worked you over as well," Albrec said. "Did a half-decent job of it, too."

Zaylus's eyes hardened. Where they were usually blue, they had darkened to the color of slate. He pulled himself up using the bed-frame, took a lurching step, and staggered as his leading knee buckled. Nameless caught him by the elbow and walked with him into the guards' room.

Zaylus snapped his head around to glare at the chest. He pulled free from Nameless and tottered toward it. "Locked," he muttered.

"Here." Nameless threw him the keys.

Albrec pressed himself against the wall beside the wreckage of the main door and glanced outside.

"How many?" Shadrak asked, rushing to the other side of the entrance to see for himself.

"Three," Albrec said. "But there's activity farther down the street."

Zaylus opened the chest and pulled out his coat, hat and sword belt, quickly putting them on. He adjusted his scabbard so it sat behind his hip.

Nameless joined Shadrak at the entrance and risked a look outside. Two kilted soldiers in bronze breastplates were examining the unconscious workmen. From out of sight, a third cried, "Guard's dead. Someone slit his throat."

Albrec shrugged. "Technically, he was strangled… with blood."

Behind them, a groan sounded from one of the guards slumped over the table.

"You didn't kill them?" Shadrak said.

Albrec frowned. "I thought I did. Must have misjudged the dose."

The two soldiers examining the workmen started straight toward the doorway.

The rasp of a sword being drawn made Nameless look behind. He tried to call out "No!" but he was too stunned to speak.

Zaylus rammed his shortsword through a stirring guard's back. The man spasmed, gurgled, and stilled.

As a soldier stepped though the debris of the door, Albrec slipped behind him and looped his cheese-cutter around his neck.

MOUNTAIN OF MADNESS

When the second soldier yelled and charged to his aid, Shadrak spun away from the wall and flung two razor stars in swift succession. One took the soldier in the eye, the other in the throat. The assassin darted in and finished him off with a dagger through the heart.

Albrec gave a final tug on the garrote and the soldier he was strangling slumped to his knees.

Nameless watched as the third soldier fled toward the Senate Building. "Time to leave," he said.

Zaylus, though, was standing over the other unconscious guard. He took a jug of water from the table and tipped it over the man's head. As the guard spluttered and came awake, Zaylus grabbed him by the hair and exposed his throat.

Nameless rushed back across the room and grabbed the knight's sword arm. "I won't allow it, laddie."

With a flash of movement, Zaylus snatched the shortsword with his other hand and hacked down at Nameless's helm. On instinct, Nameless bashed the blade aside with his axe-haft and hit Zaylus in the shoulder with the flat, spinning him from his feet.

Zaylus rolled and came up slashing for Nameless's guts. Nameless blocked with his axe, then smacked Zaylus between the eyes with the butt. The knight went down hard and hit the back of his head on the flagstones, his shortsword skittering away across the room. He blinked up at Nameless standing astride him, axe slung carelessly over his shoulder.

Zaylus rubbed his forehead. Already a knot was forming. "Why?"

"Because I remember, laddie. I remember what I did back at the ravine, and I'll not let you do the same."

There was a blur of movement, a squeal and a gasp, and the guard Zaylus had been about to kill crumpled to the floor.

"If you're gonna do a thing," Shadrak said, crouching to wipe his dagger on the guard's britches, "do it properly."

Zaylus shook his head, tried to find the right words. He gaped at the guard he'd stabbed in the back, as if he were just now emerging from a nightmare.

Nameless knew exactly how he felt.

Had it been the sword that had enraged Zaylus? That was certainly what had happened to Nameless under the sway of the black axe. But Nameless had felt that weapon's malice when he'd first seen it, before he'd grasped its haft and the world had turned upside down. He'd felt no such revulsion for the Sword of the Archon. Perhaps the change in Zaylus was due to being locked up and tortured, or seeing the Wayist, Tovin, die at the hands of the guards?

That was something Nameless could understand. If it had been him, and if Tovin had been a friend, like Thumil or Cordy, he would have done the same. But Zaylus? A man who was more priest than warrior?

"I don't want to hurry you or anything…" Albrec called from the doorway.

A horn blasted from outside. Orders were barked. Boots thumped, armor clattered, swords rasped from scabbards.

To Shadrak, Nameless said, "You three go. I'll slow them down."

Zaylus stooped to pick up the shortsword, then recoiled, sucking at his fingers, as if he'd touched a boiling pan.

He looked at Nameless in horror. "What have I done?" he asked. "In the name of the Way, what have I—?"

"Go, laddie!" Nameless said. "Now!"

In a daze, Zaylus withdrew his hand inside his coat sleeve and used that to pick up the shortsword. As he re-sheathed the blade, Nameless bustled him toward the entrance. Shadrak grabbed one of the knight's arms, and Albrec the other.

It hadn't been boots he'd heard, Nameless realized, as a platoon of soldiers in bronze helms and breastplates rounded the corner from the Senate Building: it was sandals. Rectangle shields were formed up in a wall six abreast and four deep, short stabbing swords poking through the gaps.

The four of them emerged from the doorway together, but as Albrec and Shadrak half-dragged Zaylus toward the narrow alleyway they had first approached the jail by, Nameless strode straight toward the shield wall.

It was impressive, how quickly the soldiers had responded, and their discipline would have made the Ravine Guard look sloppy.

With a roar of "Kunaga!" he raised his axe and charged.

The soldiers faltered. They hadn't expected this, but still their discipline held. Shields were braced to meet the impact. Shortswords glinted hungrily.

And Nameless veered away in a wide loop back toward the jail.

Of Albrec, Shadrak and Zaylus, there was no sign. They must have made it into the alley.

A moment's hesitation, and then a cry went up, and the shield wall surged toward him.

As he'd hoped it would.

Suddenly, the soldiers' discipline wasn't quite so perfect. Gaps opened between shields as they struggled to match each other's pace, and when Nameless doubled back and slammed into them, none of them saw it coming.

The clangor of steel on steel broke like a thunderstorm. The shield wall buckled, and Nameless was in among the soldiers shoving and pushing, using the flat of the axe like a club. Soldiers fell into one another in a panic of chaos. And then Nameless was back out and pelting toward the alley.

As he made the entrance, some inner sense sent prickles of ice along his spine and made him look up at the roof of the Senate Building.

There was a dark shape close to the edge. He could have sworn it was the same thing that been watching him outside the diner, and likely the same creature that had attacked Shadrak. It was vaguely manlike, only sleek, black, and featureless.

A thud and a clang rocked his head back and spun him round. A crossbow bolt ricocheted from the helm and clattered away across the ground.

When he angled another look at the rooftop, the creature was gone.

A second bolt glanced off Nameless's hauberk. It had come from a top story window.

Sandaled feet scuffed toward him, and Nameless whirled to confront the advancing soldiers. They fanned out in a semicircle around him.

Nameless held up a hand. "Now listen, laddies," he said. "I'm going to say this only once."

Silence.

Hard eyes glittered. As one, the soldiers started to close in.

Nameless suddenly tilted the great helm to look up at the sky. "Look out!" he cried. "The suns are falling!"

The soldiers all looked up, and Nameless pelted down the alley.

One second, two, and then there were sounds of pursuit.

But it wasn't just a straightforward alley; it was the entrance to a warren of passages between buildings, a labyrinth of byways filled with rats and refuse. Losing the soldiers was going to be easy; getting himself lost, easier still.

He barged through a gate into a courtyard garden, entered a house by way of the back door, walked to the front as if he owned the place, even waving a greeting to the startled residents, and then he was out onto a main street.

Soldiers were gathering a way off to the right, so he hugged the walls of buildings, then made a dash for an alley on the opposite side of the street. Without pause, he strode ahead, taking random turns into adjoining passages until he no longer had any idea if he was heading back the way he'd just come.

But one thing was certain: there were no more sounds of pursuit. All he heard was yelled orders off in the distance, the peep of a whistle, the blast of a horn. They hadn't given up, by any measure, but they were moving in the wrong direction.

At an amble now, he emerged from the narrow lanes onto a cobbled street and found himself staring up at a sign depicting a naked woman with a fish's tail. Above her head was the name of the establishment, painted in red: The Mermaid.

Nameless slipped inside the doorway and immediately relaxed. It was the scent of hops that did it, the aroma of pipe tobacco. The only surprise was to find a tavern open so early in the day.

"Breakfast?" a crone said from behind the bar.

The scattering of punters gave him uneasy looks, and then he remembered the helm.

"Just beer, lassie," Nameless said.

"Beer for breakfast?"

"And why ever not?"

With a sigh and a roll of her eyes, she filled him a flagon and set it on the counter before him. He paid for it with the coins Aristodeus had given him, then carried his beer to a nook over by the hearth.

As soon as they realized he meant no trouble, the punters went back to their breakfasts of eggs, ham and kaffa.

Nameless suppressed a pang of envy as he set his beer down on the table and stared into the froth.

And stared.

TWENTY-ONE

"What do you mean you can't use the sword?" Aristodeus was saying to Zaylus as Nameless entered Queenie's Fine Diner to the accompaniment of the tinkling bells above the door.

Thunder rolled outside the window and lightning sheeted upward into the sky. It had started when he left the Mermaid and begged directions to Queenie's, and yet no rain had fallen as he made his way back.

"Well?" the philosopher said.

Cords stood out on Zaylus's neck, and his cheek twitched. But despite the fact he looked ready to carve Aristodeus up into pieces, he turned away. It wasn't so much suppressed anger; it was shame.

Nameless made his way to the bar and plonked himself on a stool next to the scruffy wastrel who had been slumped unconscious in the very same position before they left to rescue Zaylus.

Rutha hovered by the latrine door. She sneered at Aristodeus, then acknowledged Nameless with a roll of her eyes.

"So, we're screwed, is what you're saying," Shadrak said. He was leaning back in his chair, feet crossed on the table. He eyed the crust he'd been nibbling, snorted, and tossed it over his shoulder.

The kitchen doors swung open, and Albrec backed out carrying a steaming dish in each hand.

"Best I could do at such short notice," he said, turning to see who was listening.

No one was.

"Did I miss anything, laddie?" Nameless whispered to the unconscious punter, who grunted and turned his head to get more comfortable.

And Nameless nearly fell off his stool.

"Rugbeard!"

The old dwarf gazed at him with bloodshot eyes. He propped his head on one arm and belched. "Do I know you, son?" He peered around at the others in the diner, taking it all in with a bored expression. "How'd you make it out of the ravine? Did anyone else survive?"

"Aye," Nameless said. "Others survived, but too many didn't."

Rugbeard's eyes grew sharper and he narrowed them. "Take that helm off, son. I could swear I know your voice."

Nameless sighed. "I can't remove it."

"How's that, then?"

Nameless didn't really know what to say. He caught Aristodeus glancing his way. Did the philosopher know? Had he known all along that Rugbeard was the man slumped at the bar, yet chose to say nothing? Nameless had to wonder, but he gave Aristodeus the benefit of the doubt; he'd not recognized Rugbeard himself until just now. The old dwarf was a mess of tangled hair and beard, a far cry from the man who used to read such fantastic stories from the *Chronicles*, or, much later, the man who had been night warden at the mines.

"At a guess," Rugbeard said, "I'd have to say you was one of Droom's boys, not just from the way you speak, but it's in the width of your shoulders. More than that, there can't be too many helms made of *ocras*. The only one I know of was in Droom's possession. But there's no way in shog's cesspit you could be Lukar. That stool you're sitting on would have broken under his weight, and he'd have been waving a book under my nose and wanting to argue. No, you have to be the other one. Thingy..." He idly picked up an empty bottle and studied the label, as if he could find the name that eluded him there.

"Lukar's dead," Nameless said.

Rugbeard dropped the bottle on the bar, then slammed a hand down over it to stop it from rolling.

"Dead?"

"You were there, Rugbeard. You must have seen the slaughter."

The color drained from Rugbeard's face. "No, I wasn't there. I got out the minute it all started. Thing is, after arguing so much with Lukar about those passages in the *Chronicles*—the ones he said were genuine but I said were fake—I went and had another look at them."

"Lukar was right?"

"No, I was. But the important thing is, stuff the fake passages said, stuff no one would have taken to be true, had been borne out by what we'd seen in the mines."

He peered long and hard at the great helm, as if still seeking confirmation that what he'd seen was true and not some booze-induced hallucination.

"Golems, son," Rugbeard said. "We'd already seen golems were real, and when whistles were peeping all the way down to the floor of the ravine, when horns were blasting, and more Red Cloaks than I've seen in my entire life were forming up on every single walkway, I knew what was coming. It was written on the page: a butchery among the dwarves so terrible that hardly anyone survived. The Corrector, the *Chronicles* said did it. A tyrant come to punish us for our sins."

"And Lukar knew this?"

Rugbeard shook his head. "He was too wrapped up in fairy stories about the Axe of the Dwarf Lords. He never mentioned no Corrector to me. I bet he didn't even read that far ahead. That's the trouble with scholars these days: too specialized. Eyes only for what takes their interest."

"I remember nothing about any Corrector," Nameless said. "Just a butcher. And people did survive. Lots of them. When we left Arx Gravis, there were Red Cloaks all over the place."

"Maybe the *Chronicles* got that bit wrong," Rugbeard said. "Or perhaps it hasn't happened yet."

MOUNTAIN OF MADNESS

"Oh, it happened, Rugbeard, I can assure you of that. Just not the same way."

Could it be that Aristodeus had averted a much greater catastrophe by placing the *ocras* helm on Nameless's head? Maybe fate wasn't set in stone after all.

Rugbeard reached over the counter for a cask of mead. Albrec scowled at him from across the room, and Rugbeard withdrew his hand as if slapped.

As the poisoner-cum-chef stalked back toward the bar to keep an eye on his stock, Aristodeus sucked in a long breath through his teeth and asked Zaylus, "What have you done?"

"Nothing I haven't done," Nameless threw across the diner at him.

Aristodeus shot him an irritated glare and then fixed his eyes on Zaylus once more.

"I killed a defenseless man," Zaylus said.

"So?" Shadrak said.

"It was more than that," Aristodeus said, taking a step toward Zaylus. "You've killed before, and the sword didn't reject you then."

Zaylus closed his eyes.

"It was the rage," Nameless said. "Same as with me."

"No," Zaylus said. "Not the same. This is the Sword of the Archon, not some demonic axe."

Albrec gave a delicate cough. "I take it no one's hungry, then. Such a waste of good chowder."

Rugbeard raised a shaky hand. "Bring it here, sonny, and grab me another beer while you're at it."

"You were not to blame for what you did," Zaylus said to Nameless. "But what I did at the jail, I did out of weakness, anger, a need for revenge. It wasn't the sword; it was me."

Rutha made a scoffing noise then pulled up a seat at the bar as Albrec plonked down the food in front of Rugbeard, then filled a tankard from a keg.

"Me too," Rutha said, rubbing her stomach and wincing.

"There is only so long I will be ignored," Aristodeus said.

"Face it, Baldy," Shadrak said, "your master plan is buggered. I

163

don't know why you didn't send an expert in the first place." He drew his Thundershot and made a show of polishing it with a napkin.

"Years and years and years," Aristodeus said, thrusting his face into Zaylus's. "Do you think I wanted to train you? Do you think I wanted to keep coming to tutor you in that stinking hovel in the armpit of the Vanatusian Empire?"

"That was it all along, wasn't it?" Zaylus said. "I always knew you wanted something from me—something very specific—but you played me so well, got me thinking you were a friend, family, even."

Aristodeus wagged his fingers dismissively. "Whatever you may think about my motives, it is imperative that you wield the Sword of the Archon. Nothing else will suffice."

"Says who?" Shadrak stood and holstered his weapon.

Aristodeus threw his hands in the air. "Are you all complete bloody morons?"

"The little fellow has a point," Nameless said. "If you have all the answers, then maybe you'd better start sharing them with us."

Aristodeus's shoulders slumped. "All I can say is that I tried once before to stop Sektis Gandaw, and I failed. I didn't factor in the power of the goddess Etala, which he had somehow harnessed. If it hadn't been for the dwarves; if it hadn't been for Maldark—"

Rutha cut across him. "So, your plan's to neutralize the statue with the Archon's sword? You want to pit sister against brother?"

Aristodeus pulled out a chair at Shadrak's table and sat down. He flashed Rutha a smile that said she'd just gone to the top of the class. "The statue really is Etala," the philosopher said. "Her fossilized essence. That was Gandaw's genius: he found a way to turn a Supernal being to stone and use her as a power source."

Albrec started to stack the plates on the table. Aristodeus snatched an olive from one of the plates and popped it into his mouth, chewing noisily. Albrec pursed his lips then offered Aristodeus the last olive, which he accepted with relish.

"Gandaw thinks he's the one in control," Aristodeus said. "He thinks he has the perfect plan to unweave the old and create the new, but he forgets what he is. He's no god. He's human, and as flawed as the creation he judges so harshly. But more than that, he's blinded by his own hubris. Yes, he can control Etala, but does he know what she really is? Do any of us, other than in some loose metaphysical sense? Deception underlies this whole bloody mess. Self-deception, yes, but a whole other layer of deception beneath that."

"The Lord of Lies," Zaylus said. "Mananoc."

"Exactly!"

"Laddies, laddies, laddies," Nameless said. "And lassie. All this peeling away the layers of the onion doesn't solve our immediate problem."

Shadrak gave a slow handclap. "At least someone's got his head out of his arse."

Another crash of thunder shook the windows, and in its wake the diner was noticeably darker.

"Basically," Shadrak said, "what you're saying is that Zaylus is the only one who can defeat Gandaw." He shook his head, as if at some private joke. "But to succeed, he needs the sword."

"If it were a simple matter of fighting prowess," Aristodeus said, "I'd have finished Gandaw when I had the chance."

"Yeah, well maybe you ain't as good as you think," Shadrak said. "Maybe I should have a crack at him."

Aristodeus slapped a palm to his forehead and pressed his lips tightly together. "Obviously, I am not making this clear enough. Etala is our problem."

"But only the righteous can wield the Sword of the Archon!" Rutha said, as if a light had suddenly gone on. "That's why..." She looked Zaylus directly in the eye. "That's why the bald bastard warned me off you."

"He what?"

"So you would remain holy," Aristodeus said.

"Well that certainly explains a lot," Zaylus said.

Aristodeus pushed himself to his feet and drew himself up to his full height. "This isn't about you, Hale. We are talking about the end of all things. Sacrifice. If there's one thing I hoped you would take from all that Wayist balderdash, it's the idea of self-sacrifice."

Thunder boomed outside, and this time rain began to pelt the windows.

"Nameless is right," Aristodeus said. "We need to deal with the immediate crisis. You are the only one remotely close to being able to wield the Archon's sword, Zaylus. I've already tried once." He brushed his palms together. "And these two"—he indicated Albrec and Shadrak—"have a trade that's hardly compatible with holiness. Rutha is… well, she's Rutha." She was pouring herself a beer from a cask as he spoke. "And as for Nameless…"

"Why not just spit it out, laddie?" Nameless said. "I'm a murderer? A maniac? What's the word for someone who attempts to butcher his entire race?"

Rugbeard stiffened, and he turned wide eyes on Nameless.

"I was going to say," Aristodeus said, "that you might have been the perfect choice, had you not had your own brush with Mananoc. I'm sorry, Nameless, but the black axe wounded you far more deeply than it did your people."

"Droom used to say…" Rugbeard said.

"Salvation would come from my mother's womb. I know." Nameless pivoted the great helm so he could stare at the wall. The rush and patter of rain echoed around his skull. It called to him, lured him back into rivers of blood.

"So, it was true," Rugbeard said in an awestruck voice. "The axe was real."

"Lukar discovered its whereabouts," Nameless said. "But the Svarks killed him. They fed him to the seethers."

Rugbeard would have known the legends about those writhing monsters. The way he put a hand over his mouth and stared into his beer showed that he did.

"But it wasn't the *Paxa Boraga*," Nameless said. "It wasn't the Axe of the Dwarf Lords."

The sound of footsteps crunching past the windows drew everyone's attention, and there was a collective intake of breath, but when the footfalls faded away, the tension left the room.

The door burst open, and Buck Fargin came in, dripping puddles on the floor. "It's all right, they wasn't looking for you."

"Whatever," Aristodeus said. "Now, Zaylus, what you need

right now—and I never thought I'd hear myself saying this—is confession."

"Fargin," Albrec said, "aren't you supposed to be keeping watch?"

"Nah, reckon you're safe enough right now."

Shadrak cocked a finger at him, and Buck rolled his eyes and went back out into the rain, slamming the door behind him.

"He can't confess," Rutha said. "There's no priest."

"Poppycock," Aristodeus said. "A good outpouring of the heart to your beloved Way is all it takes. Trust me, the rest is all smoke and mirrors."

"Rutha's right," Zaylus said. "There needs to be a priest."

"Well, what do you expect me to do?" Aristodeus said. "Rustle one up out of thin air?"

Another boom rocked the diner, this one much closer. Somewhere in the distance, glass shattered, and a gusting howl ripped through the street.

"Sword or no sword," Zaylus said, "we have to do something. Judging by the state of things out there, I doubt we have enough time to trek back to the Mountain of Ocras. Can you get us there, Aristodeus?"

"You must confess first!"

"Can you, or can't you?"

"My freedom is not as complete as it might look," the philosopher said.

"You manage to magic yourself around easy enough when it suits you," Rutha said.

"Nevertheless, I cannot penetrate the *ocras* of the mountain." Aristodeus sighed and turned to Zaylus. "If you won't do as I ask, then you have failed and you leave me no choice. Desperate times call for desperate measures. Come!" He held out a hand to Rutha.

She looked up blearily from the bar. "You're kidding, right?"

"And bring that with you." The philosopher pointed at her sword, which was propped up in the corner. Nameless could have sworn it was a curved blade before, but now she had a perfectly straight long sword in a gem-encrusted scabbard.

Aristodeus turned back to Zaylus. "Do what you can, Hale, but it's probably wasted effort without the Sword of the Archon. Just remember, this is your doing, not mine."

Rutha sauntered over, fastening the sword belt around her waist. Aristodeus grabbed her in a rough embrace, green light swirled, and they vanished.

"So, now he's gonna use the bitch to save the world?" Shadrak said. "You gotta be having a laugh."

Albrec gave a dry chuckle, but then he picked up the stacked plates and headed to the kitchen.

"I can get you there," Rugbeard said.

All eyes turned on him.

"I can get you to the Mountain of Ocras, and I can get you there real quick."

TWENTY-TWO

They left the city in a covered wagon. Rugbeard insisted on driving, despite being too drunk to walk in a straight line.

Nameless rode in the back with Zaylus, Shadrak and Albrec. After the jail break, there were patrols all over Jeridium, but Rugbeard said there was no need to worry; it was a guild wagon on loan to Buck Fargin, and the guards didn't question guild business. After all, it was the guilds that supplemented their wages and gave them gifts for their families on all the major feast days.

Once they left the shelter of the city walls, Nameless joined Rugbeard up front. Unnatural winds buffeted the wagon, and the air about them shrieked, as if it were a beast being torn apart. Lightning flashed, and every now and again the draft horse pulling them would balk and whinny.

Rugbeard was a mass of grey hair and beard tousled by the wind. He held the reins in one hand, a bottle in the other. The journey seemed to revive him, though, and he had a lot of talking to get out of his system.

"I got out of the ravine as soon as the blood started flowing," Rugbeard said. He glanced at Nameless, but if he was wary of sitting next to the Ravine Butcher, he didn't show it—probably an effect of the drink. "The Svarks and the Red Cloaks had their hands full, so I made for the mines and took the train to the headframe. There's a ghost wall in the upper cavern that no one else knows about. It leads to a fissure that takes you all the way to the hills on the surface."

Up ahead, a whirling vortex of black—Nameless could only call it light—crossed the road and went spinning through a field, carving its own path and leaving bizarre patterns in the crops. A shadow passed across the face of one of the suns, and the other sun started to strobe, making their progress appear stilted and unnatural.

"What happened, son?" Rugbeard asked. "With you, I mean. What exactly happened?"

A cold fist closed around Nameless's heart. "I'm still piecing it together," he said. "Some things I remember clearly, but others are hazy like dreams on waking. There was blood. A lot of blood. And there were demons swarming the walkways, only they weren't really demons."

Rugbeard grimaced and looked off into the distance. "Go on," he said.

"I had an axe that shone like the sun."

"But it wasn't the Axe of the Dwarf Lords," Rugbeard said.

"When I found it in Aranuin, it was made of shadows. It spoke to me, Rugbeard, in my head; and it distorted everything I saw and heard and felt. The only thing that stopped it was this helm."

"Yalla's helm," Rugbeard said. "Your ma's. A strong woman if ever there was one, and sorely missed."

"Yalla," Nameless repeated. Another name reclaimed. He asked Rugbeard if he knew what the family name was, the name of the House Yalla was descended from, but the old dwarf shook his head and frowned. "I should know it," he said, "but I can't remember. You think it's the booze?"

"No," Nameless said. "It's just gone, same as my given name."

The name-stripping had been complete, and it brought shame on his family as much as it did him. Even Droom's family name from before he was married had vanished. If the scroll of genealogy Droom had read aloud every year on the anniversary of Yalla's death still existed, it would list only given names followed by blank spaces, and in Nameless's case, there would be nothing at all.

Off in the distance, a greenish brume roiled above some hills, and the hills themselves were stretching, contorting, as if they were putty in invisible hands.

Rugbeard took a long pull on his drink and tossed the bottle over the side. "Reach under the bench, son. Grab me another."

Nameless pulled a bottle from a crate and unstoppered it before he passed it to Rugbeard. He could feel the breath of the black dog on the back of his neck. He imagined its teeth breaking the skin, its tongue lapping at his blood. Numbness spread through his limbs as if he were slowly petrifying.

"Whatever happened back at Arx Gravis," Rugbeard said, "whatever they've done to you, don't forget who you are."

"And who's that?" Nameless said bleakly.

"Droom's boy. Yalla's son. Lukar's brother. And even if you do forget, I won't."

Zaylus pushed through the canopy covering the wagon bed.

Rugbeard grew silent, but his eyes kept flicking to Nameless, as if he couldn't comprehend the magnitude of the suffering being unnamed caused him.

"How long till we get wherever we're going?" Zaylus asked.

The wagon lurched as a tremor ran through the road.

"Not long now." Rugbeard took a swig then held the bottle over his shoulder to the knight.

Zaylus waved it away.

Rugbeard shrugged, then poured the contents down his throat. He growled, shuddered, and slung the bottle from the wagon. After he'd wiped his mouth on his sleeve, he took the reins in both hands again.

A body of water glimmered some way off to the left, and there was a low range of mountains to the right.

Nameless thought he recognized the route they had taken on the way to Jeridium. "Are we heading toward Arx Gravis?"

"Them's the Southern Crags, son." Rugbeard nodded toward the mountain range. "Arx Gravis lies straight ahead, but we'll be stopping before we reach it. Once we're by the Great Lake of Orph"—he looked over toward the ever-nearing water, which was reflecting the turmoil of the skies and sending up a shimmering haze—"we'll pull up shy of the hills above the mines."

"But we've been denied access to the mines by the Council," Zaylus said.

Rugbeard chuckled. "Then it's a good thing there's more than one way into the tunnels that lead beneath Gandaw's mountain."

Nameless looked out at the boiling waters of the lake as they finally passed along its shore. It wasn't just a haze he'd seen earlier, it was steam. Heat stung the exposed skin of his arms and made him sweat within the helm.

"Is that normal?" he asked.

Rugbeard sucked in his lips and made a popping sound. "Can't say that it is. Grab us another beer, son. All that steam's drying my throat out."

When Nameless handed him the bottle, Rugbeard took a long swig. "I can't stop thinking about what you did at the mines, to that golem. Ol' Droom used to say your ma was a dwarf lord. Did he tell you that?"

Nameless sighed. "All the time."

With a raised eyebrow, Rugbeard said, "There's an ancient story recorded in the *Chronicles* about the Lords of Arnoch once killing a dragon."

"You have dragons in Medryn-Tha?" Zaylus asked.

"If we still do," Rugbeard said, "they never cross the Farfall Mountains. But my point in mentioning the dwarf lords"—he looked sharply at Nameless—"is that legends ain't the same as lies. Your brother and I agreed on that, only we disagreed on which parts of the *Chronicles* were myth and which were history."

"Are we there yet?" Albrec called from inside. "I need to pee."

"There's a bucket in the back," Rugbeard called over his shoulder. "Anyway," he said, scanning the way ahead and giving the reins a gentle flick, "the Lords of Arnoch kept watch over all the lands we now call Cerreth. They patrolled the skies in baskets hung from enormous balloons. The balloons were filled with gas that was lighter than air, but they weren't exactly safe. A single lick of flame, and that gas'd go up, boom!

"One day, a dragon was razing the fishing villages along the coast, but then he gets all purposeful and comes at Arnoch itself.

MOUNTAIN OF MADNESS

Flames charred the city walls, hundreds were killed, and just when all hope seemed lost and the city was making ready to sink beneath the waves, as it was designed to do in the worst of all perils, Lord Kennick Barg asked permission of the King to go out after the beast on his own. The King agreed, seeing as there was nothing to lose, and brave Lord Kennick goes up in a balloon, hollering insults at the dragon for all he was worth. The wyrm grew angry. It soared right at the balloon and unleashed a searing torrent of flame, and kabooooom! No more dragon. No more Lord Kennick, neither."

Rugbeard turned his gaze on Nameless. "That's our model, what we're supposed to be like. Don't believe all that rubbish about Sektis Gandaw making us dwarves by melding faen and humans. Where's the proof? In the *Chronicles*? You know yourself how much they can lie. The word of the Council? Those old bastards are always so ready to see everything as doom and gloom, and themselves as no more than the Mad Sorcerer's botched experiments. We're better than that, I tell you; and back there in the mines that day, you showed us just how much better."

They rattled along in relative silence, save for the skirling wind. Above them, both suns flared briefly then began to flicker like guttering candles. In the far distance, what looked like a third sun, though black as the Void, sent inky fractures through the surrounding sky. Rugbeard pointed out a barren hill set back a couple of hundred yards from the lake.

As they drew nearer, Nameless could see the hill was made of packed earth, as if it had been piled there during some mammoth dig. Holes pocked its surface, many of them big enough to drive the wagon through. They pulled up close, and he climbed down, along with Zaylus.

Albrec was straight out the back and rushed into the cover of some scrub, while Shadrak jumped down lithely and proceeded to check the daggers in his baldric.

Rugbeard busied himself hammering an iron spike into the ground and tethering the horse to it.

"Looks like an ant-hill," Nameless said.

Rugbeard chuckled as he slung his mallet inside the wagon and brought out a hooded lantern. "Like I said, a legend ain't necessarily a lie."

"Those holes are tunnels?" Zaylus said. "Big ants."

"Giant," Rugbeard said. "They say they never aged and died, neither, not the ants, nor the Ant-Man that Gandaw made to control them."

"And you want us to go in there?" Albrec said, traipsing back over and fastening his britches.

"The ant-hill's deserted nowadays," Rugbeard said. "Last mention in the *Chronicles*, the Ant-Man and his pets were seen near Malfen. Probably trying to cross the Farfalls to be with all the other monsters."

A muffled boom rolled across the sky, and the ground shook beneath their feet. Dirt cascaded down the side of the ant-hill.

A dark shape appeared in one of the holes, then slipped out of sight.

Nameless was already moving toward it.

"Was that an ant?" Albrec said.

Zaylus shook his head. "It was standing upright."

Nameless scrabbled up a bank of dirt until he reached the opening, Zaylus and Albrec struggling up behind him.

There were footprints leading away down the tunnel, and a smudge of similar markings around the entrance. But they weren't ordinary footprints; they were long and slender, the impressions left by the toes splayed wide.

"Looks like it was hanging around the entrance for some time," Shadrak said, coming up alongside the others. "Waiting." He exchanged a look with Nameless.

"You think it's the Ant-Man?" Albrec asked.

Rugbeard was next up, shaking his head, eyes wide and bulging. "Perhaps he came back from Malfen…"

"That weren't no Ant-Man," Shadrak said, drawing his Thundershot and slipping into the tunnel. "Wait for me here."

To the south, the black sun was wobbling, expanding, and its fractures were thrashing about like tentacles. And then, as if the dreaming god at the core of Aosia blinked, everything was plunged into darkness.

MOUNTAIN OF MADNESS

Was that it? Were they too late?

The next instant, the darkness lifted, but there was no sunlight now, only a crepuscular grey that turned the surrounding landscape dull and lifeless.

Shadrak came back down the tunnel. "Gone," he said. "The scut sure does move quick."

"Laddie?" Nameless asked.

"It was the thing that attacked me in the city," Shadrak said. He unfastened his black cloak and slung it down the hill, then took the concealer cloak from his backpack and put it on. "My advice: anything moves in there, kill it and worry about what it was later."

Rugbeard struck flint to steel and got his lantern burning and they entered the tunnel. Shadrak was almost invisible in the concealer cloak, no more than a shifting blur beside the tunnel wall. Albrec brought up the rear, fiddling nervously with his cheese-cutter.

When they reached an intersection, Shadrak took the lantern from Rugbeard and scanned the ground. "Tracks have gone," he said, raising the light to inspect the ceiling and walls. Finally, he handed it back to Rugbeard. He muttered something to himself and pulled the concealer cloak tight, merging with the gloom once more.

Rugbeard led them to a steep decline, which they had to descend on their backsides. They emerged into a mine tunnel lit by the soft green glow emanating from veins in the otherwise black *ocras*. Struts and supports lined the walls and ceiling. Iron rails with *ocras* sleepers threaded down the center of the tunnel.

Rugbeard led the way to an abandoned train. The undercarriage was of rusted iron, but the main body was a sleek silver capsule, caked in rock dust.

Rugbeard wiped a patch of grime away with his hand, revealing a row of five buttons. He pressed each in turn, and the side of the carriage slid open to admit them.

There were three rows of seats inside, each upholstered with padded leather, and at the front was an array of levers and knobs. Rugbeard toggled a switch, and a panel lit up. The smell of ozone wafted through the tunnel, accompanied by a low, pulsating hum.

"Hop in," Rugbeard said with evident relish. "This is a train ride I've always dreamed about."

TWENTY-THREE

"Keep your guard up!" Aristodeus yelled.

Rutha couldn't. Her arms were leaden, the black sword a ponderous weight in her hand. "Can't you at least open the door? It's stifling in here."

The whitewashed walls of the philosopher's tower felt as though they were closing in on her. There was no room for maneuver, and that meant the swordplay was relentless: no retreat, just parry, thrust, block, slice; either that, or receive a sharp slap with the flat of Aristodeus's blade.

"We've been going at it for hours," Rutha said. "Shouldn't the world have ended by now?"

Aristodeus sighed and lowered his sword. "As I've said a thousand times, it would not be wise to leave the tower, nor open the door—even a crack."

"But why? What's out there?"

He held up a hand. "And as for the Unweaving, consider it on hold. It's more complex than that, but let's just say time has no meaning here. We could train for days, years even, and still emerge before the end of all things. Call it a blessing. Call it a curse. Call it a responsibility."

He lunged at her, and she batted his blade away with ease.

"Good," Aristodeus said. "See, it's paying off. Still a poor substitute for Zaylus, though. If you're to have any chance, we'll need to go in together. You must be fast, very fast; and you'll need the element of surprise. Without Zaylus's sword, our chances are virtually nil, but I refuse to sit back and do nothing. If Sektis Gandaw doesn't see us coming, and if that evil-looking sword of yours can penetrate his *ocras* armor, who knows, maybe we won't need to deal with Etala."

"So, what, you just magic us in and hope he's looking the other way?"

Aristodeus shook his head and adopted a defensive stance. "I can't get us through the *ocras* cladding of the mountain."

"What, then?"

The philosopher looked up at the ceiling and sucked in his top lip. "I fought Gandaw once before, and he used Etala's power to send me here."

"But where is—"

"I have a theory," the philosopher said, talking right over her. "A desperate one, I might add. This tower is, shall we say, a construct of my will. It is all that wards us from what's outside. It is not, however, altogether stationary. It can be relocated, moved, propelled, even. You've already seen what I can accomplish with my will—how else would I have brought you here? How do you think I show up all over the place in the blink of an eye? No, just wait and see. I think I can get us to Sektis Gandaw. Now, fight!"

He launched a blistering series of attacks. Rutha parried frantically until he backed her up against the door. He pressed in close, the whiskers of his beard scratching her face. His breath stank of garlic and wine, same as last time, when she'd drunk too much and succumbed to him.

She tried to knee him in the groin, but he saw it coming.

"You lack strength, speed and stamina. We'll work on all three. But first, if you've had enough for today—and don't forget, we'll be doing this day in, day out until you're ready, no matter how long it takes—there's something I want from you, sober this time."

He pushed himself away from her.

Rutha screamed and swung the black sword with all her might. Aristodeus was quicker, though, and he grabbed her wrist and stayed the blow.

"Look at me. Look at my eyes. Are you telling me it was just the wine last time, or do you see something there, something familiar?"

She was riveted to the ice-blue of his eyes, the way they darkened at the edges like a gathering storm. How could she have not noticed before? Had it been the drink? "Zaylus," she said. "You have Zaylus's eyes."

"Oh, it's more than just the eyes, my dear."

And then he explained. Explained how he had failed against Gandaw before. Maldark might have prevented the Unweaving, but Aristodeus had been plunged into the Abyss when the Mad Sorcerer had opened up a chasm in the floor of his mountain chamber using the might of Etala. The Supernal power had been too much for the philosopher, and it would be again.

"I have outwitted Mananoc," Aristodeus said, gesturing at the walls of the tower. "Not only did I create this with my own mind, but I discovered a way to travel beyond its confines, albeit for limited periods. I can visit any place, past or present, and I have started to redress the balance in our favor."

"What did you do?" Rutha asked. "To Zaylus?"

Aristodeus smirked. "Not to Zaylus. To me. I went back to the time I was born, stole the baby that was destined to be me, and gave it to foster parents in Maranore, on the fringes of the Vanatusian Empire. I picked them myself: Jarl and Gralia Zaylus: a warrior and a woman of such piety they would have made her a luminary, if she hadn't lived in such obscurity."

"No," Rutha said. "I don't believe it. Zaylus is you?"

"How else do you think his voice awakened Nameless from the artificial slumber I placed him in?"

"Why?" she asked. "Why did you do it?"

"Because in order to face the power of Etala, I needed to be able to wield the Archon's sword. I tried once before, but the sword rejected me. I lacked the requisite holiness." He said the last with a sneer. "But I refuse to entrust the fate of the worlds to someone else. The stakes are too high."

"And you have to be the one in control?" Rutha said. "But Zaylus isn't you, is he? He led a different life. There were different people around him, different influences."

Aristodeus puffed out his cheeks and sighed. "I see that now, which is why I think Zaylus won't be enough. That's where Nameless comes in, and to be doubly sure, that's why I need you."

TWENTY-FOUR

Nameless sat next to Rugbeard at the front of the train. His ears popped as they raced along an unending tunnel. Green blurs streaked past the windows, but other than that the walls outside were black as pitch, broken only by evenly spaced grey struts.

Rugbeard was wittering on, but Nameless wasn't really listening. He turned the helm to look at Shadrak seated behind. The assassin was nervous. The creature that had attacked him in Jeridium had put the fear of shog in him, and seeing it waiting for them as they entered the ant-hill only made it worse. Not only was it stalking them, but it now seemed one step ahead, as if it knew what they were attempting to do and was planning to stop them. It was too much of a coincidence to think it was just some random predator that had picked up their scent.

Albrec was beside Zaylus on the next seat back. They were silent, Albrec fiddling with his cheese-cutter, Zaylus looking straight ahead as if he were staring at his own tomb.

Without warning, the tunnel walls bulged and contracted.

"That ain't right," Rugbeard said.

The tunnel began to twist and turn like a writhing serpent.

Rugbeard raised his hands. "Ain't right, I tell you. These tracks are supposed to run straight as the crow flies."

It had to be the warping effects of the Unweaving.

They were running out of time.

There was a muffled thud from the roof of the train, a frantic scrabbling and scratching.

Everyone looked up, but there was nothing to see. Shadrak's pink eyes glanced Nameless's way, and he drew his Thundershot.

The undulations stopped as quickly as they had started, and the train picked up speed.

"Hold on!" Rugbeard called out. "Some shogger's left a mine cart on the track."

The undercarriage screeched and juddered, and the train came to a faltering stop.

Rugbeard hit a switch, and the door slid back, revealing a stone platform lit from above by flickering strips of crystal. Something dark streaked past the opening.

Shadrak was out like a shot, leading with his Thundershot. Nameless climbed out after him, holding his axe in a death-grip. He scarcely dared to breathe as they waited and watched, but there was nothing.

In front of them was a mine cart filled to the brim with chunks of *ocras*. They had missed it by a hair's breadth.

Rugbeard jumped down from the train. "Ain't nothing short of dangerous, is what—"

There was a whoosh of air farther along the platform, followed by a resonant clang.

"I thought this tunnel wasn't in use," Shadrak said.

"It ain't," Rugbeard said. "Dwarves haven't come to the Mountain of Ocras in a very long time."

Albrec gingerly stepped onto the platform as if it might sprout teeth and bite his legs off. Zaylus emerged last and walked straight past them. Nameless exchanged a look with Shadrak, then they set off after the knight.

Zaylus waited for them before a huge circular portal that must have been thirty-feet in diameter. Its center was a swirl of steel petals surrounding an aperture no bigger than a coin. There was a panel of dark glass to one side.

"This is the way?" Zaylus asked.

"Right into the roots of the mountain," Rugbeard said. "Back in the day, the ore would've been dropped off here, and Gandaw's creatures would take it inside."

Shadrak pushed past Rugbeard and glared at the panel.

"It'll take more than lock picks for that," Albrec said. "I suppose you could blast it, if you had any more of those blasty things."

Shadrak placed his fingertips on the glass, each one touching a glowing shape. When he traced his fingers along the surface, the shapes moved with them. With a quick succession of swipes, he rearranged the patterns, and they started to flash green. There was a sharp rush of air, and the petals of the portal retracted until the aperture filled its circular frame.

Shadrak stepped away from the panel, a befuddled look on his face.

"Laddie?" Nameless said.

Shadrak waved him away. He shut his eyes and pinched the bridge of his nose. The assassin looked like he had no idea what he'd just done, or how. Not for the first time, Nameless saw him as a faen. It would explain a lot: the lore craft, his appearance, the way he'd just worked out the panel, but it left a lot unanswered, too. If Shadrak was a faen, how come he didn't know it?

"Come on," Shadrak said. "Let's get this over and—"

Zaylus pushed past the assassin and stepped through the opening. The instant he crossed the threshold, a red light started to wink on the panel. Before Nameless could say anything, Rugbeard had gone after the knight.

"So much for caution," Albrec said.

There was a fizzing crackle from beyond the opening, a burst of light, and a scream.

"Rugbeard!" Nameless cried, already running through the entrance, Albrec and Shadrak right behind him.

Nameless was met with the impression of a vast space and the stench of roasting meat. Something silver flashed above him. He roared and flung his axe. Metal struck metal, and sparks flew. The axe clanged to the floor, and the silver sphere it had struck whirred and gyred away. It spun in a wide arc, steadied itself, then dived toward him.

Shadrak's Thundershot bucked in his hand. It boomed, there

was a blinding flash, and silver rained down in a thousand shards.

Shadrak threw himself into a roll and came up beside a pile of black ore, Thundershot held out before him.

Zaylus and Albrec stood staring down at the charred and smoldering body of Rugbeard.

Nameless dropped to one knee and let out a long, keening moan. In his mind's eye, he saw a stretcher laid out on the floor of the hearth-room back home. His pa was upon it, covered in rock dust from where the mine gallery had collapsed on him.

He cradled Rugbeard, rocking him back and forth. The old dwarf had been there when the miners brought Droom home.

His focus snapped back when he heard Shadrak's boots crunching as he came round the ore stack. Nameless lay Rugbeard down, gently closed his eyes, then stood to retrieve his axe.

The chamber was so massive, he could barely see the far wall. There were heaped piles of *ocras* all over the floor. He'd never before seen so much of the precious ore in one place.

A metallic rasp turned his head, and he swore as the petals of the door snapped shut. High above, red lights blinked like evil stars, and smoke began to rise through grilles set into the floor.

"What's happening?" Albrec said.

Zaylus was staring at the smoke coiling about his boots like a man consigned to the Abyss and despairing that anything could be done about it.

"We have to get out," Shadrak said, sprinting for the door. There was a panel on the inside. The assassin ran his hand over it, but nothing happened. He stepped back and fired the Thundershot. Sparks flew, smoke plumed from the panel, but the petals remained shut.

"Now what?" Albrec said.

It was hot. Too hot, and the soles of Nameless's feet were blistering through his boots. And then he remembered: *ocras* absorbed force. It was virtually indestructible, and it was the perfect insulator.

"To the ore stack!" he bellowed. He lunged for its base, and the minute his feet touched *ocras*, the sizzling stopped.

Albrec made a beeline for the stack, but Shadrak veered toward

Zaylus, grabbed the knight's coat sleeve, and dragged him to safety. Zaylus offered no resistance, but neither did he seem to appreciate the danger he was in.

It was a brief respite. The heat continued to rise, and the air grew thinner. High above, another silver sphere swooped into view and began to circle the ore stack. A nozzle emerged from the sphere, and searing light streamed from it.

Nameless swept his axe up. Light bounced from the blades, sent burning heat into his palms. He let go the haft and the axe clattered to the ore stack, glowing red.

The sphere circled them and then soared toward Albrec.

Shadrak let rip with three blasts from his Thundershot. The first two ricocheted from the outer casing, but the third sent the sphere whirling and shrieking to the far side of the stack.

"Bugger," Albrec said, pointing at the far wall.

Brownish-yellow gas was cascading down from vents and rolling out across the floor.

"What is it, Albrec?" Shadrak demanded.

"If you get a whiff of horseradish, ask me again. Although, if the concentration's high enough, you might not get the chance."

Nameless pivoted to take in the rest of the room through the eye-slit. There was no way out he could see, no exit save for the petalled door, and that was a dead end.

A whining, droning sound reached his ears, and the silver sphere spun into view. It dropped a few feet, righted itself, and then started to rise in fits and starts.

A carpet of dirty gas was inching its way across the chamber, and more of the stuff was flooding out from the far wall.

Albrec clambered up the ore stack toward its summit some twenty feet above the floor. "Once there's enough volume, it'll start to rise," he said.

Zaylus curled his fingers around the hilt of his shortsword. He winced and gritted his teeth. He tried to draw the sword but finally let go.

Nameless glanced at the gas roiling toward them, then at his axe. There was no way in shog he was leaving it behind. He grabbed the haft and felt the skin of his palm bubble and blister.

With a curse, he started to climb after Albrec, but Zaylus was in a daze at the bottom, staring blankly at the gas now swirling about his boots. As Shadrak came up, Nameless went back down, grabbed the knight by the arm and made him follow.

At the top, he leaned back to look up. The ceiling was maybe fifty feet above, crisscrossed with girders, and there was a circular opening just shy of the ore stack, toward which the silver sphere was heading.

Shadrak saw it, too. He holstered his Thundershot and leapt from the summit, catching hold of the sphere. It spat fire at him, singeing the hood of his cloak. Grabbing the nozzle, he ripped it from its socket amid a spray of sparks. The sphere emitted an earsplitting shriek and shot upward, and Shadrak clung on by the tips of his fingers.

The assassin's boots disappeared through the opening, and a blast sounded from his Thundershot, another close behind—too close, as if two such weapons had fired at virtually the same time. There was a rustle of movement, a dull thud.

"Laddie?" Nameless called up at the opening.

Nothing.

"Shadrak!" Albrec cried. "The gas is still rising!"

The murky cloud was up to Nameless's knees.

From above came a succession of wet stabbing sounds, a grunt of effort.

Something dark dropped through the opening. It made a pulpy splat as it struck the ore stack, then bounced down till it vanished beneath the carpet of gas.

It had been a head. A featureless head, sleek and black as tar.

"Lovely!" Albrec called up. "Now get us out of here!"

The gas reached Nameless's chest.

"Shadrak!" Albrec's voice was shrill.

"Laddie?"

As the gas continued to inch upward, Zaylus still seemed unconcerned. He looked numb to what was going on, turned in on himself.

A silver disk floated down from the aperture in the ceiling.

"Get on!" Shadrak yelled down through the opening as the disk alighted atop the ore stack.

"It's below the level of the gas," Albrec called back. "What do we—?"

"Get the shog on!" Nameless barked, stepping to where the disk had sunk beneath the gas and taking Zaylus with him.

Albrec jumped and then did as he was told.

"All right, laddie," Nameless yelled. "Bring us up!"

The metal beneath their feet vibrated as the disk carried them upward, out of the mist. It came to a hover a few feet above the opening. Directly overhead was another circular aperture, through which the disk could presumably rise further.

To one side lay a glistening black creature, viscous fluid pumping from the stump of its neck. Its limbs were long and slender, its legs articulated backward like a bird's. Silver glinted from its torso: dozens of daggers nestled in some kind of harness.

On the other side, Shadrak lay slumped in a heap, barely visible in his concealer cloak. Blood stained one shoulder, and his pallid face seemed a whole shade whiter.

Albrec stooped over him and prodded him with a finger. "Shadrak?"

"Laddie?" Nameless said. "Laddie, are you all right?"

Zaylus knelt beside the assassin's head. He pulled out his book and opened it to read.

Shadrak cracked an eye open. "Oh, no," he rasped. "No you sodding don't."

He tried to move, but Albrec leaned in close and restrained him. "I can stem the flow of blood. Just keep still."

Albrec unclasped the concealer cloak and took a knife from Shadrak's baldric to cut a strip from the fabric.

"That's the creature that was watching me in the city, right enough," Nameless said. "Looks a shog sight better with its head off. Where's its thunder weapon?"

"Gone," Shadrak grunted. "Turned to dust. Shot me first, though. I'm done for."

"Don't be so silly," Albrec said. "You're coming with us. No one else knows how to use these panels." He nodded to a plinth beside where Shadrak lay. A red light winked atop it.

"Too weak," Shadrak said. "Find Gandaw. Stop the Unweaving."

Nameless walked over to the opening and peered down. "The gas has cleared," he said. Then he got on his belly for a better look. "And the door with the petals is open. Was that you?"

Shadrak nodded. "Just don't ask me how."

Zaylus stood and put his book away. He seemed there all of a sudden, back from whatever inner torment possessed him. Nameless knew that feeling well, knew how the black dog could pounce when he least expected it, then retreat to the corners just when he thought it would never let him go.

"Can you send this disk down again?" the knight asked.

"If someone holds me up long enough to work the panel," Shadrak said. "Why?"

"Albrec," Zaylus said. "Think you can drive the train?"

Nameless climbed back to his feet.

Albrec scoffed. "If a drunken sot like…" He glanced at Nameless and winced. "I think so."

"Take Shadrak back to Jeridium. There's nothing more he can do here."

"And I'm a useless waste of space?" Albrec said, finishing packing Shadrak's wound and starting to wrap strips of concealer cloak about it.

"It's for the best, laddie," Nameless said.

"And what about Zaylus?" Albrec said. "What about the sword he can no longer use?"

"We'll deal with that when we have to," Nameless said.

Once Albrec had finished tying off the improvised bandages, Nameless helped Shadrak to stand over the panel.

"When we're on the disk," the assassin told Zaylus, "slide these two symbols together. They should turn green, then swipe them toward the bottom of the glass like this." He demonstrated without actually moving the symbols.

Zaylus nodded that he understood, and then Albrec helped Shadrak onto the disk.

"Just you and me now," Nameless said, as the disk disappeared below.

MOUNTAIN OF MADNESS

This was it, he knew with sublime certainty. The moment he had been awakened for. His chance to atone for what he'd done. And if he couldn't atone, if his crimes were simply too much, he could at least do what Aristodeus had asked of him, and keep Zaylus alive long enough to reach Sektis Gandaw.

Zaylus's eyes met Nameless's through the eye-slit, still riddled with uncertainty, still more grey than blue.

Albrec called up from below that they had cleared the disk, and Zaylus's fingers danced across the panel.

As the disk came back up, Nameless's guts sunk to his boots. The brief snatch of purpose he'd found dispersed like clouds in the wind.

Zaylus clamped a hand on his shoulder and once more met his gaze. This time, the knight's eyes were glittering sapphires, and his touch imparted strength. More than that, it conveyed gratitude.

And then they stepped onto the disk.

TWENTY-FIVE

The roots of Sektis Gandaw's mountain were a warren, though it was a warren with design. The halls were the hubs, with the corridors the spokes, uniformly grey and flanked by an endless succession of sliding doors. Soft light bled from glowing panels, and strips of crystal glared starkly overhead. Ribbed tubing of some sleek material ran the length of the ceilings, and at every intersection a silver globe hung down from a sinuous stalk, each with a winking red light.

Nameless stomped ahead, the clangor of his footfalls on the cold steel floor like a bell tolling the end of the worlds. He heard a clatter and a rattle, the whoosh of air. He stopped dead and pressed himself against the wall. Zaylus did the same.

A faen came through an open door, pushing a metal trolley. He was dressed head-to-foot in grey. A white mask covered his mouth and nose, and his eyes were enclosed in clear goggles. Surgical instruments lay atop the trolley, and on the shelf beneath there was pink-stained tubing and a glass bell jar smeared with blood. Something red and misshapen lay within, but before Nameless could get a good look, the man wheeled the trolley down an adjacent corridor.

"Look," Nameless said. "The shifty little shogger's left the door open."

The instant he crossed the threshold into the vast room beyond, Nameless was freezing. Frost rimed the walls, and set into the ceiling there were blue crystal globes and vents that gusted down chill air. The floor formed a walkway around a massive domed cage made from *ocras*.

Within the cage, a red-scaled and winged reptile, easily the size of a wagon, lay curled up and unmoving. One plate-sized eye was half-open, the sclera yellow, slit down the middle by a purplish pupil. Fangs like scimitars protruded from either side of its jaws. Low, rumbling breaths sent faint shudders through its scales, and plumes of steam rose from its nostrils.

"Poor old Rugbeard was right," Nameless said. "Seems there are dragons, after all. Have to wonder, though..." He pressed up close to the bars.

"About what?" Zaylus said.

"If there really was a Lord Kennick Barg to blow that dragon up with his balloon. If there really was an Arnoch."

Lacerations crisscrossed the dragon's thorax, and a fresh incision that had been stitched with thick twine weeped blood and pus. Its forelegs had been hobbled, and its frost-dusted wings hung limply, pierced with sparking rings. Gossamer threads pulsing with beads of light trailed down from the top of the cage and attached to the rings.

Zaylus moved around the walkway to the other side, and Nameless followed.

Half the dragon's skull had been removed, replaced with glass, and within, glowing worms of violet burrowed in and out of its exposed brain.

Nameless clamped a hand on Zaylus's shoulder. "Come on, laddie. I've seen enough."

They continued past row upon row of sealed doors. Muffled noises came from behind some of them—chirps and growls, moans and gurgles. A few of the doors had windows, and through them they could see all manner of aberrations: tentacled things with human heads; giant clams that emitted dark vapors as they opened and closed; four-legged fish with cloven hooves; spiders with wings. In one cell-like chamber, there was an enormous bear with a glass bowl for a head, within which the brain had been divided into segments connected by copper wire.

When they reached a stairwell, Nameless led them up to a sprawling hall where dozens of faen zipped around on silver disks. If the creatures spotted them, they didn't show it, and Nameless didn't let Zaylus linger long enough to find out. They were immediately off into yet more labyrinthine corridors until they reached another stairwell leading up to the next level.

Nameless's knees ached, and his calves were burning by the time they reached the top and came to an open doorway with a silver trolley outside. There were a number of steel implements on the trolley—forceps, tweezers, a miniature saw—and a yellow sack of some shiny material hung from a hook at the top.

Nameless stepped through the doorway, straight into the stench of rot and decay, and something astringent that made his eyes water inside the helm.

Tiny bodies hung from meat hooks.

Babies.

More were laid out atop burnished steel tables, and still others had been crammed into jars filled with a greenish liquid. The lid of a long metal chest was partially open, with an infant's foot sticking out of it.

He backed straight out of the room, retching and groaning.

"What is it?" Zaylus said.

Nameless waved him away and bent double, clutching his stomach. After a moment, he let out a long sigh and straightened up. "Laddie, you don't want to go in there."

But Zaylus was already at the doorway. "In the name of the Way!" he said, covering his mouth and nose. Inch by inch, the knight crept into the room.

Nameless stood on the threshold, cradling his axe, drinking in the abomination. Was this what Sektis Gandaw saw as work? Was this how he whiled away the centuries? It wasn't enough that they called Gandaw the Mad Sorcerer. This was evil.

Zaylus turned back to the tables, studying their contents with an expression of horror and disgust. Nameless edged into the room to stand at his shoulder.

There was something about the bodies lying upon the tables: their necks were arched at unnatural angles. Zaylus stepped in close and touched his fingers to a livid cheek, so he could move the head. He flicked a look at Nameless, as if communicating his revulsion could somehow lessen it.

The baby's spinal cord had been snipped just below the base of the skull. Same with the others. And they were all so tiny, smaller than any newborn Nameless had ever seen.

"Are they...?" Zaylus started, but he seemed unable to form the rest of the question.

"No, laddie, I don't think so." Nameless lifted a baby's waxen arm and examined it. "Proportions are wrong for one thing, and dwarves are born with beards. They're human."

But the babies had no hands, just bloody stumps with protruding nubs of jagged bone. The feet were missing, too, as if they had been crudely hacked off.

Zaylus took hold of the table to steady himself, then moved toward the chest Nameless had seen coming in.

When the knight lifted the lid, the foot that had wedged it open dropped to the floor with a dull thud. There were hundreds more inside, frozen in ice that had a pinkish tinge from the blood.

Zaylus lowered the lid and fell to his knees. He dipped his head and clasped his hands in an attitude of prayer. His chin trembled, and cords stood out on his neck. His breaths grew faster and faster, but when the explosion came, it was with a whimper.

"Why?" he muttered in the voice of a child. "Why take their feet?"

Nameless staggered. Ice cracked deep within him, and a thousand malignant faces spilled out, swirling about his mind like leaves churning in a gale. Demons assailed him from every side: red-winged demons with blazing eyes. Shadow-formed devils descended from overhead walkways on strands of spider web. They clawed and raked and slavered. The axe in his hands came down, chopping and hacking. Blood ran from the walkways to pool at the foot of the ravine and turn the waters of the Sag-Urda red.

Nameless let out howl full of despair.

It was no longer like hearing about the butchery secondhand. He relived it fully now, as if he were there once more, yet this time with sober vision, not the illusion fostered by the black axe. And he felt the terror of the dwarves he slaughtered, felt the horror, and above all else the shame.

His anguished cry reverberated through the room, and his axe clattered to the floor.

"I killed them, Zaylus," he said. "It didn't feel real until now. Gods of Arnoch, I killed my own people. But not children. Not babies. I should have been stronger. Strong enough to resist. But no matter how weak I was, not even the black axe could have made me kill a child." But he didn't know that for sure; he just needed to believe it.

He heard a scuff of movement, then Zaylus laid a hand on his shoulder. "You would have resisted it," the knight said. "From everything I've seen of you, you would have beaten it."

Nameless looked into the knight's eyes, seeking something, though he had no idea what. Forgiveness? That wasn't Zaylus's to give. Hope? Maybe, but all he saw in Zaylus's face was the look of a man who had lost his way.

Zaylus took a step back, then averted his gaze.

"Pray, laddie," Nameless said. "To this Way you worship. Pray for yourself, and while you're at it, put in a quick word for me."

Zaylus made a scoffing noise and shook his head.

"It's what's needed," Nameless said, "if we're to put a stop to this madness. Pray for forgiveness, if that's what you need. Pray that you break free of this stupor that's followed you all the way from the jail. But most of all, pray that you see Sektis Gandaw's evil for what it is and have the courage to destroy it, right down to the roots." He pointed at the shortsword sheathed at Zaylus's hip. "With the tools you've been given."

Zaylus turned to him, red-faced and glowering. "Oh, I'll fight evil, all right. With my bare hands, if I have to. But prayer… Even if I still thought there was anyone listening, I wouldn't hold my breath for an answer. And as for forgiveness…!"

"So, what you did to that guard back at the jail," Nameless said, "are you saying there's no forgiveness for that?"

Zaylus sneered, and his eyes roved around the room, drinking in the senseless death, as if it somehow affirmed him in his guilt. "How could there be?"

"So, what about me?" Nameless said. He thrust the great helm up close to Zaylus's face. "If you're beyond redemption for losing control, where does that leave me? You only murdered one man. I slaughtered hundreds."

"It's not a numbers game," Zaylus said. "It doesn't matter how many you killed, how many I killed."

"It matters to me."

Zaylus grimaced. "What I meant was, I acted from within. It's who I am. Who I really am. All this... This..." He fumbled his book out of his pocket and held it up. "This nonsense is just to keep me reined in. Only, back at the jail, after what they did to me, and to Tovin—the Wayist those bastards tortured to death—it would have taken a damn sight more than pious scriptures to hold me back."

"No," Nameless said, walking away to the far side of the room and facing the babies impaled on meat hooks. "There's more to it than that. There has to be." He moved a couple of bodies to one side, and peered behind them, pointing out the closed door he had uncovered.

Zaylus nodded that he'd seen.

"Thumil's no fool," Nameless went on. "He'd not waste his time reading the *Lek Vae* and praying if that's all it was about."

"I agree," Zaylus said, slipping the book back into his pocket. "But it's beyond me right now. I don't even know who I'm praying to anymore."

"Maybe you don't need to know. Just pray, laddie. Head to the heart, Thumil used to say." He bent down to pick up his axe, spat on the blade and gave it a quick polish. "To be honest, I thought Thumil was just drunk and rambling most of the time, but I'm starting to see the sense of some of the things he said."

He swept the axe up and brought it down hard on a table. It left a huge dent in the surface.

"This," Nameless said, stroking the head of one of the babies, "is evil. That's enough to tell me we're on the right side. Are you sorry for what you did to that guard? Really sorry?"

A knot of emotions warred on Zaylus's face, but when he lifted his eyes to the great helm, they were glistening with unshed tears.

Nameless made way for him as Zaylus leaned over the baby, touched two fingers to its forehead, and uttered a prayer.

Tension sloughed away from the knight. He lingered a moment longer, then tipped his hat to the child.

"Ready to go on?" Nameless asked.

Zaylus's hand strayed to the hilt of his shortsword. He flinched, as if expecting it to burn him, but then he curled his fingers around it and let out a sigh of relief. "Ready," he said.

TWENTY-SIX

Nameless pushed through the babies on hooks till he came to the door. He angled the helm to try to get a good look at the panel beside it through the eye-slit. All he saw was a blur of symbols. None of them made any sense to him.

"Let me," Zaylus said.

The knight pressed a glowing triangle, and the door slid back.

"I would have had it in another second or two," Nameless said.

The room beyond pulsed with a soft amber glow. An elliptical track ran round the center of the ceiling. Dozens of women were hung spread-eagled from it by metallic cords around their wrists. Their ankles were secured to a similar track on the floor. Their eyes were completely white, their mouths gaping. They each had the pallor of death, and yet their bellies were grossly distended, as if they were heavily pregnant.

The tracks carried them forward a few feet and clunked to a halt. Snaking tubes rose from the floor and inserted into their abdomens, delivering a brownish fluid before retracting. The tracks moved them on another few feet, and the same thing happened again.

"Let's not linger here," Nameless said, indicating a door on the far side.

This one slid open as they approached.

Nameless led the way into a hall so large, he couldn't see the far side. All around the walls at ground level there were frosted oval windows. Each was as tall as a human, and behind them, shadowy forms were moving.

"Not sure I like the look of this," Nameless said. "Back the way we came?"

Zaylus nodded.

But the instant Nameless turned around, the door slid shut.

Zaylus raced to the panel on the inside. He pressed the dark glass, gave it a slap, but nothing happened.

"Uh, laddie..." Nameless said.

The frosting was melting away from the windows, and in some cases the glass—or whatever it was—was starting to bulge, where hands pressed against it.

An arm burst through a window, pale fingers clutching at the air. There was no shattering of glass, just the tearing of a clear membrane. The head was next out, stretching the membrane until it split.

The face was human, though bloodless, and white eyes roved sightlessly back and forth. Where there should have been hair, wires were bundled up around the cranium, and a single red light was nestled in among them. The second arm punched through, this one an articulated silver tube that ended in a metal hand. Enough of the membrane had fallen away to reveal a shallow alcove behind it.

Nameless hefted his axe and Zaylus drew his shortsword, as all about the room more limbs ripped their way free of confinement. Dozens of the things—half-metal, half-human—were stepping from their alcoves as far into the distance as Nameless could see. Those closest started lumbering toward them on legs braced with steel struts.

"All right, that's far enough," Nameless growled.

He rushed forward, swinging his axe in a murderous arc. The blades sparked across metal and threw up shreds of grey flesh that didn't bleed.

Zaylus darted in, hacking at an arm, and the shortsword sliced through dead flesh and steel with no resistance. The limb fell twitching and grasping to the floor. A slash across the neck sent the head flying, and the body crumpled.

Nameless brought his axe down with all his weight behind it, ripping through a shoulder and sending a metal arm skimming across the floor. He rammed the butt of the haft into the man-thing's nose, then powered the blade right through its jaw.

Zaylus struck to his right, but a bloodless fist caught him on the left temple. He stumbled, reversed his sword, and stabbed back into pliant flesh. Spinning, he ripped the blade up through the creature's torso and split it in two all the way to the head.

Nameless went down beneath a barrage of blows, his axe clattering to the floor. He grabbed two of the creatures by the ankles and surged upright, flipping them into the throng. Retrieving his axe, he staggered backward, flailing about wildly.

"Run!" Zaylus yelled.

"You run," Nameless said, swaying on his feet.

Zaylus rolled his eyes, and they fought on, backs to the wall, where at least they couldn't be surrounded.

A glimmer of movement drew Nameless's eyes to the ceiling. Fifty or so yards ahead, a disk was coming down, a lone faen standing on it and watching them intently. He wore a grey tunic and britches. His hair was an oily black and far too perfect to be natural.

As the disk reached the floor, the faen jumped off and tapped at a vambrace on his wrist. The mass of creatures fell back from Zaylus and Nameless, leaving a corridor that led to the disk.

Zaylus saw the opportunity first and practically flung Nameless ahead of him into the opening. "Go!"

This time, Nameless obeyed.

Already, the channel was closing up, and he had to duck and dodge grasping fingers and clubbing blows. Zaylus came with him, cutting and thrusting with deft precision.

The faen stepped away from the disk and weaved his way into the mass of metal and flesh until he was lost from sight.

Nameless's feet were starting to drag, but he was seconds from the disk, when a huge bloodless man stepped from an alcove and raised a metal arm with a barbed spear tip in place of a hand. With a sound like the crack of a whip, the spear flew at him, trailing a length of chain. Nameless twisted at the last possible instant, but the tip tore through his side in a spray of blood and the clatter of broken links from his armor. Pain flared beneath his ribs, and then the creature yanked on the chain and reeled him in like a fish.

Nameless stumbled onto his knees and slid toward it, one hand clasping the base of the spear jutting from his side. His vision started to fade, but then fire ignited his blood. Just as the creature reached out to grab him, he swung his axe with the other hand, hitting it in the chest with more force than he'd have believed possible, shattering its ribcage. The chain slackened, and with a sickening roar, Nameless tried to pull the spear tip out. The barb caught, and his roar turned into a scream as he slumped to the floor.

He dimly saw Zaylus arrive ahead of the lumbering crowd. The knight swung for the creature, and its head bounced away.

"Grit your teeth," Zaylus said, kneeling beside him.

Nameless grunted and shuddered as the knight pushed the spike out through his back. When the barb emerged, Zaylus swept down the shortsword and sheared it away. Sheathing the sword, he placed one hand on Nameless's shoulder, and with the other pulled the chain out through the front. Nameless bucked and gasped, and when the chain came clear and snaked to the floor, he bellowed, "Shog, shog, shog!"

"I can heal you," Zaylus said, starting to draw the Sword of the Archon again, but Nameless put a hand over his.

"No, laddie. No magic. Not from that thing. I saw how it sliced through those shoggers like they weren't even solid. It has the feel of the black axe about it."

Zaylus hooked an arm under Nameless's shoulder and helped him to stand. "But you'll bleed to death."

"Come on," Nameless said, scooping up his axe and limping toward the disk.

Zaylus supported him on one side, casting wary looks at the creatures behind.

The instant they reached the disk, the horde grew frantic. Those in the front ranks parted to admit three more massive men, steel glinting against pallid flesh. They each raised metal arms and launched spears that trailed chains.

MOUNTAIN OF MADNESS

Zaylus threw Nameless to the platform and dropped on top of him. There was a succession of impacts as the spears struck some invisible barrier, and the chains clunked heavily to the ground.

The faen appeared off to the right. He gave a single nod and tapped at his vambrace.

With a whir and a shudder, the disk lifted into the air. As it passed through a hole in the ceiling, it gathered pace, shooting up through level after level.

Nameless moaned as he was rocked from side to side. He had one hand vainly trying to staunch the flow of blood, the other draped over the haft of his axe. After what seemed an age, the disk entered a metal shaft, shook violently, and came to a halt.

The disk had come to rest in a silver-walled cubicle, where it fit seamlessly into the floor. One of the walls had a hairline crack down its center, and there was a panel adjacent to it. Nameless could hear someone running about on the other side. There was a clang of metal, a searing hiss, and beneath it all, a sound like the roar of flames.

Zaylus placed a hand on the wall.

"Heat," he said.

Stepping away, he bent to examine the panel. "It looks unlocked, if I understand the symbols correctly."

"Boot, laddie," Nameless rasped. He held out his leg. "I'll plug the wound with a sock." The warm seep of blood flooded the disk beneath where he lay.

Zaylus took hold of the boot, but before he could pull, Nameless heard a man say something from beyond the cubicle, not loud enough for him to make out the words, but the timbre of the voice was somehow familiar.

"Is that Baldilocks?"

Zaylus stiffened, straining to hear.

Another man spoke, the sound clipped and toneless.

There was a cry and a clash, then a boom rocked the cubicle.

Zaylus ducked instinctively.

Nameless tried to roll onto his side, let out a gasp, and lay back. His chest fluttered as it rose and fell, and his breaths rattled around the great helm.

"Think I'll take the magic, after all," he said. "If you don't mind."

Moving aside Nameless's blood-soaked hand, Zaylus touched the shortsword to his wound. Golden light flowed down the blade.

Nameless cried out, and his back arched. Searing heat cauterized the flesh. He winced at the sensation of muscle and sinew knitting back together. And then Zaylus withdrew the sword.

"Thank you, laddie." Nameless yawned, suddenly overcome with fatigue. "Just thirty winks and I'll be right as—"

A woman screamed.

Zaylus whirled toward the crack in the wall.

Another scream, and this time Zaylus cried, "Rutha!"

Nameless struggled to rise but slumped back down. "Go, laddie. I'll follow… when… I…"

His words trailed off as blackness claimed him.

TWENTY-SEVEN

Nameless had no idea how much time had passed. As he rolled his head from side to side, he heard the scrape and grate of the helm on the floor, and his eyes snapped open.

He was lying on his back, staring at a silver ceiling. With a start, he sat. Ahead of him was the open doorway Zaylus had headed for. A flickering orange glow came from the other side, and with it a blast of warm air.

He tried to stand, but swooned and had to lie back down. The healing had worked, but he felt as though he'd fought ten bouts in the circles.

He heard Zaylus's voice. Aristodeus's, too. And there was a third man speaking, in a tone that was cold and rasping.

He rolled to his front and crawled toward the doorway, dragging his axe with him. It was hard going, and the blood he'd lost smeared as he passed through it.

He crossed the threshold into a chamber like the inside of an enormous cone. Blood pounded in his ears from the effort of moving.

Tiers of walkways, each with banks of flickering mirrors atop steel desks, wound all the way up to the apex of the cone. Naked women with wings like a bat's were hunched in front of the mirrors, watching the moving pictures playing across the glass.

Crimson footsteps led across the floor—Zaylus's, from where he'd stood in Nameless's pooling blood.

A flame-filled chasm rent the chamber in two, and from within its maw, the top of a slender tower poked, its ivory walls blackened with soot.

Aristodeus was staring wide-eyed from an open sash window just below the tower's turreted roof, and Nameless followed his gaze to where Rutha was suspended in midair, a silver sphere hovering above her, bathing her in blue light.

Even more shocking, though, was how different Rutha looked. She was armored in dark leather, with black boots all the way up to her knees. Her hair was pulled back in a braided tail, and where her arms were exposed, they looked harder, more defined. Her eyes glared defiance, and not a little frenzy. Her sword—with a start, Nameless saw that the blade was black—was directly beneath her feet, lodged in the fizzing and sparking shell of a metal crab the size of a pony. More of the crab-things were heaped around the room in smoking piles.

Zaylus stood off to one side, staring at the heights. He didn't look like a man who had come to fight. He seemed bewildered. Out of his depth.

Nameless rolled to his back so he could look up more easily. At first, all he saw was an inky cloud belching waves of blackness near the cone's truncated ceiling; then, within the miasma, he could make out the form of a serpent with glowing amber eyes and fangs like jags of lightning. It had to be the Statue of Etala. Atop its head, a crown of pulsing threads sent a constant ring of sparks up through the ceiling. At the center of the circle they formed, a single mirror glared down, showing nothing but a black hole that seemed to beckon and tug.

A disk drifted out from behind the serpent statue and made an arcing descent until it hovered twenty feet above Zaylus.

A man stepped to its edge and inclined his head to look down with eyes of incandescent blue. His face appeared grey, mask-like, beneath black hair as slick and unnatural as the faen's had been. He wore a long brown coat, beneath which Nameless glimpsed dark metal greaves and cuisses. One hand was gloved in black, but the other looked desiccated. Ribbed tubing ran from the knuckles up under the coat sleeve.

The Mad Sorcerer.

Sektis Gandaw.

Zaylus threw a look at Aristodeus, who shrugged and turned his palms up. A ripple passed through the philosopher's body, and he flickered. If Aristodeus noticed, he didn't show it.

Sektis Gandaw, however, did, and he narrowed his eyes. "How did you get here?" he asked the philosopher. "Stolen lore, no doubt."

Nameless rolled to his side until he could see Rutha hanging beneath the sphere. She hadn't moved since he'd entered the chamber. Was she even breathing?

"You are quite wrong, Sektis," Aristodeus said. "It was not lore that brought us here, merely an act of will."

"Spare me," Gandaw said. "There is no hidden power of the mind that allows you to teleport, let alone move an entire tower. I don't care how ancient you are and how inflated your ego, you are either lying or deluded. Now, let me see…" The Mad Sorcerer's eyes alighted on the chasm the tower had presumably emerged from.

"Last time you tried to thwart the Unweaving all those hundreds of years ago, that very same chasm opened up and swallowed you, Aristodeus. All I did was unleash the power of Etala, and she did the rest. What happened next was as unexpected to me as I'm sure it was to you. I confess, I should have investigated the phenomenon, and it's been niggling away at the back of my mind ever since. But I recently had something of an epiphany: There are two imponderables in this miserable universe that I've not set my scalpel to. I realized I'd been deceiving myself—about the Abyss, and that." He jabbed a finger toward the lone mirror at the top of the chamber.

Its hungry emptiness hit Nameless with sudden clarity. Somehow, Sektis Gandaw had a mirror showing that which shouldn't be seen—couldn't. He realized with a primal dread that he was gazing directly into the Void.

"They didn't fit into my grand hypothesis," Gandaw said, "and so I ignored them. Maybe you've done something similar, or maybe someone's been pulling the wool over your eyes. Could it be that your flickering presence here is but an illusion—to you as much as to the rest of us?"

"Flickering?" Aristodeus said, glancing at his hands.

"Could it be," Gandaw continued, "that your true being is elsewhere, kept by a master who allows you a long leash?" He looked at Zaylus. "You holy types invented the myths. What do you think? Is it possible that the impeccable mind of Aristodeus has fallen prey to the deceptions of Mananoc?"

A haunted look passed across Aristodeus's eyes, and his mouth hung open. Then he clamped it shut, and his face grew as mask-like as Gandaw's.

"You don't believe that, Sektis. All this speculation is hardly your style. What are you up to? Stalling?"

A faen stepped out of a wall and pattered across the floor. It was the same one that had given up his disk for Nameless and Zaylus, and rescued them from the flesh-and-metal creatures below.

"Ah, Mephesch," Gandaw said. "Re-route enough of Etala's power to close that rift, would you?"

When the faen looked at him blankly, Gandaw said, "The serpent goddess opened the exact same chasm when this upstart philosopher plunged to what should have been his death."

"Hundreds of years ago," Mephesch said, "and yet he doesn't look a day above seventy."

Aristodeus frowned at that, but he was as rapt as everyone else.

"My point, Gandaw said, is that if Aristodeus has found a way to re-open the rift that Etala once created, it stands to reason that she can seal it again."

"But the Null Sphere…" the faen said.

"A minute's delay, at most. Just do it."

Aristodeus started to protest as the faen leaned over the shoulder of a bat-winged woman and tapped at its mirror.

A brilliant burst of amber lanced down from the serpent statue's eyes.

Nameless rolled back to his front, got onto his elbows, and tried to drag himself forward. He grunted with the effort and slumped back down. He'd not even moved an inch.

MOUNTAIN OF MADNESS

"No!" Aristodeus cried. "Zaylus!"

The philosopher fell back from the window as, with a shake and a rumble, the white tower sank beneath the flames and the chasm closed over it. When the tremors subsided, the metal floor looked as good as new, as if the tower had never been there.

Sektis Gandaw's disk hovered closer to Zaylus. "I met Aristodeus only once—well, twice, if you count his ill-fated attempt to stop the Unweaving last time round. He was sent to see me in Vanatus, at the behest of some obnoxious ethical commission or other cobbled together by the insipid Wayists. I forget what they were called—one of the curses of longevity for an imperfect organism. They had grown concerned at my success with melding."

When Zaylus frowned, the Mad Sorcerer explained:

"Fish with beast, plant with man, that kind of thing. It was early days and inestimably crude, but we all have to start somewhere. The Wayists' strategy was that a face-to-face meeting would render me vulnerable to Aristodeus's silver tongue. Find out what your opponent wants, they believed, and you can talk your way into a compromise agreement. I imagine Aristodeus underestimated my goal, and the ethics commission overestimated his capacity for debate.

"But enough of him. You, Hale Zaylus, have been quite the nuisance, coming all the way from Vanatus and trespassing within my mountain. Aristodeus must have high hopes for you. Misplaced, but high nevertheless." He jerked his head toward Rutha. "Mephesch, the woman next. Get rid of her."

"As you wish," Mephesch said, rapidly tapping at his vambrace and raising it to his mouth.

"Rutha?" Zaylus said. "But she's already in your power."

—A furnace burst into life at Nameless's core, and lightning arced through his veins.

"She won't feel a thing," Gandaw said. "And besides, in a few more minutes everything she's ever known will cease to exist, so think of this as a mercy killing."

—The Slean's five walls dropped down around Nameless. There were seven Red Cloaks. One of them touched Cordy...

A nozzle emerged from the silver sphere holding Rutha aloft.

—He hit the shogger. The rest turned on him. That was the first time his blood had flared…

"No," Zaylus muttered. And still he seemed incapable of acting.

Nameless surged to his feet, and in the same movement, he flung his axe with such force, it streaked like a comet.

Metal clashed with metal, and the sphere holding Rutha exploded in a shower of sparks. Silver shrapnel clattered down, and the axe fell with it, clanging as it struck the floor, and skittering off till it came to rest against a wall.

—Seven Red Cloaks down and bleeding. Cordy aghast. Later, she joked he was a dwarf lord, like his pa claimed his ma was. But everyone thought Droom was just a doting husband who placed his wife on a pedestal…

Rutha seemed to hang in midair for a second, then she dropped like a stone. Zaylus lurched toward her, but she was too far away. She tucked her knees in, rolled as she hit, and came up smoothly.

She moved like a cat, and the veins along her biceps stood out in ridges as she took hold of the black sword and wrenched it free of the metal crab-thing.

The fabric of Gandaw's coat ripped as he swelled from within. His entire frame shuddered, and then he expanded again. The coat and the grey tunic beneath disintegrated, swirling about him in a cloud of dust. Where his chest should have been, there was a black breastplate, flecked with green. His legs and arms were encased in *ocras*, too, and the air around his head grew denser, solidifying into a clear, crystal dome.

"Lassie," Nameless said grimly, "pass me my axe."

Rutha backed away to the wall, black sword held in white-knuckled hands. Without taking her eyes from Gandaw, she used her foot to shunt Nameless's axe across the floor to him.

As the faen, Mephesch, ran for cover, Sektis Gandaw raised his gloved hand and extended the palm. The glove smoldered and fell away to reveal metallic fingers, each tipped with fiercely sparking crystals. Lightning arced between them, and the hand glowed white-hot. With quick stabbing motions, he aimed first at Rutha and then at Nameless.

TWENTY-EIGHT

Balls of fire streaked from the Mad Sorcerer's metal hand. Rutha dived, but the blast drove her head first into a black mirror, shattering the glass amid a spray of sparks.

Nameless could barely walk, never mind run, but he saw the fireball coming a mile off and ducked. It sped over his head to explode against the floor.

Gandaw spun toward Zaylus and unleashed a barrage of missiles. The first was wide. Zaylus sprinted for a desk and hunkered down behind the bat-winged woman seated there. The second fireball struck where the knight had been standing a split second before.

Zaylus emerged from cover and held the Sword of the Archon in front of him. When the third fireball hit, the blade threw the full brunt of the blast straight back at Gandaw. It exploded against the edge of the Mad Sorcerer's disk and sent him plummeting toward the floor. Grapnels shot out from Gandaw's armor and snagged the rail that edged a walkway, reeling him in. Effortlessly, he took hold of the rail and vaulted over it, landing on the walkway with a resonant clang.

"Interesting," Gandaw said. "A sword that absorbs and redirects energy. More stolen lore?"

"Don't answer, laddie," Nameless told Zaylus. "He's stalling." The Mad Sorcerer must have needed more time to complete the Unweaving.

Gandaw stepped back from the railing and cast his eyes back and forth. For a moment, he took on the appearance of a cornered rat. Within seconds, though, he resumed an air of calm confidence. With the ghost of a smile, he said, "Mephesch, the bat-meldings. Release them."

The faen popped up from behind a steel desk and ran his fingers over its mirror.

Nameless cursed. He'd thought Mephesch was helping them earlier. But wasn't that just the way of the faen—to betray and to deceive?

Zaylus started to run at Mephesch, but he was too late. With a cry, he flung the shortsword like a javelin. The faen ducked behind the console, and the sword flew overhead.

The women hunched over the desks with the mirrors jerked and unfurled their wings. As Mephesch got up and ran, Zaylus's shortsword turned in a wide arc and shot toward him. Mephesch dived—and passed straight through the wall, as if it weren't there. The shortsword drew up sharp, then reversed direction until it slapped back into Zaylus's palm.

The bat-meldings' wings flapped furiously, lifting them a couple of feet above their chairs. They shrieked as the cords that connected them to their desks ripped free in sprays of blood.

"Gandaw, laddie!" Nameless cried, seeing the Mad Sorcerer hurrying along the walkway above. "Your sword!"

This time, Zaylus simply slackened his grip, and the Sword of the Archon launched itself through the air.

Gandaw threw up both hands and instinctively ducked, but even before the blade reached him, it struck something solid and rebounded. A sphere of blue light flickered around the Mad Sorcerer.

Zaylus snatched the returning shortsword from the air as the winged women on the lower levels flew at Gandaw. More of the creatures flocked overhead in a tightly packed wedge, then dived.

Gandaw scattered them with a fireball, and the few that pressed their attack squawked as they struck his shimmering barrier. With a great cacophony of beating wings and cawing cries, the bat-meldings spiraled about the chamber in a frenzy, crashing into walls and bumping off the apex.

"I should have seen that coming," Gandaw said through gritted teeth.

He exploded a fireball against the ceiling, obliterating the lone mirror that hung there. Half a dozen winged women dropped, smoldering and lifeless, bouncing from railings, then hitting the bottom with a thud.

The rest descended like a murder of crows onto the ground floor desks. Their caws turned into mournful wails, and they started to rip out tufts of their own hair with long-taloned fingers. They scratched at their breasts, leaving trails of crimson down their torsos.

Gandaw detonated another fireball, above and behind the bat-meldings. The women let out a collective squawk and took to the air once more. They wheeled as one toward the Mad Sorcerer, then shied away, instead swooping toward Rutha's unmoving body.

Zaylus started to run, but Nameless had already seen it, and he was closer.

He barreled in among the winged women, scything about with his axe. Each swing drove them back a few paces, but they instantly flapped closer again. Talons slashed at him. Fangs snapped.

Zaylus hurled the shortsword, shearing the head clean off a bat-winged woman. As the sword returned to his hand, he reached Rutha and dragged her back from the desk, letting her slump to the floor at his feet.

Nameless burst through the cloud of wings, whirled back to face it, shook his axe, and roared.

The bat-meldings dispersed, but then they flew behind him in an arc and came down at Zaylus.

"Sorry, laddie!" Nameless yelled above the din. "Unintentional."

The Sword of the Archon was a dazzling blur as Zaylus cut and chopped, hacked and slashed in every direction. He ducked, wheeled, and spun, taking in every move the meldings made, predicting every attack. The sword seemed featherlight in his hand, yet each blow he delivered was brutal, solid, and utterly devastating.

Nameless's axe rose and fell, but for the most part he was just hitting air as the women flapped and fluttered away from his strikes. But then he found his timing and started to aim a little ahead of, a little behind, the target. Blood showered down on him. Women screamed. Bat-wings shivered.

On the next tier up, Gandaw rushed along the walkway toward a metal staircase. He was heading back to the top.

A bat-woman raked her claws across Zaylus's coat collar, narrowly missing his throat. He backhanded it away, and as it gathered for a renewed attack, he plunged the shortsword between its breasts.

"Get Gandaw!" he yelled at Nameless.

Clutching his axe to his chest, Nameless dipped his helmed head and charged through the chaos of wings.

A bat-melding followed him, clawing from behind, but Nameless twisted, turned, and swung for it with almost casual grace. The woman fell to the floor in two pieces, and Nameless reached the steps and started upward.

As he made the next walkway, he glanced down.

The meldings assailing Zaylus rose into the air. At first, Nameless thought they were coming for him, but then they began to circle, cawing mournfully at the mass of dead bodies heaped on the floor.

Nameless pounded along the walkway. Gandaw was already halfway up the steps to the next level.

Down below, Zaylus dragged Rutha from beneath a pile of bat-meldings. He steadied her by the elbow and shoved her toward the steps as the winged women dived once more. He hacked one out of the air as it sped at Rutha, but another made it past. He called out a warning, but Rutha was already in mid-swing, and the black blade sliced into human flesh, exiting through the leathery membrane of a wing.

Gandaw reached the top of the steps as Nameless started up them, axe clattering against the railings. Gandaw let off a fireball, but Nameless swayed aside, and coruscating sparks sprayed across the walkway below.

A reverberating clunk sounded from above, and the room was suddenly plunged into shadow.

The bat-meldings squawked and flew toward the ceiling.

Mephesch was standing at a desk on the floor of the chamber, fingers dancing over a bank of winking crystals.

Above, Sektis Gandaw stopped and stared up at the ceiling with a look of horror on his usually impassive face.

A hole had opened in the apex, and the walls at the top of the cone started to retract into the level below.

"No!" the Mad Sorcerer cried. "Mephesch, we are not shielded!"

A fierce wind blew down the funnel, buffeting the bat-meldings as they swarmed through the widening aperture and out into the darkness beyond.

Because that was all Nameless could see: a sphere of absolute blackness hanging above the Mountain of Ocras, pulsing like a gigantic, malevolent heart. With every beat, it swelled and grew denser. Its oppressive weight was almost tangible, and a sickening wave of wrongness rolled through Nameless, sending him reeling back against the railing.

Beneath him, Rutha stumbled and clutched her stomach as she gazed up at the burgeoning dark. Zaylus looped his arm in hers, and his face hardened with resolve.

The walls of the cone continued to retract. As they passed beneath Zaylus and Rutha, Nameless saw just how dense the walls were, each level sitting within the one below in concentric circles, each with its own rooms and passageways sandwiched between twin walls of *ocras* at least ten feet thick.

Down and down the walls went, level by level, until the heart of the chamber, with its tiered walkways and flickering mirrors, was little more than a skeletal framework, completely exposed to the raging elements.

Nameless looked down over the railing and felt himself swaying.

They were hundreds of feet up, atop what was now the truncated summit of the Mountain of Ocras. Far below, bone-white sands swirled into vortices that spun wildly in every direction.

MOUNTAIN OF MADNESS

Mangroves at the edge of a swamp were stretched to impossible heights and bowed beyond breaking point. The bruised skies were fractured like broken glass, and way off in the distance, a cordon of shimmering fog whirled dizzyingly up into the heights, ever expanding to engulf more and more of the hazy, unreal landscape.

Gandaw was transfixed by the scene. Transfixed and appalled, judging by the way he just held the railing and gawped. Everything he had worked for was coming to fruition outside, but he was mortified to be caught up in it himself, stripped of the protection of his *ocras* mountain and whatever lore had warded it before Mephesch lowered the defenses.

Nameless hurtled at Gandaw and swept his axe down. There was a blinding blue flash, and the axe head lodged within the shimmering egg of blue light that surrounded the Mad Sorcerer. Nameless hung onto the haft with both hands and pushed his boots against the sphere in an effort to free the axe.

Gandaw swung his metal hand around. Lightning arced between crystal-tipped fingers. Flame swelled upon his palm, and Nameless winced in anticipation of the impact.

A blur of gold streaked past him and struck Gandaw. The Mad Sorcerer's protective sphere spat blue motes, buckled, and fizzed out. Nameless yelped as he fell on his arse, still clutching his axe.

Gandaw stepped back against the railing, staring wide-eyed at the Sword of the Archon as it reversed its course and sped back through the air to Zaylus's waiting hand.

Nameless rolled to his feet and attacked once more. A coil snaked out of Gandaw's armor and wrapped around Nameless's ankles, tripping him and whipping him into the air. Nameless hacked through the coil with his axe and hit the ground hard.

And then Rutha was there, helping him to stand, even as Gandaw fled upwards to the next level. Rutha ran after him, taking the steps two at a time, and Nameless stumbled behind her, shaking his head to clear it.

When she made the walkway, Rutha yelled and charged. Gandaw hadn't seen her coming, but he still managed to get off a shot. Rutha must have predicted it, for she rolled beneath it and swung the black sword.

A coil snapped out of Gandaw's armor and caught her wrist, locking the sword in mid-swing. Gandaw brought his metal arm round till it was directly in Rutha's face.

Nameless saw the opening, and flung himself at the Mad Sorcerer, swinging his axe for all he was worth. It struck the *ocras* armor like a thunderclap—and shattered.

"Oh, shog," Nameless said, as Gandaw aimed his metal hand at him instead.

Fire blasted from the palm, and there was no missing this time. On instinct, Nameless ducked into it and took the full brunt of the explosion on his great helm. There was a muffled boom, and flames flared briefly, but then fizzled out as if they had struck water. Nameless fell like a plank, and the back of the helm clanged against the metal of the walkway.

He tried to get straight back up, but the walkway careened in his blurred vision. He saw Rutha's hazy form kick out at Gandaw. The Mad Sorcerer swung his arm back toward her, but before he could fire, Zaylus was there, slamming the shortsword into Gandaw's transparent helm. The crystal cracked, and Gandaw gasped. The second blow sheared right through the metal hand, and Gandaw screamed.

Nameless blinked until his eyes came into focus. He was stunned, and every limb, every organ felt like it had been tenderized or crushed to a pulp. But it was more from the impact with the walkway than the exploding fireball. He thanked shog for his ma's *ocras* helm. Without it, he would have been dead.

Sparking tendrils thrashed from the stump of Gandaw's wrist. Zaylus drew back the shortsword for a thrust, but the coil holding Rutha reeled her in and smacked her against Gandaw's breastplate. Another coil sprang out and wrapped around her throat.

Nameless struggled to rise, but it was as if he had no bones. He was sprawled in a heap, utterly flaccid, and he started to panic that he might have been paralyzed.

Gandaw took a few steps back. His blue eyes blazed fiercely with either fear or rage, but within moments they dulled. A halo of soft light irradiated the crystal helm, and the crack Zaylus had made melted over until there was no sign of it.

MOUNTAIN OF MADNESS

Gandaw raised his remaining hand. At first, Nameless thought he was surrendering to Zaylus, but then he saw the flashing red light on the Mad Sorcerer's vambrace.

A silver sphere rose into view from somewhere outside and soared to a position above Gandaw's head. A beam of blue light shot from it and bathed Gandaw and Rutha, lifting them high into the air and bearing them toward the Statue of Etala. The black sword fell from Rutha's grasp and clattered to Nameless's walkway.

He heard Zaylus curse, and looked back. The knight started for the steps, but two more silver spheres sped straight at him, unleashing streams of fire. Zaylus threw up the shortsword, and it answered with a surge of golden brilliance that sent the beams back on themselves. The silver spheres erupted in flames and clattered and clashed against the walkways as they dropped.

Nameless glanced up at the black sphere gyring above the Mountain of Ocras, swollen and about to burst. Lightning arced upward into the sky. In its wake, a purplish vortex materialized and spun along the fringe of the swamp, tearing up grotesquely distorted mangroves and flinging them far and wide.

The silver sphere carried Gandaw and Rutha into the inky cloud beneath the spinning void and brought them alongside the serpent statue. Glowing tendrils sprouted from the Mad Sorcerer's armor and inserted themselves all over Etala's petrified body.

Prickles of pain ran beneath Nameless's skin. Heat surged through his veins, but it was weaker this time. He twitched his fingers, but that was as much as he could manage.

A flare of golden light drew his eyes upward. Zaylus's shortsword was lit up like a sunburst. It suddenly launched itself into the air, and the knight clung on with both hands.

Gandaw looked up as Zaylus reached his height. Rutha twitched against the Mad Sorcerer's breastplate, her face bloodless, lips tinged with blue.

Light pulsed along Gandaw's tendrils, and Etala's fangs blazed amber. Flame gushed from her maw and struck the bottom of the chamber. The mountain shook, and with a succession of tortured cracks, a fracture worked its way across the floor, until it yawned into a gaping chasm—the same as had swallowed Aristodeus, only, this time there was no white tower. This time, gigantic ribbons of shadow quested forth like avaricious fingers. They brushed against Nameless, tugged at him with irresistible force. He flipped onto his side and slid inexorably toward the edge of the walkway.

As he shot over the side, he grasped the railing and clung on. Desperate, he cast a look above, but there was no help there.

The coils holding Rutha released her, and she fell. Zaylus let go of the Archon's sword with one hand and reached for her, but it was no good. She plummeted toward the rift.

Rutha's screams swirled away in the chaos of snaking ribbons. Zaylus screamed, too, and Gandaw laughed.

White brilliance sparked and sputtered behind Nameless's eyes, seeped into his veins. Holding onto the railing with one hand, he lashed out with the other and snagged Rutha. Her hurtling weight almost dislodged him. Daggers of pain sliced through his shoulder, but he held on. The strain was unbearable. It wasn't just Rutha, the momentum of her fall; it was the infernal force dragging them both down.

Veins stood out along his biceps as he drew her closer. His grip on the railing began to uncurl. He reinforced it by wrapping his fingers over the top of his thumb—the hook grip he'd always favored on his heaviest dead lifts back at the Slean. He twisted his upper torso, pulling with everything he had.

Little by little, he curled his forearm toward his biceps, bringing Rutha with it. His hook grip held, but pain lanced through his shoulder, his elbow, his wrist.

A flash of gold made him glance above. Zaylus was still holding onto the shortsword as it hovered level with Gandaw, but the tip of the blade was now aiming straight at the Mad Sorcerer.

With a sudden surge of movement, the Sword of the Archon rushed forward with Zaylus clinging on, and embedded itself in the silver sphere above Gandaw. There was a burst of flame, a thunderous roar, and Gandaw fell. Tendrils ripped free of the statue and flailed around him as they retracted into his armor. Again, grapnels snagged a railing and reeled him to the safety of a walkway.

MOUNTAIN OF MADNESS

Down below, the chasm trembled and then snapped shut like the jaws of a monstrous beast.

Instantly, the relentless tug to the bottom ceased. Still gripping Nameless's hand, Rutha swung back and forth to gain momentum, then flipped herself over the railing. With a grunted, "Thanks," to Nameless, she snatched up the black sword and sprinted for the steps up.

Nameless hung on for a moment longer, then climbed back onto the walkway. He glanced around for something to use as a weapon, then simply bunched his fists and went after Rutha.

As they reached the uppermost level, Gandaw turned to a metal desk and made a series of swipes and taps on its dark mirror. The Statue of Etala descended toward him, the crown atop its head still ablaze with sparks that stretched into strings of fire and fed into the base of the black sphere.

Clinging to his sword, Zaylus matched Etala's descent, and he reached out to grab the statue, but Gandaw got there first and plucked it from the air.

"Seconds to go!" the Mad Sorcerer raved. "Seconds!"

Above them, the black sphere ballooned and shuddered.

Tendrils reemerged from Gandaw's armor and penetrated the statue. Instantly, Etala was irradiated with fire, then blazed like a small sun. Zaylus was thrown back, but golden light exploded from his shortsword and met Etala's assault force for force. Flames and light burgeoned into a conflagration that consumed Zaylus and Gandaw.

It made no sense. Scorching heat from the flaming sphere forced Nameless and Rutha back, and yet within its ambit Nameless could see two silhouettes—Gandaw and Zaylus—locked in sorcerous combat.

"Nameless!" Rutha cried. "We have to help him."

She stepped forward, arm covering her face. Sweat poured from her. Dark flames danced along the blade of her sword. She took another step, then cried out and backed away. Her hair was smoldering.

"Deadlocked," Gandaw said to Zaylus from within the fiery barrier. The Mad Sorcerer glanced up at the black sphere shaking violently and growing denser by the second. "Let me raise the walls to shield us, otherwise we'll all die."

"Isn't that what you want?" Zaylus said.

"Not me," Gandaw wailed. "Not me!"

The Sword of the Archon bucked in Zaylus's grip, and golden light slammed against amber fire, neither holding sway.

"Please," Gandaw cried. "Lay down the sword!"

"Don't do it, laddie!" Nameless yelled.

"No, Hale," Rutha said. "Don't stop!"

A low drone came from the black sphere, growing in volume. The sound reverberated through Nameless's bones, pressed on his skull, threatened to crush it.

"You're a holy man," Gandaw said, barely visible through the blaze coming off the serpent statue in his grasp. "If you can't trust me, place your faith in your wretched Way. Lower the sword."

Inch by inch, Zaylus brought the shortsword down.

"No!" Rutha cried.

Nameless snatched the black sword from her and ducked into the conflagration, trusting the *ocras* helm to absorb at least some of the heat.

Vileness crept into his veins from where he gripped the sword. His muscles contorted into knots of pent-up violence. He felt once more the malice of the black axe, the need to kill, to slaughter, to triumph.

The flames about him parted around the great helm, but still his skin started to blister and his hair and beard smoldered. He inched forward a step, then another. It was like walking into a hurricane. The black sword in his hand strained toward Gandaw. It hungered. It thirsted for the Mad Sorcerer's blood.

"Fight, laddie!" Nameless yelled at Zaylus. "Fight!"

But the knight released the shortsword, and it clanged to the walkway.

Its light died instantly.

Etala's attack petered out as Gandaw whirled around to the desk behind him and tapped its mirror. With a rattling hum, the walls of the chamber began to rise, and when Gandaw made a few more passes across the mirror, they raced upward and closed the chamber tight against the Unweaving.

The instant the ceiling snapped shut, blocking sight of the black mass that was about to end all things, Gandaw turned back in triumph.

The hum from beyond the apex rose to the roar of a thousand waterfalls. The walls of the chamber warped and buckled, and time seemed to stand still.

Gandaw's mouth opened and closed with macabre slowness. "Yeeeessss!" slewed from his lips in an endless stream.

"Nooooo!" Nameless cried, heat erupting from his depths, not exploding this time, but slowly blooming. But then it hit his veins and he was moving fast against the lagging tide. The black blade in his hand shrieked for blood, and he lunged forward with all his might.

Sektis Gandaw screamed, and greenish fluids misted from his mouth as he stared almost disinterestedly at the sword embedded to the hilt in his chest. The black blade had penetrated *ocras* as if it were skin. The same green blood gushed from the mortal wound to drench Nameless's hand. It was colder than ice, and he let go of the sword.

"No…" Gandaw gasped. His hand fell open, and the Statue of Etala dropped to the floor.

It didn't shatter on the walkway as Nameless had expected. It hit with a soft thud, then began to writhe and grow.

A wheezing breath escaped Gandaw's lips. He tried to speak, but all that came out was a rasp.

Etala reared up, swelling to a monstrous height. The serpent goddess dashed her sparking crown against the ceiling, crushing the pulsing tendrils linking her to the black sphere, and then, with a second blow, the crown shattered.

The chamber stilled, and from outside came nothing but a deathly silence.

Gandaw staggered back, remaining hand clutching feebly at the black sword jutting from his chest, but Etala's tail whipped around his legs and held him fast. Coil upon coil she wrapped around his body, until all that was visible was the Mad Sorcerer's head, greenmisted breath smearing the inside of his crystal helm. His lips moved faster now, and a babbling stream of pleas left them.

Etala's jaws opened, her head snapped down, and she swallowed him whole, along with the black sword.

Nameless watched in fascinated horror as a bulge passed down the serpent's throat. Amber eyes turned toward him, and he braced himself. Etala's head bobbed atop her neck, and it seemed to Nameless that she nodded. Then, with a flick of her tail, the serpent goddess vanished.

The Archon's sword flared golden for an instant, then started to flicker, and then it too winked out of existence.

"Sweet Way!" Zaylus was saying, voice quavering from just how close they had come to the end of all things. "Dear, sweet Way."

Nameless slumped to his knees, and old darkness washed over him. His hands shook, and his eyes stung from unshed tears.

Rutha's hand on his shoulder made him look round at her through the eye-slit of the great helm. "It's all right," she told him. "You did it. It's going to be all right."

But Nameless was trembling from the way the black sword had made him feel, sickened by the rage that had given him the strength to win through in the end.

He was caught up in memories of Arx Gravis.

Next thing he knew, Nameless was being helped to his feet, Zaylus on one side, Rutha the other. Mephesch's head poked above the walkway, and then the faen rose into view atop a floating disk. Mephesch was beaming from ear to ear. He stepped off the disk and set about swiping symbols on the mirror Sektis Gandaw had so recently been using. With a clunk and a hum, the ceiling snapped open a crack, and then the walls began to sink once more toward the floor.

The black sphere was gone, and instead, a ray of sunlight lanced down through the opening. Motes of dust danced along its length all the way to the floor of the chamber.

MOUNTAIN OF MADNESS

The receding walls gave way to skies of brilliant blue dotted with gossamer wisps of cloud. High above the Mountain of Ocras, the twin suns blazed with newfound health and vitality.

Mephesch hopped back onto his disk and descended through the ground floor into the roots of the mountain.

Outside, a greenish light flared amid the white sand of the Dead Lands and a figure stepped out of it. Nameless blinked against the glare, seeing little more than a silhouette, but Rutha tutted and went to lean out over a railing to watch the figure approaching.

Even without seeing him clearly, Nameless knew who it was. It was starting to seem that nothing—not even the gaping maw of the Abyss—could stop Aristodeus from returning like a fly to a pile of dung.

The philosopher opened his arms and quickened his pace, and Mephesch ran to him. As the two of them walked back to the disk, Rutha shouldered her sword and headed for the steps down.

"Nameless?" Zaylus said warily.

"Gods of Arnoch, laddie, we did it!"

Zaylus hesitated for a moment, and then gripped Nameless by the wrist. "I did nothing. At the end, I didn't know what to do."

It was the truth. Nameless and Rutha had fought tooth and nail, and were both nearly killed in the process, but then Zaylus had lowered the Archon's sword, as if he had given up.

"You did what you thought was right," Nameless said.

"And I was wrong."

Zaylus looked away, down into the open chamber, where Rutha stood waiting as Aristodeus and Mephesch came up through the floor on the floating disk.

TWENTY-NINE

The cart pulled up just shy of a crater-pocked plain that stretched away from the road.

"This it?" Shadrak said. "Where you left my lore craft?" He scratched inside the sling holding his injured arm tight to his chest. The blasted thing was infested with lice, he was sure of it. Either that, or Albrec had cut it from Buck Fargin's shite-encrusted loin cloth.

Buck looked over his shoulder from the driver's seat. "It's where I found him."

Albrec didn't look so sure. The poisoner was seated in the back with Shadrak, a half-eaten pastry clutched in his pudgy hand. He stood and turned a slow circle, using his spare hand as a visor. "They all look the same to me," he said.

Shadrak grunted as he rolled forward from the crate he'd been using as a seat. Pain lanced down his arm, all the way to the fingers. "Find it." he said.

"You find it," Albrec said, taking a bite of pastry.

Shadrak knew it was the pain, knew it was the annoyance of being injured, but he was right out of patience. A couple of day's practice, and he was as good with the left hand as the right. He drew his Thundershot, twirled it once on his finger, and took aim.

Cramming the rest of the pastry in his mouth, Albrec shuffled to the end of the wagon bed and sat on his arse so he could climb down. The wagon bucked when he dropped off the end, the horse

MOUNTAIN OF MADNESS

nickered, and Fargin cursed. Then Albrec was trudging off over the plain like a chastised kid, waving his arms and swinging his hips. He blundered first one way, then the next, without a clue where to look. Suddenly, he stopped and waved excitedly, then squealed and ran off toward a hole. Shadrak could just about make out a brown-stained piece of cloth fluttering in the breeze that Albrec dashed toward and snatched out of the air. Another one of Fargin's?

"Yes!" Albrec cried back at him. "Papa's hanky! I dropped it here. Now I know we're in the right place."

Shadrak leapt from the wagon and winced at the jolt of pain from his shoulder. He made his way over to Albrec and started feeling in front of him with his fingers splayed out. Together, they swept the rocky landscape while Buck looked on from the cart, shaking his head.

"Got it!" Shadrak said at last, finding the invisible recess. A glowing panel appeared at his touch, and he tapped out the entry code.

The door slid open to reveal a rectangle of stark light hanging in midair. A burnished silver corridor led off beyond it.

"Well," Albrec said. "I guess that's it, then. Nice working with you, Shadrak. Give my love to the rest of the scum back in Vanatus."

"Won't change your mind, Albrec? About coming back with me?"

Albrec sighed and glanced at the wagon, where Buck Fargin was growing impatient. "This place is perfect, Shadrak, and I've already made connections. Enemies too, now that Senator Rollingfield has woken up, but he'll come round in time. What would I go back to Vanatus for when the guilds of Jeridium are just crying out for someone like me to lead them?" The poisoner started back toward the cart.

Shadrak watched him go, wondering if Albrec didn't have a point. But still, Vanatus was what he knew.

Before he could step across the threshold into the lore craft, a voice spoke—a voice like the rustle of dry leaves.

"Shadrak."

He froze, and his hand went to his Thundershot.

"Shadrak the Unseen," the voice came again. "You must not leave."

There was no one there. Shadrak shook his head.

The air before him shimmered, and a brown-robed figure appeared. White fire suppurated from beneath an all-enveloping cowl.

"This Nameless Dwarf you have befriended," the figure said. "I need you to keep an eye on him."

"What makes you think I give a stuff about what you want?"

"I am the Archon."

A tingle of dread crept beneath Shadrak's skin. "So?"

Ribbons of white flame streamed from beneath the Archon's hood. "While this dwarf lives, thousands yet may die."

"Not my problem," Shadrak said.

"Then think of it as one part of a contract."

"You got money?"

"What I have is this."

Another figure appeared beside the Archon.

Shadrak gasped as he recognized the creased dark skin, the beaded grey hair, and those eyes of sparkling green that could warm his soul, no matter how far he fell.

"Kadee," he breathed.

The Aculi woman who had raised him.

A solitary tear tracked down Shadrak's cheek.

"I will not stand idly by this time," the Archon said. "This Nameless Dwarf has already killed before. Hundreds were slaughtered in the ravine city. Aristodeus persuaded me to stay my hand—him and the Voice of the Council. And now the philosopher is working on a plan to free the Nameless Dwarf from the *ocras* helm that contains him. In his arrogance, Aristodeus thinks he can destroy the black axe that was the cause of the massacre. He thinks he can outwit my brother, Mananoc."

Shadrak wasn't listening. He couldn't take his eyes off Kadee. "How?" he asked in a voice choked up with grief. "How are you here?"

"Fellah," Kadee said.

He winced as if she'd struck him. How long had it been since he'd heard her voice?

Her people were superstitious savages, through and through, but Kadee hadn't been like the rest. She'd lived among the city-folk of Vanatus. Said she'd done that so she could raise him. He'd never understood why a woman would do that for someone else's child.

"I've missed you," he told her.

"I know."

"I've grown rotten without you. Turned into everything you hate."

"But I will never hate you, my fellah."

Shadrak shook his head. "You're dead." He'd nursed her as she wasted away, held her when she gave her last shuddering breath. "How can you be here?"

"Death is not the end for everyone," she said. "For some, it is worse."

In her somber eyes, Shadrak caught a glimpse of skeletal trees and mountains of obsidian. A black sun hung in a granite sky.

"Enough!" the Archon said.

And with that, Kadee vanished.

"Work for me, and I will show you how to find your foster mother," the Archon said. "Do we have an agreement?"

Shadrak drew his Thundershot and cocked the trigger.

"If you know how to get me to Kadee, then do it now."

The Archon threw back his hood, and white flames roared forth. Shadrak fell to his knees, blinded by the blaze.

"You think you can harm me?"

Shadrak's hand holding the Thundershot began to tremble. Under the Archon's glare, he felt as insignificant as an ant.

"What do you want me to do?"

The flames retreated within the Archon's cowl. "Nothing you're not used to. Wait. Observe. And when the time is right"— the Archon twitched his index finger—"pull the trigger."

And then he was gone.

The clatter of the wagon pulling away snapped Shadrak back to full alertness. He cried out for Albrec and Buck to stop, but when they didn't hear, he let off a booming shot in the air.

The wagon lurched to a standstill, and Shadrak waved. Albrec clambered down and hurried toward him.

"Give me a minute to get some supplies from inside the lore craft," Shadrak said.

"You're staying?"

"Albrec, someone had better warn the guilds of Jeridium, because if you and me partner up, they are going to be well and truly shogged."

Nameless woke to the sound of the door swishing open. He was reclining on a padded black chair in the center of the room Aristodeus had taken for his study. It had apparently been Sektis Gandaw's, but now there was a new lord of the Mountain of Ocras.

His chainmail hauberk was up around his waist, and a tube ran into his stomach from a silver bag on a metal stand. Liquid passed from the bag along the tube with a steady drip.

Rutha had her feet up on a low table and her arms crossed over her chest.

Aristodeus was seated at a desk on the other side of the room from her, rattling through some glass tubes in a case, occasionally taking one out to look at more closely. Directly above him, suspended in midair, was a long crystal case, from within which Nameless could just about make out the shadowy form of the black axe.

Zaylus was standing in the open doorway. The knight paused there for a moment, taking everything in. When he crossed the threshold, the door slid shut behind him.

Aristodeus spun round on his chair. "Now, Zaylus," he said, "I expect you're wondering what I've been up to these past few days."

Rutha snorted.

"Not really," Zaylus said. "I'm more interested in getting back to Vanatus."

"I figured as much," Aristodeus said. "Which is why I've been working with the faen to find a way that will save you weeks at sea—if you can find a ship willing to risk such a perilous voyage."

"You've not had any trouble popping up here, there, and everywhere," Zaylus said. "So why not us?"

"I travel from A to B," Aristodeus said, "and the effort is prodigious. More so when there are passengers." He cocked a thumb at Rutha. "Given that we are currently at B, it would be necessary to return to A prior to predicating a new B."

Rutha dropped her boots from the tabletop and stood, the empty scabbard that had once held the black sword at her hip. "What he's saying is that he would have to take you to his poxy white tower first."

"Because A's the Abyss?" Nameless said. "You travel back and forth from the Abyss?"

Aristodeus closed his eyes and took a deep breath. "Don't you worry about that. That is a problem for minds far older and wiser than yours. It's an ages-long campaign, a battle of wills, but given our progress here, I'd say at last I have the upper hand."

"Can I get up now?" Nameless asked.

Aristodeus came over to the stand and squeezed the bottom of the bag. "A few more dregs, and you'll be good to go."

"Well?" Rutha said. "Are you going to tell Zaylus why I can go with you and he can't?"

Something was communicated between them.

Nameless had no idea what it was, but it made him edgy.

"It's too risky, Zaylus," Aristodeus said. "You and I being in the same space within the Abyss. I cannot place all my eggs in one basket. If we were to both be slain…"

Rutha sneered. She knew more than she was letting on, and Nameless didn't like it. Neither, apparently, did Zaylus.

"Right now," Zaylus said, "I couldn't give a damn if you win or lose. Just get me home, and then find yourself someone else to manipulate."

Rutha gave a slow handclap. "I'm sick of it, too. So, whatever you've got planned to get Zaylus home, I'm going with him."

Aristodeus whirled on her but then instantly softened. "Very well," he said. "I suppose I could countenance that."

"You suppose you could what?" Zaylus said. "Who do you think you are?"

"You really want to know?" Rutha said.

Red flooded Aristodeus's face, and he clenched his fists. "This is not about megalomania, Zaylus! Can't you see that? Did I waste all those years educating you, teaching you to think? Gandaw was the control freak, not me. Do you think I want to fight this battle? Have you any idea how long it's gone on for, how many centuries? I am pivotal, Zaylus. Understand? Pivotal. And I am getting close."

Zaylus narrowed his eyes. "Close to what?"

"Freedom, of course. And after that, turning the tables on Mananoc and sending him back where he came from."

"I remember thinking I was ridding Arx Gravis of demons from the Abyss," Nameless said. "And we all know how that turned out."

"This is not the same!" Aristodeus thundered. He wrenched the tube out of the bag and rapidly coiled it up and lay it on Nameless's belly. "Tape," he muttered. "Tape, tape, bloody tape." He located what he was looking for on a desk and began to tear off strips from a spool which he used to stick the coiled tube to Nameless's skin. "There, you can go now. Just remember, once a month—"

"Yes, yes, back here for dinner. I'm already salivating at the prospect."

Nameless jumped up from the chair and tugged down his hauberk. He clasped Rutha's hand. "Don't forget what you did, lassie. Makes this old dwarf proud to have been there with you."

Then he offered his hand to Zaylus, who hesitated to take it, as if he still believed he had failed in some way, and so Nameless drew him into a fierce hug. "You did well, laddie, and if anyone tells you otherwise, they'll have my axe to answer to."

Then realization struck.

"Shog, the blasted thing broke." He turned the eye-slit of his great helm up to where the black axe lay encased in crystal. "Don't suppose…"

"No!" Aristodeus said, rushing over and ushering him toward the door.

MOUNTAIN OF MADNESS

"Just joking," Nameless said, tapping the side of his helm. "The ol' bucket's still working."

Be that as it may, he still felt the pull of the axe, though it was diminished. It would have taken far more willpower to resist a pint of Cordy's Arnochian Ale, or a flagon of Ballbreaker's. In the scheme of things, his desire for the black axe was about as strong as his yearning for Ironbelly's.

The door slid open, and Nameless stood there for a moment. "You have a plan, though? So we can destroy the axe and get this thing off my head?"

"Yes," Aristodeus said, "but you'll have to be patient. There are a million and one other things to do, but I'm already working on it."

"Till we meet for dinner, then," Nameless said.

He waved at Rutha and nodded to Zaylus as he stepped outside, and then the *ocras* door slid shut behind him.

Cooped up in the ravine all his life, Nameless had never seen much more than chasm dogs and goats, and the flocks of birds that made their home on the Sward where he'd lived. But here, in the upperlands of Medryn-Tha, there were so many things to see, and first off, he was going to start with the Sour Marsh.

When he reached the mangroves skirting the swamp at the edge of the Dead Lands, he cast a look back at Sektis Gandaw's mountain, once more sheathed in its *ocras* cladding. They had indeed done well—him, Rutha, and Zaylus. Shadrak and Albrec, too. Rugbeard. But for Nameless, it wasn't enough. It could never be enough to atone for what he'd done back at the ravine.

He felt the black dog mood creeping from the back of his mind. For a moment, he was tempted to greet it as an old friend, simply sit down and let it numb his brain, petrify his limbs. A dwarf with no name, after all, was a dwarf most shamed. What was there left for him to live for?

But then a rustle of the mangroves snapped him out of it. A

thrill of excitement ran through his nerves. Had there been something watching him from the edge of the Sour Marsh?

He entered the mugginess of the swamp and found himself some deadfall weighty enough to serve as a club. His boots squelched on the boggy ground as he edged deeper into the mire. His heart was a bracing tattoo that grew louder and faster with every step. He knew it was here somewhere, whatever it was that had been spying on him.

A sucking, squelching noise came from behind. He spun round and staggered back in horror.

A mound of mud and vegetation surged up from the marsh floor to loom over him. I was shaped like a man, woven from swamp grass, dirt, and twining creepers. Its head was a twisted knot of fungi. It glared down at him with emerald eyes, then took one shambling step, followed by another. Slime dripped from its rotting maw, and it let out a gurgling roar.

"Yes!" Nameless cried. "Shogging yes!"

And with the fire of battle coursing through his veins, he lifted his improvised club and charged.

The story continues in…

SOLDIER, OUTLAW, HERO, KING:

ANNALS OF THE NAMELESS DWARF

BOOK THREE

CURSE OF THE BLACK AXE

Please support independent authors by leaving a brief review of MOUNTAIN OF MADNESS both at the retailer of your choice and at Goodreads.

Thanks for reading!

Please stay in touch at www.dpprior.com and sign up to my mailing list for new releases and special offers.

Connect with me on social media at:

Twitter: @NamelessDwarf

Facebook: @dpprior

Instagram: namelessdwarf

Printed in Poland
by Amazon Fulfillment
Poland Sp. z o.o., Wrocław